Black Rose

A Stella LaRosa Thriller

Book 1

L.T. Ryan

with

Kristi Belcamino

LIQUID MIND MEDIA

For information contact:

contact@ltryan.com

https://LTRyan.com

https://www.instagram.com/ltryanauthor/

https://www.facebook.com/LTRyanAuthor

The Stella LaRosa Series

Black Rose

Red Ink (coming soon)

Join the L.T. Ryan reader family & receive a free copy of the Rachel Hatch story, *Fractured*. Click the link below to get started:

https://ltryan.com/rachel-hatch-newsletter-signup-1

Love Hatch? Savage? Noble? Maddie? Get your very own L.T. Ryan merchandise today! Click the link below to find coffee mugs, t-shirts, and even signed copies of your favorite L.T. Ryan thrillers! https://ltryan. ink/EvG_

1

A MOURNFUL FOGHORN SOUNDED IN THE DISTANCE. MARK Bellamy felt a sliver of unease as he walked alone in the night, his ridiculous dress shoes clicking and echoing in the deserted downtown San Francisco streets.

It felt like the dark was closing in on him and the hairs on the back of his neck were standing up even though his senses were not picking up on any evidence of a threat. He was trained to scan his environment for anything like that. But this was different. This was a feeling deep down in his core.

Maybe the feeling of dread had to do with his meeting the next day, he thought. Or maybe it was the bone-chilling cold that seemed to seep into his bones and take root there. He'd grown up in upstate New York where cold meant you could spit and it would freeze before it hit the ground, so it was just *stupid* that he felt chilled in California in the middle of July Why he'd ever thought it was a good idea to walk back from the Top of the Mark to his hotel without a coat was beyond him. His excuse was that with his bulky bodybuilder physique, any type of coat felt like a straitjacket.

The band of fog that had seemed to roll through the city right when he turned onto the empty streets of the business district not only made it colder, but also disorienting, making it difficult to gauge how far away sounds were. When Bellamy first left the strip clubs and crowds in Chinatown for the darker streets of downtown, he'd heard a woman's peal of laughter that sounded like it was on the same block. He swore the musky scent of a woman's perfume had mingled with the salty brine of the ocean breeze that ruffled his thick head of hair. However, when he'd turned, he was greeted by an empty street. But now he'd heard something else.

Footsteps.

Something was there. *Someone* was there. A quick glance back revealed nothing but the low roiling fog that stretched for half the block, leaving the other half hidden in the white mist. He began to walk faster, treading lightly, cursing the loud clopping from the fancy dress shoes he'd worn to the gala at the Mark Hopkins Hotel. Of course, they matched the monkey suit Julia had begged him to wear. From the second he met her a year ago, he could never say no to that woman.

He heard a sound again, and he turned to look but saw nothing but mist. He ducked into a dark doorway, pressed his back to the cold glass door, and listened. His fingers curled into fists and his eyes searched the dark alcove for a weapon. There was nothing. But Bellamy had been trained to make his own body the deadliest weapon of all.

In the distance, he could hear the soulful wail of the foghorn. Then utter silence.

Whoever was following him was good.

He should've taken a cab. He could've avoided all this drama. He was tired and a little tipsy. He just wanted to get to the hotel and crawl into bed with Julia. But no, he'd thought the night walk would be good for him, help to clear his head.

One of the men at the gala had made a comment about military operations overseas, and some unbidden dark memories had risen from the depths. Bellamy had found himself growing angry and

2

excused himself, saying it was late and that he needed to head back to his hotel. Now, that peaceful walk he'd envisioned had turned into a major pain in his butt. He'd been certain that he was going to end his night hurting someone.

But he'd rather not.

He scolded himself for not packing heat. Waving a gun around, even if he didn't have to use it, would scare any would-be mugger away. He'd grown somewhat careless after coming back to America. When Julia had asked him to please not bring his gun on this trip, he'd agreed. Julia hated guns. He loved them. But he couldn't tell her that. Not now.

She couldn't know his past. Nobody could. It was too dangerous. And the last thing he would ever do is put her in danger.

Once he met with his contact the next day down by the water-front, it would all be over. He and Julia could fly back to their ranch in Montana and build their life together. Tomorrow's meeting would mark the closing of the door to his former life.

It would be a smidgen of balm on the festering wound of guilt he would carry around for the rest of his life. That anguish had nearly overcome him until he'd met Julia. This final meeting would make things right. Or as right as they could be in such a horrific situation. After turning over what he knew, he'd be done with it once and for all.

Duty to his past life would be over, and he'd be ready to start anew with Julia. He'd do almost anything to make her happy. Her comfort and safety were of the utmost importance. That's why he'd sent her home when her migraine came on. She'd insisted Bellamy stay, reminding him as he'd put her in the hired car that if he was serious about making the old ranch into a resort, then he was going to have to do some networking. Of course he was serious, he didn't want to be a kept man. So, he stayed and schmoozed the hoi polloi.

Now, tucked into this doorway, unease rolled across his taut body. Usually a mugger or junkie wouldn't be so stealthy in stalking their prey, especially if they were just looking to score some easy cash. He was starting to wonder, what if it was something else? Something else from his past had found him, someone else who knew about his meeting the next day.

Impossible.

Bellamy had been careful. Oh, so careful. He was the best of the best. Nobody could ever find him unless he wanted to be found. And he wasn't worried that his contact had given him up, they wanted the information too badly.

Another sound. A clanging, metal striking metal reverberated throughout the silent night and then echoed, fading off in increasingly quieter waves. But it wasn't close. It had to be down the street from him. It meant he had time to act.

Time to end this game.

He'd confront the person and finish it so he could get back to the hotel, and to Julia.

Bellamy poked his head out of the doorway, barely registering a dark silhouette standing before him before feeling a crushing blow to his jaw. Even so, he managed to land a solid blow to the other man's midsection before pivoting away.

The attacker charged. The large man in the ski mask threw powerful punches but few hit home. Neither did Bellamy's parries. Both men managed to dodge the other's blows with skilled precision. The fog-shrouded street echoed with the sounds of heavy breathing and the smack of fists hitting flesh from the few strikes that landed.

Bellamy managed a powerful, bone-crunching blow to the other man's kidney, but instead of crumpling, the masked man retaliated with a looping hook that sent him reeling backward. Stumbling to regain his balance, Bellamy charged and tackled the other man to the ground. They fell hard, each grappling to gain control.

Bellamy broke free and scrambled to his feet. Again, he launched himself at his assailant. The sole of his shoe connected with the masked man's head. The impact sent the other man reeling, but then he was back. For a brief second, the two circled each other, panting, bloodied fists clenched.

"Who are you?" Bellamy asked, his voice labored. "Take off your mask, you coward."

Instead of answering, the other man sprang forward, triggering another bout of fists flying. Then, somehow, the masked man broke through Bellamy's guard and pummeled him with a crushing right hook to the jaw.

As he flew through the air, knocked off his feet Bellamy saw that the fog had lifted, revealing a night sky that engulfed him completely as all went black.

* * *

The first thought Bellamy had when he regained consciousness was that he'd gone soft. Two years back in America, and he was as helpless as a civilian. The next thing he thought was curiosity as to why his attacker had on a ski mask still. Bellamy scanned his prison and looked for an escape angle.

The man in front of him wore a black turtleneck and black jeans. The ski mask covered his entire head, but his dark eyes glittered when they caught the light from the bare bulb hanging from the low ceiling.

The room was a small subterranean space, no bigger than ten by ten feet. The stone walls dripped with condensation. After memorizing the layout, Bellamy scanned his body. His head ached and his wrists were stinging. He realized they had been bearing his full weight, connected to a metal ring in a concrete wall about waist level. He'd been hanging by the handcuffs. No wonder they stung.

As the attacker took a step forward, Bellamy noticed something familiar about the man. Was it his gait? Bellamy didn't know. What he did know was that this wasn't an ordinary mugging. This was something else. Something much, much worse. This was his past come back with deadly consequences.

"You going to torture me or what?" Bellamy asked. "What's all this about?"

"If I have to."

The voice. Bellamy *knew* that voice. That's why the man wore a mask. They knew each other. His face scrunched up as he tried to place the voice.

"Where are your other team members? I need exact locations."

"I don't know where they are. We're not in touch, man."

"I don't," the man paused, "believe you."

"I can't tell you what I don't know."

The man screwed a silencer onto the end of a pistol, a Glock 19. A gun every operative carried.

"I'm going to give you another five minutes to tell me where they are. If you don't, I kill you."

"What if I told you I was already dead?" Bellamy said.

"Quit delaying," the man said. "Tell me where they are. Where is the Black Rose?"

A shiver of dread raced down Bellamy's spine at that name. This was bad. Really bad. He gritted his teeth as he spoke. "I told you I don't know."

"Then you die." The man lifted the Glock. "But first I will make sure you don't know."

He pulled the trigger. Bellamy screamed as his knee shattered and an intense pain began spiraling up his leg. Sweat poured down his face now, and his breathing was labored. He told himself not to look at his knee.

When he regained a semblance of calm, he looked back at the gunman. "If you're going to kill me, at least be a man and let me see your face."

The man squeezed the trigger again, this time into Bellamy's left arm. He shouted out in pain and squeezed his eyes shut. He fought to keep his voice calm. "I didn't tell anyone. Nobody else knows. You can believe me or not, but that's the truth."

"You're wasting my time," his assailant said. "I'm going to ask you one more time. Where are they?"

"I told you, man. I don't know."

"You still don't get it, do you?"

Bellamy knew then it was over. He had mere seconds to live. This man knew about the meeting. This man knew everything.

"Who are you?" Bellamy said, as the acrid taste of fear filled his mouth. He'd escaped a lot of near-death situations over the years, but he'd always held out hope. Not this time. He knew this was the grand finale.

The other man stepped closer.

The end was near.

The most Bellamy could hope for was saving the others. They deserved that. He'd brought this all on himself.

"Nobody else knows a thing," Bellamy said. "What I know goes to the grave with me. What do you want? I'll tell you everything you want to know, but nobody else on the team had anything to do with this. This was all me. I swear it."

"Why should I believe you? Would they do the same for you?"

"Yes."

The assailant shook his head and plainly, simply said, "No."

Bellamy finally gave in to the fear crawling up his throat. Had someone on the team betrayed him and that's why he was going to die in a damp torture chamber? He shook away the thought. No. No way.

Then, the man ripped off the ski mask and walked toward him.

Bellamy's mouth dropped open in surprise, but before he could speak the gun was shoved in his mouth. The last thing he heard was the sound of his cell phone ringing in his pocket. It was playing Journey's "Faithfully" — a special ringtone he'd set up.

Julia.

2

STELLA LaROSA IGNORED THE WHISPERS IN THE newspaper's gym as she stripped off her sweaty workout clothes. One woman had even gasped as Stella ripped off her shirt. Her body was lean and toned, so it was unlikely the women were criticizing her physique. She knew exactly what had caused the interest, and it wasn't the Phoenix tattoo that spanned her back.

It was the scars. Three jagged white lines of tissue crisscrossed her back against her Mediterranean skin. A half-dollar-sized indentation with a rippled border was prominent on her left abdomen and marked where she'd caught a bullet in Mogadishu. On the back of her right calf, an angry looking zipper-type scar.

Even if she had the money for cosmetic surgery, Stella would never get rid of them. They were a visible memorial of what she had lost. They were also a reminder that although her body was scarred, it was still walking above ground, breathing. That was something she would never take for granted.

Inhaling deeply, the locker room smell—a potpourri of sweat, damp, and disinfectant—made her nose wrinkle. Once upon a time, she hadn't even flinched at the smell of a decomposed body. But that was a lifetime ago.

Ignoring her fellow reporters, Stella left her clothes in a puddle at her feet and walked naked across the room to the showers. As she did, she heard the whispers. Even though she couldn't hear what the women said, the murmuring still stung a little. The scars proved she was different from these women who would go home to their happy suburban world where the only scars they bore were from C-sections.

Standing in front of the mirror naked for one brief second, Stella envied these women their seemingly carefree lives. She reminded herself that, just like her, they might have horrific scars that nobody else could see. Ones hidden deep inside. Those were the worst scars to carry.

She didn't work with these women, these reporters who covered restaurants and bestselling books and award-winning movies. They were feature reporters. Stella, however, was the new night police reporter. She took the job specifically so she wouldn't have to interact with anyone except a few nightside editors and photogs. Editors were assholes, but she had always gotten along well with the photographers.

As she stared at her reflection in the mirror outside the shower, Stella was disoriented. Barely recognized herself. For the first time in years, she looked healthy. Her cheeks were flushed pink from her workout, her black eyes no longer bearing dark shadows under them. Her dark hair was long and silky instead of tangled and greasy. Life back in America was good for her once she'd stopped drinking herself to sleep every night. Even though she seemed healthy on the outside, the inside was still shredded, barely held together. Those unseen scars were embedded and twisted within her.

Stella stepped into the shower to let the hot water beat down on her skin and drum away the dark shadows of memory that always threatened to overwhelm her. Turning the tap as hot as it would go, she relished the feel of the near-scalding bullets of water pummeling her back. As she lathered her hair, the air filled with the smell of eucalyptus. It reminded her of a day with her team in Cyprus. Brushing the memory away, instead, she closed her eyes and gave herself a pep talk about having a good attitude in the newsroom that day.

There were about three hours where her shift intersected with some dayside reporters, and one reporter in her department seemed to think that Stella was her bitch. From the first minute they met, Marilyn had tried to palm off some lame stories to Stella-— construction on a bridge, beef between city council candidates, community uproar over a new bar in their neighborhood. It was a far cry from covering war-torn countries overseas.

At first, Stella was amused. She could understand why the woman thought Stella was a rookie reporter. After all, the night police reporter shift was the most entry-level reporter job you could work. Barely a step above intern, but not always.

A company-wide email on Monday introducing Stella had blathered on about her decade overseas and the many award-winning stories she'd covered. Even so, Marilyn still treated her like her personal assistant. On her way out of the newsroom on Tuesday, Marilyn had stopped at Stella's desk.

Stella waited a few minutes before looking up. The woman was bird-like, with sharp features and beady eyes. Her blonde bob was streaked with gray, and she wore very stylish huge, black-rimmed glasses. She wore all black every day, a pencil skirt with a black sweater and chunky jewelry.

"I emailed you some stories that need to be in tomorrow's paper." Marilyn's voice was perfectly modulated. Stella wondered if the woman had ever spoken a curse word in her life. "I don't have time to get to them today." Marilyn tapped one manicured nail on her chin, waiting for a response. Stella remained silent.

"The one we need to cover," Marilyn said, "is how the secret tunnel between the B.A.R.T. train tracks was made public by urban explorers, and now gang members are congregating down there at night and killing each other. They just found a body there last week. It's a small tunnel between the two tracks where maintenance people can go. They offered to give a tour tomorrow night, but I'm not working nights like you."

Stella was surprised. For once, a story Marilyn had pitched was good, but she couldn't do it. Underground. Tunnels. No way in hell. She'd stared at Marilyn until the other woman had grown uncomfortable, huffed, and walked away, leaving a cloud of patchouli in her wake.

Now it was Friday and Stella was ending her first week in the newsroom. Every afternoon in between, Marilyn had pummeled Stella's email inbox with stories she hadn't had time to finish. None of them were as intriguing as the gang activity in secret underground tunnels. After the first one on Tuesday, Stella didn't even bother opening the emails. Just deleted them. At 3 p.m., Stella stopped outside the door to the newsroom warily, her eyes darting to Marilyn's desk. It was empty. Good. The silver-haired bulldog reporter was gone for the day.

This newsroom had been in the same high-rise building for fifty years. It used to take up five floors, now it was contained to one floor. The vast array of windows overlooked the city. This floor, she'd been told, once only housed the newsroom. Now, various corners were divided up to also encompass advertising and administrative workers.

Pausing in the doorway, Stella inhaled. It smelled like home. Newsroom smell was so familiar: fresh coffee, faint odor of cigarette smoke from a bygone era, the smell of black ink on fresh newspapers, and the strange, slightly sweet scent emanating from the endless stacks of yellowed newspapers.

Stella had worked out of dozens of newsrooms in her career, mostly overseas. The one thing they'd all had in common was that persistent buzz that made you feel like you were at the epicenter of everything. It didn't matter if it were a tiny hole in the wall in

Beirut or a makeshift office in an ornate flat in Paris. The energy of a newsroom was addicting.

During her days as a war correspondent, fellow reporters became like family. They often slept in the small newsrooms and woke at reports of violence, donning flak jackets, hard hats, and sometimes even goggles before rushing out.

She was jolted out of her nostalgia by her editor, Jack Garcia, shouting across the newsroom.

"Collins! What's the word on the street?"

Stella smiled, then realized it was the first time her face had cracked that way all day. She liked Garcia. He was a no-nonsense newspaper man. Jack was short and wiry, and always wore a white dress shirt and loose tie as a nod to some long-forgotten formality.

During her job interview, his face had scrunched up in confusion when she told him her intentions. Stroking his close-clipped goatee, he had examined her. "Are you sure you want that beat? You know we have an investigative reporter opening, too."

She met his gaze with a stone face. "I want night cops."

She didn't tell him why. The less she interacted with any other human beings, the better. She wanted friends but was also terrified of letting anyone in again.

Chewing on his inner lip for a while, he held up her resume. "With your experience, you could call the shots." She pretended to think for a moment before replying. "How about I fill your night cops position and if it's slow, do some of those investigative pieces?"

Garcia shook his head, looked up at the sky, and made the sign of the cross. "Who sent you? Of course, the job is yours. You start Monday."

"Thank you."

As she turned to walk out, he called after her. "Collins? You didn't ask about salary. The pay is dismal. A complete joke. You can still back out. If I don't see you Monday night, I won't hold it against you."

Without turning, she waved her hand in response.

Now, on her fifth day of work, she swung by Garcia's desk on the way to the cop reporter corner. A corner with a whiteboard and police scanners that were more relics than anything else since most of the police channels were encrypted nowadays.

"Hey, Garcia," she said. "I heard something on the scanner while I was working out in the gym. Something about a dead body found near the waterfront?"

She didn't tell him she'd cut her workout short when she'd heard the scanner traffic on her phone. It was something about the cop's voice. Stella had heard scanner traffic about dead bodies all week long, but this one seemed different. The cop who'd called it in on the radio had seemed shaken.

"Josh is already on his way," Garcia said. Josh was the daytime cops reporter.

Disappointment filled her. So far, she hadn't had any good crime stories to cover. Just a few robberies and car crashes. She lingered at Garcia's desk until he finally looked up.

"I'm impressed you heard about it, though," he said. "You must already have some sources if you heard about that around the same time Josh got his tip. He's been working the crime beat here for years. How did you hear about it, anyway?"

Wouldn't he like to know? Stella smiled to herself. An old friend with the C.I.A. had given her the secret police scanner channels and told her how to access them on her phone when he'd heard about her new job. Good old Harry.

When Stella didn't respond, Garcia just smiled and said, "I'm not going to ask you to reveal your sources."

There was an uncomfortable silence.

Garcia attempted to fill it by clearing his throat and saying, "Josh also mentioned something about a body found over by the stadium. If you feel like getting out of the newsroom, you might want to check it out. The only reason I think it might be worth running out to is because it was found outside that new flour plant. Probably just a vagrant, but worth checking out."

13

Last year, protestors had locked themselves to the chain link fence in protest of the construction company who'd built the facility, alleging the company was racist. After one incident of violence, the protestors had given up and the flour plant opened six months later.

"I'm on it," she said.

"Be sure to log your mileage."

"Yeah, whatever."

"Also, if you take B.A.R.T. for any reason, we have petty cash, or you can get reimbursed."

Stella would not be taking the Bay Area Rapid Transit. In Europe, she'd forced herself to take the subway, but going underground in a small, contained tube was high on her list of things that might make her freak out. B.A.R.T. actually traveled under the San Francisco Bay. Even thinking about it freaked her out. She had started to leave, but she turned back around. "Have you thought about the story I mentioned?" she asked. "The oil one?"

"It might be over our heads, Collins. I know you're used to the big stories, but this one's bigger than us." He began his signature stroking of his goatee that indicated, Stella realized, deep thinking.

"This one might win you your first Pulitzer," she responded. Stella turned around and headed back to the elevator.

"Hey!" Garcia yelled after her. "How do you know I don't already have one?"

* * *

Stepping outside onto the sidewalk, Stella looked around and felt a small flush of joy seeing the sunshine pouring through the puffy white clouds above. The emotion felt unfamiliar but welcome. Most of the day had been gray and dreary and cold, but the fog had lifted and revealed brilliant blue skies and ethereally lit clouds for the last few hours of daylight. The sun was setting, and the entire city was glowing. Off to the north, the Golden Gate Bridge was lit up in all its splendor. She'd missed the beauty of the city during her stint overseas.

Inhaling deeply, Stella felt energized, alive, and free. Then a wave of survivor's guilt washed over her. She had no right to be happy.

3

RORY MURPHY LOOKED AROUND THE WINDOWLESS ROOM that lay deep within the Pentagon. It was oppressive and smelled like furniture polish and old books. He wasn't sure if he felt trapped because he knew they were deep underground, or because of the men who were inside staring at him.

Rory had known from the beginning he was in way over his head. As a congressional aide, he was to keep his mouth shut and his head down. Rory was good at both. But something about this room felt dangerous. He was only there because his boss, Representative Alec Walker, had been running late due to a delayed flight. Rory was supposed to fill in for Walker at this top-secret meeting. He'd been so anxious he'd locked himself in a bathroom and worked on slicking down the unruly cowlick in his red hair. That cowlick was the bane of his existence. Every time he tried to look mature and professional, that stupid thing would act up and make him look like a toddler who just awoke from a nap. The only thing worse than inheriting the hair from some distant Irish relative was the fair skin that colored nearly every time he felt any hint of emotion. It was going to ruin his career, he was certain. He never could play poker.

Also, he had a nervous habit of smoothing his cowlick, and did so when he walked into the bunker-like room. His hand fell to his side as a man with a swarthy complexion, square jaw, and full head of dark hair told him to sit down.

Rory eyed the long, well-worn wood table. There was one empty seat, and he headed that way.

"Wait right there young man," a silver-haired man in a suit said.

Rory froze.

"Congressman Walker gave you clearance to take notes and report back to him," the man with the square jaw said. Only about five foot ten, he had the body of a swimmer with muscular arms and a large chest. "This goes against my better judgment, but since some of us are leaving the country this afternoon we are relying on you. You see, the information we have to share cannot be conveyed in any way that could be compromised, such as in electronic form."

"Are you sure about this, Kam?" the silver-haired man asked. "This seems like a bad idea to me. Why would Walker grant clearance to an aide? For something like this? This is top secret. There are rules governing this. We can't just say it's okay because we feel like it one day."

"We don't have a choice. Both of us are getting on a plane in an hour. It's either meet this way or not at all. We can't have a meeting without Walker. Those were the rules. So, it's his choice and prerogative to appoint a proxy."

"Well, I still don't like it," the older man grumbled. "He's a kid. A congressional aide for crying out loud." He looked around at the other men at the table as if for support, but nobody answered.

Rory knew why he'd been the one granted this top-secret clearance. He was Walker's bitch. Two months ago, he'd asked Walker for his daughter's hand. He was going to be Walker's son-in-law by next spring.

"I spoke to Walker myself," Kam said, then looked at Rory.

"Give me your cell phone."

Rory fished his phone out of his pocket and handed it to him.

"Sit there." Kam pointed to the empty spot. "With that legal yellow pad and pen, you'll take notes. Then we will seal your notes in an envelope that you will hand to Walker."

"Okay," Rory agreed, sliding into the seat with the pad and pen in front of it.

"And you'll forget everything you've heard today."

"I will?" Kam shot him a look. "I will." Rory nodded his head.

"Well, I'm still going to use some code words that only Walker will know," the silver-haired man said with a slight huff.

"When don't we?" another man asked, clearly irritated.

Then the men began the meeting. Rory took notes, but realized they hadn't been kidding about using code.

"I called this meeting because the threat I mentioned last week has been eliminated," Kam said.

"That was too close," another man said. Rory looked over at him. He looked a lot like an F.B.I. agent Walker had introduced him to once at the country club. The more Rory thought about it, the more certain he was that the man in the dark blue suit at the far end of the table was F.B.I.

"How can we be sure that nothing was revealed?" the silver-haired man cast a glance at Rory, who noticed it out of his peripheral vision. He was trying to be as invisible as possible, keeping his eyes trained on the notes he was taking.

"We don't know," Kam said. "We have activated some sleepers to tie up any loose ends."

"There should never have been any loose ends to begin with," the F.B.I. agent said. "How on earth did this ever get out?"

"We're still figuring that out. It might have to do with, uh," Kam hesitated and looked at Rory before continuing. "It might have to do with our friend overseas."

"He knows that he's in as much danger as us if this falls apart!" the older man said.

"Maybe," Kam said.

It went on in this cryptic way for quite some time with Rory scribbling notes, trying to document the conversation verbatim.

"You getting all this kid?" Another guy with blond hair to his right asked him once.

"Yes, sir."

By the end of the meeting, Rory had pages of notes, but still no idea what the meeting had been about. He tucked his handwritten notes into the envelope, sealed it, and then stuck it in his breast pocket. Before he walked out, Kam stepped in front of him.

"Walker told me you're engaged to Isabel."

It was a statement.

Rory nodded.

"Just to be clear about what you heard here," Kam continued. "If any of this information gets out, you are endangering your future father-in-law's life, and most likely your future bride's life. Do you understand?"

A dark chill raced down Rory's spine. What had he gotten into? But Rory nodded solemnly and said, "I do."

Then he left. He was going straight to the airport to wait for Walker's flight to land, and then he would hand over the envelope immediately.

But as he drove to the airport, he thought about what he'd heard. As far as he could tell, these men were part of a secret government program that Walker wasn't a part of, but he was privy to their operations. It was called Headway.

One of the men had let the name slip. Rory had picked up on the panicked looks that had flown around the room, but he had kept his eyes on the notepad continuing to take notes, so they didn't notice how he had felt the import of the name being spoken.

It involved sending special forces to countries to do things that the U.S. government couldn't do out in the open without causing problems for the country. There was talk about how information had somehow been leaked about what the program did, and it had put "countless lives" in danger.

One part of the conversation had been bothersome. The silver-haired man had frowned and asked, "How do we prevent more bloodshed?"

"It's them or us," Kam replied.

4

THE SUN HAD DIPPED BEHIND THE SKYSCRAPERS, CASTING A chill on the waterfront area facing Oakland near the baseball stadium. At first, Stella had a hard time finding the address of the flour factory, but after doubling back she saw a large open metal gate. Beyond it, she saw a road that led down to a large warehouse. Slowing, she spotted a few police vehicles and a dark blue coroner's van parked near the warehouse.

The wind from the bay whipped her hair through her open car window as she drove down the driveway. Salty air was laced with the smell of grains from the flour factory. As she navigated the driveway, she leaned forward, keeping her eye on the scene at the bottom.

It definitely didn't look like a murder. Only a few police squads. No crime scene tape marking off the entire block. No perimeter set up. No plastic numbers set up on the ground indicating evidence.

This wasn't a crime. Just a D.O.A. Josh was the one who got to cover a homicide today. Not her.

Stella was able to drive her Jeep right up to the scene and park it behind the other vehicles. As she got out, two men with navy blue jumpsuits with the word "Coroner" on the back, walked past her hefting a gurney with a body under a sheet. A gust of wind from the nearby bay blew the sheet off the man, revealing his face.

Her reporter instincts kicked in, and Stella began to catalog everything she saw and what it might mean. It was hard to tell because life on the streets prematurely ages most people, but he looked like he might be in his late fifties. His face was lined with deep wrinkles, and he had the beginnings of a silver five o'clock shadow. The guy was homeless, but he seemed to still care about things like shaving and bathing Stella thought. His clothes looked halfway clean as well.

They continued loading the gurney into the back of the van.

Stella walked toward the rear of a large building where it looked like the man had lived—and died. Crime scene tape was strung from a utility pole to a chain-link fence marking off a triangular area with the wall of the building making up the third side. The enclosed area was a patch of dirt strewn with cigarette butts, empty booze bottles, and a small tarp that must've been the man's shelter. It was strung between two stacked piles of bricks, like someone had allowed this man to stay here.

His makeshift home was not only against the new building, but there were also jugs of water lining the wall. He had lived behind the locked chain-link fence that protected the plant. Interesting. Which must have said something about his character, and about whoever ran this facility.

Stella logged all of these details into her memory. It was unlikely she'd do a story about the death of a homeless guy—happened too often to be newsworthy—but you never knew. She'd poke around some more. For instance, she'd like to know what the man's simple shelter contained.

The wind from the bay had picked up, and a faint odor of urine and perspiration mingled with the salty smell of the ocean. Stella held her dark hair back from her face as she approached a cop taking down the crime scene tape.

"Closing up shop already?"

"Sarge is over there," the officer said without looking her way.

Turning, she saw a cop with sergeant's chevrons standing by the driver's side window of the coroner's wagon. He was short and stocky, with a thick head of brown hair and a gigantic Mario Brother's inspired mustache.

"Mind if I take a look, since it's not a crime scene?" she asked the officer.

He shook his head. "Go ask the sergeant."

Stella pivoted to talk to the officer in charge when there was a sound from the living space. Whining. Without thinking, she was kneeling down in the blue-infused light under the tarp. A brown dog was curled up on a folded sleeping bag. A small plastic water bowl was near a neat stack of clothes. A pile of packaged food in another corner.

"Hey there," Stella crooned softly.

The dog's tail thumped on the fabric of the sleeping bag, but it also gave out a low growl.

"Hey!" It was an unfamiliar voice.

Stella straightened up. The sergeant, with his black mustache and thick head of black curly hair hovered above her.

"You the new reporter at the *Tribune*?"

"That's me," Stella said, standing and wiping her palms off on her black jeans before sticking out her hand.

"That's all fine and dandy, but there's nothing to see here," the sergeant said, ignoring her gesture. "Nothing that will make your readers buy your paper, that's for sure. Not even a crime scene. I know how you guys work—if it bleeds, it leads."

Stella narrowed her eyes. Another ignorant cop. Wasn't the first one she'd worked with over the years. This one was American and spoke English, but that didn't mean he would understand her job any more than the ones who carried AK-47s and worked for corrupt warmongers.

"I could care less about selling papers," she said and arched one eyebrow.

"Whatever," the sergeant said. "Time to go. We're clearing out and you need to clear out, too."

"I'm not done here," she said.

"Yeah. You are. Not sure if you noticed, but at the head of the driveway it said this was private property. You're trespassing."

"Oh yeah?"

"Yeah."

Just then, the coroner's wagon pulled away, heading toward the main road.

"What about his dog?" Stella asked.

"What about it?"

"You're just going to leave it here," she said as a statement, not a question.

"It's homeless. Like its owner. What do ya want me to do, lady?"

"It's going to die out here if you leave it."

"Not my problem."

"Glad to see one of San Francisco's finest has such a big heart."

"What's your name?" he said and scowled. "Who said you could even be at my crime scene?"

She glanced at his badge, "You told me yourself it wasn't a crime scene."

He glared.

The other police officers snickered.

He turned toward them. "What are you still doing here? The scene is cleared. Go see what's happening in the waterfront precinct. Heard they might need back up."

Stella tried to act nonchalant, busying herself flipping through her notebook, but listened intently. The waterfront precinct was where Josh was. That's where there was an *actual* homicide.

"What's going on over there?" she asked, trying to make it sound innocent.

The sergeant shook his head. "Nice try. You want info on that, you're going to have to talk to our P.I.O."

Stella nodded. She already knew that anything that came from the public information officer meant she was lucky if she got half the story. The air grew colder as the sun finally set.

Stella held her breath as she turned her back on the sergeant and headed toward the tarp. The dog had whined again.

She leaned down. "Come on buddy. It's okay. Come on out now."

A large streetlight had kicked on illuminating the warehouse parking lot in an orange glow, but this small corner tucked up against the building remained in shadows. She waited, but the dog didn't budge.

"Come on, baby."

She sensed the sergeant before she heard him. He'd followed her to the tarp. Interestingly, he wasn't yelling at her to leave. Stella smiled to herself.

"Come on," she made a clicking noise. She heard movement on a vinyl sleeping bag. Then a black nose poked out.

"Good boy," Stella said. "Come on out now."

As she held her hand out the dog stepped outside, only a few inches away from her hand. She waited, holding her breath as it leaned over and sniffed her hand.

"Okay, I get it–you're a bleeding heart, but this could take all night," the sergeant said. "I've got places to go." The dog visibly startled at the sergeant's booming voice and backed up but didn't go back into the shelter.

"Don't worry about me," Stella said. "I'm not leaving this dog here alone. You're going to have to arrest me for trespassing."

"I'm not leaving a woman out in this neighborhood alone at night."

"I'm sure you'll find this hard to believe, but I've been in much worse places than this."

"Oh yeah?"

"Yeah," Stella said. "I'm not going anywhere until I make sure this dog is going to be okay."

"I'll call the damn pound. They'll come get 'em. That make you happy? Dog's got a better shot of surviving out here on the streets than in the pound. That place is overflowing."

Stella looked up, surprised. There was some feeling in his voice.

"Don't call anyone," she said. "I got it handled."

Crouching, she held out her hand again.

"Thing's probably got rabies. Bite you and you get the shots in the stomach. I've had them before. It's not worth it, lady."

"Name's Stella Collins," she said and straightened.

"Tommy Mazzoli."

Italian, she thought. Good. It was that or Black Irish. She hadn't been sure but knew his type all too well.

"Nice to meet you, *paesano*."

"You Italian with a name like Collins?" he asked, his eyebrows knitting together.

"On my mom's side."

"Good. Was worried you were Sicilian."

"Hell no," she said and laughed.

"Let me help you get this guy in your car. I've done this a few times."

"So, you're not such a heartless tough guy, after all?" she said in a teasing voice.

"Don't you say a word about this," he frowned.

"Your secret is safe with me."

5

STELLA WALKED INTO THE FOURTH-FLOOR NEWSROOM carrying the dog in her arms. Once she'd gotten the dog into her passenger seat, she'd driven through a fast-food restaurant and bought a few cheeseburgers and a cup of water. She ate her burgers, and he ate his, and they were both happy.

After that, they'd become fast friends. He sat upright in the passenger seat, staring at her. Whenever she glanced over at him, he'd wag his tail. In the light, Stella saw he was brown with some black and beige patches. He looked like he was a mix of a collie and lab, weighing about thirty pounds. He'd been pretty good during the drive, if maybe a little hyper, jumping from the front passenger seat to the back until she pulled to a stop in the newspaper parking lot.

As soon as the car stopped moving, he began to whine and pace. When she opened the door and called for him, he stayed out of reach, huddling against the other side. She had to get into the newsroom and this was taking too long so, hoping he wouldn't bite her, she crawled into the backseat and cornered him, scooping him into her arms.

"What on earth is that?" Garcia said when she walked past his desk carrying him. He stood up. All 5'6" of him.

"A dog."

"I see that. Why the hell is he in my newsroom, Collins?" He sounded pissed, and for a second Stella felt a twinge of guilt.

"He belonged to that dead homeless guy."

Garcia recoiled. "He looks like it, too. That thing probably has rabies and most definitely has ticks and fleas."

"Probably," Stella said. "I'm just going to settle him under my desk until my shift ends then I'm taking him to the vet to get checked out."

"Lyme disease is a thing," Garcia said. "There's no way that thing doesn't have ticks on it. And that means you probably do, too."

"Yeah, I've dealt with worse."

Stella realized that was her new response to everything. She'd already said it twice in the past two hours. It was bitter and jaded. Like her, maybe? But it was the reality of her life now—whatever nonsense flew her way she'd already dealt with worse. It helped her maintain perspective.

"Hate to ruin your fur baby plans but I need you to head down to the precinct. They're doing a presser on the homicide."

"Josh isn't covering it?"

"Seems his kid is in a play tonight or something. I don't know. I told him you'd take over. He wrote up the initial story and you can add anything worthwhile from the press conference, which will most likely be nothing. Believe me, they won't tell you jack. Maybe give you the exact time or whatever. They are less than helpful."

"What else is new?"

Stella wasn't surprised. What surprised her was that Josh, the paper's main crime beat reporter, wasn't all over this homicide. As a police beat reporter, homicides were the biggest stories you covered. He seemed to disagree. Or maybe that's what it was like being a reporter when you had a family and kids weighing you down.

Stella cringed at her own thoughts. A family and kids weighing you down. At those words, the dark shadows circling her began to close in. Once, a few years ago, she'd imagined giving everything up to be a mother, but then realized that she couldn't reconcile an innocent baby with the life she'd led. She was too haunted by the things she'd had to do.

Shaking those memories away, she turned her attention to the dog. It looked up at her lovingly. "What a good dog."

Garcia raised an eyebrow. "The presser is in twenty minutes. It'll take you eighteen to get there."

"You're going to have to watch him then," Stella said and set the dog down. It crawled under Garcia's desk and curled up in a ball. The editor jerked his chair back like the dog had burned him.

"You're kidding, right?"

She didn't answer.

"Listen," she said to the dog, stooping down to look at it. "You need to stay. Sit. Stay."

Reaching into her messenger bag, she pulled out a bag of carrots and celery she'd had in there for two days. "Give him these if he tries to bolt. Also, he's thirsty. Maybe you can find a bowl in the break room to put water in."

"Seriously, Collins? You're kidding, right?"

But she was already out the door.

* * *

An empty podium with the police department logo on its front was positioned near the front door at the top of the stone steps leading up to the lobby. A bevy of TV reporters had formed a semi-circle around the podium with their cameras mounted on tripods. Stella grabbed a slim white reporter's notebook out of a stack that Garcia had given her when she started and got out of the car. She made her way up the steps, keeping to one side.

The female broadcast reporters were obvious by their heavy

makeup. The male reporters had hair that most women would envy. But there were two other people off to one side. One had a huge microphone and a recording device hanging from a shoulder strap. Radio guy. Another man had a lanyard with a huge, laminated ID that read Associated Press.

When she met his eyes, he gave her a nod. She jutted her chin back in acknowledgement. Getting out her phone, she got ready to make a video, but then frowned. She hadn't covered a press conference like this in more than a decade.

The work overseas was always on the tightest, most chaotic deadlines. The quotes she got from people were ingrained in her head. But she didn't trust her memory as much nowadays. Not after what had happened leaving Syria. As she was deciding how to cover the press conference—taking unreadable chicken scratch notes or recording it on her phone, there was a flurry at the door. A half dozen people streamed out of the lobby doors.

A short, fit, bald guy with an easy smile wore the chief of police uniform.

He was flanked by a lieutenant and sergeant. Beyond them was a woman in a beige pants suit and a man in a black suit. The last two were either public information officers or detectives.

Stella squinted at the man in black. He was partially blocked by the others, so Stella couldn't tell for sure, but the short glimpses she caught made her wonder if she knew him. He was a pretty boy. His cheekbones were chiseled, full lips adorned his face, and dark eyes peered from under his brows. As he turned to say something to the woman beside him, his jacket opened. He had a gun, and a badge attached to his belt.

Detective.

The woman approached the podium. She must be the P.I.O.

"Sergeant Miller, can you pass out the press releases?"

The sergeant passed them to the reporters. Stella scanned hers. There it was. All the info she needed. She put her phone and notebook away and crossed her arms.

"Everyone ready?" the woman asked.

"Yes. Can you start by spelling your name?" a TV reporter beside Stella asked.

"I'm Maggie O'Connor," the woman said and then spelled her name. "I'm the public spokesperson for the department. Everyone ready?"

When everyone nodded, she began, reading from the press release.

"Unfortunately, our city has seen another senseless death today. This marks the tenth homicide of the year. Another family is grieving tonight. At 15:30, our officers were called to a report of a shooting in the 1300 block of Waterfront Road. When they arrived on scene, approximately ten minutes after the call, they made a horrific discovery."

Stella shot a look at the A.P. reporter. He made a face. Horrific was an interesting word choice. Usually the P.I.O.'s stuck to hard facts. Stella looked at the press release. Yep, there it was in black and white.

The woman in the beige suit continued. "A man had been killed. Because of the circumstances of the death, we are investigating it as a homicide."

As the public information officer droned on, Stella's thoughts wandered. She wondered how the dog was doing and what she was going to do with it.

The P.I.O. ended her statement and said she could take a few questions.

"Is there a threat to the public?"

"Are there any suspects?"

"Is the man a San Francisco resident?"

She answered all of them with a curt, "That's still under investigation."

Stella cleared her throat. "How was he killed?"

The woman turned her gaze on Stella, and something flashed

across her face before she responded, "That's still under investigation."

What the hell was that look about?

"That's all for tonight. We'll put any new information on X."

Stella shot the A.P. reporter another sharp glance. *On Twitter?
Or X or whatever they were calling it now.*

As the broadcast reporters began to pack up, the A.P. reporter
came over.

"Stella Collins." It was a statement, not a question.

"Have we met?" she asked.

"Your reputation precedes you."

"Jesus," Stella said and began to make her way down the steps.
"None of it is true."

"Probably a bit different covering a city police department press
conference instead of warlords and mass destruction?"

Stella glanced at him, but he wasn't being rude or sarcastic, he
was sincere.

"It's weird. Like when did cops start tweeting to convey
information?"

"It's not only weird, it's absurd." He stuck out his hand. "Wade
Swierczy."

Stella took his hand. She yawned and gave a wan smile. "Still
getting used to night shift."

Wade laughed. "There's a gas station a block away. You wouldn't
know it, but the coffee there is pretty damn good."

"Thanks," she said. "Nice to meet you."

She needed to stop and get a coffee on the way back to the newsroom. She could use some espresso to make it through the rest of
the night. She'd get Garcia one, too, and put in the cream and sugar
he'd loaded it with during her job interview. It would be a way to
thank him for watching that damn dog.

She'd just reached her own car when she felt someone
beside her.

"Hey."

It was the attractive detective. As soon as she heard his voice and saw him up close, she knew exactly who he was.

Oh. No.

In her imagination she placed him in a T-shirt and baseball cap, like he'd looked the night she met him at the bar. More than a year had passed since she'd first come back to America and had been constantly drunk. That night she'd been pretty intoxicated, but she still should have recognized him.

A one-night stand. A good one. But she'd never gotten his name or profession, as it hadn't mattered at the time.

During her year of being drunk, as she called it, she'd had a few one-night stands. Usually men she met at the bar near her friend's apartment, but she also should have recognized the only one who'd stayed the night. She'd been pissed off when she woke and found him in bed next to her. After they'd had sex, she'd rolled over and told him to lock the door behind him. But he'd stuck around. She'd woken up the next morning and ripped the covers off him in an attempt to get him out.

"It's time for you to leave," Stella had said. "And do yourself a favor and forget this ever happened."

Without waiting for him to answer, she'd stood up and stalked into the bathroom. She slammed and locked the door behind her before getting into the shower. When she came out of the bathroom, naked, and drying her hair, he'd been gone.

Good.

Now, after seeing him again, she couldn't shake the feeling gnawing at her gut.

"You didn't tell me you were a reporter," he said and frowned.

"And you didn't tell me you were a cop," she said and yanked open her car door.

"You seemed pretty angry the next morning."

"Because you were still in my bed. I'd asked you to leave."

"Maybe we can start over? I'm Rob Griffin. Detective Griffin."

For a second, Stella considered not answering, but realized that was a bad play since she was going to be covering the cop beat and he was a homicide detective.

Nodding, she said, somewhat reluctantly, "Stella Collins. I'm with the *San Francisco Tribune.*"

"Nice to meet you," he said. "For some reason, you look familiar?"

"I do?" Stella decided to play along, pretending they just met.

"Yeah," he said, squinting. "If you have a phoenix tattoo on your back, we've definitely met before."

Despite herself, she smirked.

"After that night you disappeared," he said. "I tried to call you. But you never picked up. I even went back to that bar every night for two weeks. When I went to your apartment, your roommate said you'd moved."

Every night for two weeks?

Pausing, he waited for a response. She wasn't going to give one. Stella lived her life without any explanations. To anybody. Ever.

But this guy? He could be a source. Once she'd stopped drinking, she also stopped sleeping around. It had been a while. At least six months. Maybe this Griffin could help her out in more ways than one.

"Nobody can say you're not persistent, but you also aren't a good listener," Stella said, considering her options. "I told you not to stay the night, you stayed the night. I told you not to call, you called. To me, that screams major boundary issues. I was raised that when a woman says something, a guy better listen and respect it."

Griffin put his hands up, palms facing her.

"Listen, I apologize if it came across that way. One reason I became a cop was to make sure guys do exactly what you just said, or they pay dearly for not doing it. But I think this was a misunderstanding."

That's one reason he became a cop? Stella was interested.

"Go on," she said and crossed her arms across her chest.

"I was going to leave, but I fell asleep. I was pretty hammered. I didn't think it was a good idea to drive home. I know that's an awful excuse for not doing what you asked."

"You could've called an Uber."

He nodded. "I know. Like I said, falling asleep because I was drunk is a crap excuse."

"And you kept calling."

"Okay, hear me out," he said. "I was drunk that night but sober the next morning when you kicked me out."

"And?"

"And I've got a pretty good memory, and I don't remember you ever saying I couldn't call you."

Stella gave an exasperated sigh. He was right. And that was infuriating.

"I didn't. But I did say I didn't want to see you again, so the no calling part was implied."

He waited for a beat and then said, "So, am I forgiven?"

Stella paused. This had to be played just right. She wanted him to trust her. She needed him to know that Stella Collins, the journalist, never gave up her sources. From the minute she was born, the importance of loyalty had been drummed into her. Her family would accept no less. She would go to jail before revealing her sources.

Gaining Griffin's trust so he could help her out covering the crime beat was the main goal. A proficient lover would be the cherry on top.

Stella turned and said over her shoulder. "Do you still have my number?"

He nodded.

"I get off at 11."

Slamming her car door, she drove off without waiting for his response.

6

REPRESENTATIVE ALEC WALKER STIFLED HIS IRRITATION AS he attempted to weave through the throngs of amateur travelers navigating their way through Ronald Reagan International Airport. Sometimes it seemed as if he were the only one in the world with any sense of urgency.

An elderly woman was tottering along. A young man with headphones was shuffling slowly, as if he were sleepwalking. But it was the family with what looked like six kids trailing behind them who were really holding up the show. They were taking forever to figure out how to get on the goddamn escalator. The mother was holding one boy's hand and encouraging him with a smile to take the first step.

Other people seemed to find this scene heartwarming. Walker gave a long indulgent smile to his fellow travelers as they exchanged glances, waiting at the top of the escalator for the kid to step onto the moving silver steps. Walker tamped down his impatience. As a father, he knew kids were quirky and caused delays. Although Margaret, his wife, would have just plunked the kid on the step and pushed him along. Then the mother, thank goodness, had suddenly become self-aware and saw the crowd bunching up behind her and her son. She picked him up with an apologetic smile and the bottleneck opened.

As he made his way through the crowd, Walker maintained a tight smile. You never know who might recognize him. He nodded and grinned at passersby who looked up at him in surprise and recognition. He could almost always tell if they knew who he was, or if they just thought he looked familiar.

Finally, he was through the stifling crowds and stepped outside. He paused and glanced around, immediately spotting his ride. The big black sedan with the dark windows was parked illegally in the airport drop-off zone, which showed Walker that his protegee had some promise.

Walker took his time coming out of the airport doors leading to the pick-up zone, giving the young man a chance to hop out of the car and deal with the luggage situation. But by the time Walker ambled past the crowds of people hailing cabs and lugging fleets of suitcases onto airport shuttles, the damn kid still hadn't noticed him.

As he grew closer to the sedan, he saw that Rory was on his goddamn phone. He yanked his suitcase to the back of the sedan and jerked the door open.

Rory jumped. "Crap!"

Walker slid into the seat and slammed the door, his silence expressing his irritation.

"How was your flight?" Rory said and pressed the ignition button.

"My suitcase," Walker said.

In the rearview mirror, Walker could see the young man's cheeks flush.

"Oh right, sorry," he said. "I was texting Isabel about tonight. I wanted to see if I should stop and bring wine. I already got flowers but ..."

"My suitcase," Walker said.

The young man threw open his door and ran toward the back of the sedan. Walker did some deep breathing. The boy was still getting trained, but he needed to know sooner rather than later that texting Walker's daughter was not a valid excuse for his lack of attention. For crying out loud, wine? Like the kid would even know what type of wine to bring. And even if he knew what type of wine, he couldn't afford it. Not on his salary. It wasn't his fault. The kid should be saving money to buy Isabel's wedding ring, not buying her cheap flowers from a sidewalk flower stand.

Walker scanned emails on his phone and distantly noted the trunk slamming and Rory climbing into the driver's seat. Out of the corner of his eye, he saw something and glanced up in irritation. Rory had turned around in his seat, holding an envelope out toward him.

Walker frowned and didn't immediately reach for it.

"It's from the meeting this morning."

Only then did Walker reach for the envelope. He put it on the seat beside him as the sedan navigated the idiots attempting to leave the airport and merge south onto George Washington Memorial Parkway.

Walker waited until the sedan hit the open highway before he reached for the envelope that Rory had given him. Before he read it, he glanced at the rearview mirror. Rory quickly looked away, but Walker saw the young man's cheeks turn a little red.

He was a good kid. Dumb, and a bit distracted, but loyal. A lot like the Irish Setter that Walker's family had growing up. Come to think of it, they both had the same hair color, fur, whatever. The stupid thing ended up getting hit by a car trying to save his sister's life. It was a waste, really, since Carly ended up dead in a car accident ten years later anyway. Her death had been awful, but he had to admit that it happening in the middle of his campaign for governor had sealed his victory. His public grief, and subsequent platform to crack down on drunken driving, had convinced all those secret bleeding-heart liberals—who had been on the fence—to vote for him.

Now, in the back of the sedan, he forgot about his future son-in-law as he skimmed the yellow legal pad pages. The Headway program had been his brainchild a decade ago. The idea of Headway had blossomed when the vice president mentioned needing an off-the-books covert team to take out threats to the U.S. government. If any of the operations were exposed, the U.S. government would disavow the team and all its members.

Walker had come up with the idea that the team would be composed mostly of SEAL Team Six members. And then, for the coup de grace, each member had been wiped. Each had been declared KIA. Gone. They were nobodies now.

During the first year, there had been an unforeseen roadblock during many of their missions. For instance, once the team was having trouble infiltrating the Saudi regime. They needed a scout, someone who already had connections and sources. Someone to do reconnaissance. Preferably a woman. Someone who could blend in, someone who could feasibly have a good reason to be there asking questions.

Walker had sat up in bed one night when the solution hit him. He'd recruit the niece of an old family friend: Stella LaRosa. She was a vetted experienced war correspondent who had access to places and people the team didn't. She could go in, gather intel, and then the team would go in after her.

But he knew enough to not approach her with the family angle. She had gone overseas to escape her family. He had to be smart about it. So, he told the team leader, Nick, to run into her at a bar in Morocco and befriend her. It had worked out better than he had imagined. Nick and Stella had become lovers, and she joined the team not long after.

Now, as he read the report, he shook his head. The program had been a good idea at the time, but it had served its purpose. It was going to implode and take them all out with it. He had to distance himself from Headway or he was going to go down with the rest of them.

As it was right now, if even one person revealed what had taken place in Syria, the repercussions would be devastating. Something had to be done right away.

"We're here, sir," Rory said.

Walker had been so lost in thought he hadn't realized they were driving down his long, winding driveway. Rory put the sedan in park and hopped out to get the luggage.

Taking a compact mirror from his briefcase, Walker smoothed his thick head of blonde hair in place. The transplants had been worth every penny for that head of hair, he thought. It shaved ten years off him for sure. The permanent bags under his eyes would be next. And maybe a bit of the jowls he saw forming.

"Sir?" It was the damn kid.

"Coming." He tucked the mirror away.

By the time Walker gathered his overcoat and briefcase, Rory had carried the suitcase up to the front door.

"Let's go eat. I don't know about you, son, but I'm starving." Walker said.

He watched Rory's cheeks flush at the word he had used for the first time. Deliberately. The boy was all right. Kind of funny looking with those freckles and red hair. A ginger. Oh well. Isabel thought he was something else. He couldn't understand it, but that was fine. The most important thing was that the kid did what Walker said.

Rory reached for the door, but Walker held out his arm to stop him. "You know what you heard today is top secret, correct?"

"Yes, sir."

"Let's keep it that way. Family is family and even though there hasn't been a wedding yet, you are considered family now. That's why I sent you there today."

"Thank you, sir."

Walker gave a tight smile and opened the front door. Rory gestured for him to enter first. As he went in, Walker felt relief. It had been risky sending the kid to the meeting, but it had been necessary. If word ever got out about the secret meeting that had been held today and the fallout from it, Walker could honestly say he had not been at the meeting and that he'd never received the notes about it from his congressional aide.

Isabel might be heartbroken for a while, but she'd get over it.

7

BACK IN THE NEWSROOM, THE LARGE WINDOWS FRAMED the downtown skyline with all the tiny windows on the skyscrapers brilliantly lit up against the black night. The distant murmur of a few reporters on deadline talking urgently into their phones competed with the chipper voices of news anchors reporting the latest on the newsroom's wall-size television. Other smaller T.V.s hung strategically throughout the newsroom.

Stella paused in the doorway and drank in the atmosphere. The energy of a newsroom on deadline was unlike anywhere else. She loved it.

Making her way through the office cubicles, Stella beelined for Garcia's desk, juggling her coffee and his. When she stood beside him, he didn't look up. He was engrossed in what was on his computer screen and didn't notice her at first.

"Here's your fancy schmancy girl coffee," Stella said, setting it on his desk. The enticing aroma wafted up, and she took another sip from her own cup. The A.P. reporter was right, the gas station had surprisingly good coffee.

"Thanks. Be with you in a sec. I'm just finishing up Akeem's school board story before the first print deadline."

Frowning, she leaned down to look under his desk. "Where's the dog?"

"Sleeping," Garcia pointed. The dog was curled up in a ball on a coat in the corner of the cubicle.

"That your coat?"

Garcia was distracted, rubbing his short goatee. "Uh, yeah," he said without taking his eyes off the screen.

"Now you got fleas and ticks too," she said and grinned.

"Just get me your story. We need to file for the first edition in twenty minutes."

"Yes, sir," she said and gave a jaunty salute. "Won't be much. You were right, there was almost nothing new from the presser. I'll have it for you in eighteen."

"Flesh out Josh's story if you can. We moved it to A1. It's a slow news day."

"Will do," she said.

Back at her desk, Stella flipped through her notebook and added a few lame quotes from the press conference to Josh's story. When she was done, she gave the story a quick read. It was a nothing story. Nothing about nothing. Incredibly frustrating.

The cops barely even acknowledged there was a crime: A body was found in a warehouse near the waterfront, blah, blah, blah. Police revealed few details about the crime but said they were investigating it as a homicide. They had no leads. An adult male. Yada yada.

So lame, she thought.

The story she really wanted to cover was the possible corrupt oil company merger. She'd start on it right after this story was filed.

After adding in details from the press conference, she was about to send it to the edit file when she thought of one more way to beef it up for the front page. She'd need help. Glancing at her watch, she saw it was only ten. *Not too late to call a fellow reporter, right? And*

43

plus, his kid's play must be over by now. Didn't kids go to bed at eight or something?

She'd give Josh a byline. When she'd first started out as a reporter, she'd wanted—maybe needed—all the glory. Those days were long gone. She no longer needed the ego strokes. Nowadays, she just wanted to write the best story she could.

And tonight, that meant hitting up a colleague.

She dialed Josh's number.

"Yo." He sounded sleepy, but too bad.

"It's Collins," she said.

"What's up?" He was speaking in a low voice.

"I went to the presser for the homicide, but it was a bunch of nothing. I'm wondering if we can add any crime scene details into your story. Garcia wants to put it on A1. Maybe just some scene setting stuff. I'd go out there, but we've got ten minutes to file."

"I don't have any color."

"Come on," Stella said. "Give me something. Talk it through with me. What did you see when you got there? Tell me like you would your wife."

"You're joking, right?" he said. "You think I talk about any of this? And even if I did, I would never talk to her about what I saw today."

"Bad, huh?"

"You know what, Collins? You know what I saw? Something I shouldn't have."

She heard a woman's voice in the background saying something.

"I got there early. I got a tip from a source. I beat the homicide detectives. I know the two beat cops who were on duty. Crooked as hell. They were making jokes about the victim. Saying some crude things. I gave them a G-spot to let me go look at the body."

He paused, and Stella heard him inhale sharply. Stella sat back in her chair impressed and took another swig of her coffee, savoring the black sludge. Maybe being a daddy hadn't ruined Josh's reporting skills.

"And?"

"Dude's head was blown clear off. The bottom half of his face was missing. Just gone." Josh's voice wobbled. "I wish I'd never been there. I can't get that out of my head. I'm laying here in bed and that's all I can see."

Stella tried to muster up some sympathy for what he'd witnessed. After her stint overseas, she was much more hardened about gruesome crime scenes. Not everybody was, though.

"Can you at least describe what you saw?" she probed.

"You're kidding, right?"

"No,"

"I saw a dude with his head blown off! And then I didn't see anything after that because I ran out of there, puked my brains out, and then got in my car and drove home."

"Okay," she said. There was a pause.

"You're probably judging me because I puked," he said. His voice wasn't angry or confrontational. It was more resigned. A little sad even.

"Maybe you're used to seeing dead bodies," he continued. "But I'm not. And I don't ever want to be used to it. Do you think that makes you a better reporter than me?"

Stella was quiet for a few seconds and then said in a low tone, "No. No, I don't think that at all." She hung up the phone before he could respond.

Stella didn't think she was any better than anyone. No, what she'd thought was that she was a total mess. Slightly less of a mess than she was a year ago, but still a disaster.

8

BRILLIANT SUNLIGHT FLOODED THE WHITE WALLS AND bounced off the smooth wood floors. There were no blinds, and it was just the way he wanted. The room he'd rented in the residential hotel was nearly empty. Lately he'd found that too many colors, shapes, and objects made him feel unsettled and restless, and even a little crazed.

So, his room was bare except for a thick stack of disassembled cardboard boxes that he used as a makeshift bed. One wall was lined with jugs of purified water. A black college footlocker with a lock held his assortment of weapons—knives, grenades, pistols, assault rifles, ammo, brass knuckles. The small closet held his spare outfit, identical to the one he wore every day. A pair of black cargo pants, a black long-sleeve t-shirt, and a lined jacket. It also contained a few spare pairs of white briefs and socks. A black back-pack hung on a hook inside.

Now waking from the morning sunlight as he wanted so he would be in tune with his circadian rhythm, he was in desperate need of the bathroom. But in this residential hotel, the closest bathroom was outside his room and down the hall. The pressure on his bladder was intense. After all, he'd drunk twenty-four ounces of water from one of the jugs last night before bed. Acknowledging the pressure meant a simple awareness of the discomfort.

He relished it. It was part of his daily discipline practice. He controlled his body; it did not control him. Pain, being uncomfortable, and unease were all part of what made him as powerful as he was. No longer was he driven by desires of the flesh: lust, hunger, and thirst. They had controlled him for far too long. Now he had utter and complete control of his own body and mind.

Instead of leaping from his bed, he forced himself to sit there and meditate while he was still prone. His mind dropped into his physical body and scanned it, starting from the top of his scalp and moving slowly down until he reached the soles of his feet.

He practiced moving a ball of white-hot heat across his body until he was certain he could feel it nearly burn him. Then he drew himself up to sitting with his legs crisscrossed as he once again imagined the next kill in utter, excruciating detail.

Down to the feeling of hot blood splattering on his face.

This is what Olympic athletes did. They imagined every lap in the pool, every launch of the javelin, every stroke of the ski poles. Like them, he was also the best of the best. It's just that his accomplishments needed to remain underground.

After doing a series of stretches and yoga poses, he stood, pushing himself off the small stack of cardboard boxes. Neatly folding the scratchy wool blanket, he placed it precisely on the corner of the bed. Stepping into his pants, kept neatly folded by his bed, he pulled the footlocker over to him and spun its lock.

Inside was a beat-up shoebox. It was where he kept all the details for his ops—pictures, printed documents that provided details the average person would never know. He studied each target until he knew them as well as a close friend. Right now, the box contained pictures and documents pertaining to the individual Headway team members. He studied them one by one yet one more time. He had already put a large red X through the one of Mark Bellamy.

Now, he flipped through the rest, pausing on two of them—the two women—Jordan and Stella. First, he looked at Jordan. A full body shot. Her short spiky blonde hair showed off her cut-glass cheekbones and Slavic slanted ice blue eyes. She wore a tank top with small shorts and tennis shoes. It looked like she'd been caught just coming back from a run. The outfit displayed her toned body and the well-defined muscles in her legs and arms. Her long and lean physique was a deadly weapon.

The only anomaly to the team, she hadn't been a SEAL. She was a former Army Ranger. One of the first—and undoubtedly the best —to graduate from the elite training. From there, she had honed her skills as an assassin until they were nearly unparalleled. He figured that was why she'd been brought into the mostly former SEAL group.

His only chance at defeating her would be if he had the element of surprise on his side. That's why he had to act fast. If she received word of Bellamy's murder and prepared for his visit, it would be a battle to the death. That's why he would leave today. That's why she had to be next on the list.

He tucked her photo into his back pocket. But before putting Stella's photo away, he stared at it for a long time. Her photo was different. Instead of capturing her in action like Jordan's, this picture was like a mug shot. Stella stared defiantly into the camera. Eyebrows arched, her black eyes glared, wild and dangerous and deadly. Her dark hair was pulled tightly back away from her face, lips full and naturally pink.

Unlike Jordan, Stella was curvy but also strong and fit. He stared at her curves.

No. No. No.

He no longer acknowledged cravings of the flesh, though it didn't mean it was always easy. Hand shaking, he put the photos back into the box in the order they had been in when he first retrieved them. He then locked the footlocker and finally headed to the floor's shared toilet to relieve himself.

Stepping out of his room and, making sure he had the key, he pulled the door closed behind him. He heard the lock engage. Halfway down the hall a door opened. It was that crazy hooker with the curly hair. At one point he'd have wanted to explore her body, but now he had evolved past that.

Now, the only lust he had was blood lust. No longer did he crave seeing a woman's pleasure. He would gain more pleasure from seeing her pain.

She had a human cage inside her room. He'd seen it once when her door was open. He'd entertained thoughts of her inside that cage but knew there was no time for that until his mission was complete.

"Oh!" she said when she saw him approaching in the hall. She was wearing a short nightgown that left little to the imagination. As he passed, eyeing her openly, she posed in the doorway with one arm reaching above her and smiled. "Looks like you beat me to the bathroom."

Grunting instead of answering, he kept walking. She scowled. Maybe he had time for her before his mission. Maybe she would be the appetizer.

9

STEPPING OUT INTO THE NIGHT, STELLA LOOKED UP AT THE velvet navy sky. It was dotted with silver stars. Because San Francisco was so often shrouded in fog or a glowing orange cloud cover that reflected the city lights, she didn't get to see the stars as often as she liked.

For a few seconds, she took in the beauty of the night. In the distance, she heard music and laughter from a strip of popular restaurants some blocks away. She loved how the city was so vibrant and alive. Her new life here didn't involve much socializing, but she never felt alone or lonely.

She'd had such mixed feelings about running home to San Francisco, like a dog with its tail between its legs, but being here felt right. Stella was less haunted by her dark memories when she was back here, enveloped in the comfort of her hometown. The nightmares still came, but she figured they always would. Long and torturous dreams about being trapped in tunnels that closed in upon her as dismembered bodies chased her.

Now, in the night, she shook off those thoughts. Out in the fresh air the dog stayed right beside her as she walked him over to a small patch of grass across the street from her building. After he urinated, he looked up at her and whined.

"Okay, buddy, we'll go home now."

High above her and across the street, the floor with the news-room glowed with its lights. She'd left Garcia there, finishing up some editing. The guy worked too hard. He was a great boss and a great editor. It was good to be reporting again.

After the adrenaline rush of the past ten years, the stories she'd had her first week at the *Tribune* had been boring as hell, but maybe that's what she needed right now. Anything to keep her out of the neighborhood bars. It gave her life some purpose. Helped her to focus on something else besides her dark memories. It was healthier than the way she'd been dealing with her past—drinking herself into oblivion. But hey, it was Friday night, and nothing was stopping her from drinking tonight.

For a second, Stella felt a tiny bit of joy. But it disappeared as she remembered she had no right to be happy. Her face flushed with anger. Happiness was for other people. People who lived in a fairy tale. People who hadn't been touched by tragedy.

"Come on," she said a little too sharply to the dog as she started toward her car and instantly felt guilty. Reaching down, she scratched him behind the ears. Stella had just slid into the driver's seat when her cell phone dinged.

She glanced at the time, 11:10 p.m. Couldn't say the detective wasn't punctual.

The message read, "Reno Room?"

She'd forgotten about him, but now his text was a welcome diversion. She gave the message a thumbs up reaction before starting her car. The bar he'd suggested was walking distance from her new place, which was perfect. She could settle the dog into her apartment before beginning their drinking session.

But the dog had other ideas. He eagerly followed her out of the car when she parked and was right on her heels all the way up the stairs to her fourth-floor walkup. He burst through the door of her apartment the minute she unlocked it. She flicked on the lights. The dog had immediately jumped on her couch and curled into a ball. This was going to be easier than she thought.

Stella took out a bowl and filled it with water before placing it on the floor in the kitchen. Then, she found another bowl and put in some leftover rice and peas. Stella peered into the living room. The dog hadn't budged.

"Hey there," she said. "I've got food for you." He looked up at her with his head resting on his paws and his tail wagging but didn't move.

In her bathroom, Stella yanked off her black tee-shirt and pulled on a scoop neck top. She swiped on some red lipstick, yanked her long dark hair out of its ponytail, and brushed it with her fingers. It felt a little greasy, but it would have to do.

"You and me both need our hair washed," she told the dog.

When she opened the front door to leave, the dog was at her heels. She tried to sneak out the door, but he managed to squeeze himself through the narrow opening and into the hall with her. It had already been forty-five minutes since the detective had texted her. Any longer and she wouldn't blame him for bailing.

After two more attempts to get out the door without the dog, she put it in the bathroom and closed the door. As soon as her apartment door closed, she realized that wouldn't work. The dog began barking and howling.

"No!" she said, unlocking the door and running back toward the bathroom. Last thing she needed was to get evicted for having a dog.

Exasperated and tired, she grabbed her phone and dialed. As soon as the detective picked up, she blurted out, "Any chance they let dogs in there?"

She heard the noises of a crowded bar and a few seconds later. "Just asked. No chance."

"Damn. I really need a drink, but I got this problem."

"Problem?"

"It's a dog."

"Oh." After a pause, he said, "How about I bring the drinks to you?"

Which is exactly what Stella had been leading him to say, but she still thought it was fair warning to tell him where she got the dog.

"So, one thing you should know. This problem I mentioned? He might have ticks and fleas."

Silence.

"And rabies."

"Oh, yeah?"

"Yup. The vet doesn't open until morning, so I really don't know."

The detective laughed.

"I'll take my chances. Text me your address and your drink of choice." He hung up.

Bulleit on the rocks, she typed along with her address.

See you in fifteen.

Stella lit half a dozen exotic smelling candles and then unearthed her laptop to get online to find out more about the homeless guy and homicide victim. No other news outlets had posted anything more than she had. She'd have to wait for the cops or the morgue to identify the two men before she could find out more. Or she could go to the warehouse on Monday morning. The homeless guy was clearly welcome at that spot since it was behind a locked gate and on private property. That might be a story in itself.

By the time she buzzed the detective in, she was yawning. What else was new. She slept nine hours each night but was constantly exhausted from the nightmares that kept her tossing and turning all night long.

When she opened the door, she saw Griffin had a bag of ice and an unopened bottle of Bulleit.

There was a sexy smirk on his face. His eyes under their dark brows took her in slowly. She didn't mind. In fact, she liked it.

She smiled.

"Come in."

As soon as he stepped inside, there was a low growl.

"Your problem?" he asked.

"He was. But he's not anymore."

The dog had taken over the couch again and stood up as Griffin passed to go to the kitchen. He began to bark loudly, his hackles rising.

"Damn," Stella said. "I'll take care of him."

She went over and petted him, and he calmed down some. She didn't know if it was because she soothed him or because Griffin was now out of his sight. She heard the detective in the kitchen humming a little song and opening and shutting cupboards and the sound of ice plinking into crystal as he made their drinks.

When Griffin poked his head back into the living room with two tumblers of the bourbon on ice, the dog went nuts again.

Griffin looked at her. Well, it was too late to be coy, she thought. That ship had sailed last year when she first met him.

"Go back in the kitchen, take the first right and close the door," she told him. "I'll be right there."

He disappeared.

"Now you stay here," Stella said as the dog settled back in, tucking his nose under his back leg as he curled up into a tight ball. She gave the dog one more look as she headed into the kitchen. It looked up and thumped its tail. Grabbing the bottle of bourbon, she headed into the bedroom.

10

As soon as he walked into the house, Alec Walker had disappeared up the wide staircase leading to the bedroom area of the home, leaving Rory standing there with the suitcase.

"Hello?" he'd called out, glancing around.

He was starting to get used to the opulence of the Walker house. The foyer had a black marble floor, glittering chandelier, a plush upholstered bench for removing shoes during the winter, and walls filled with oil paintings. The other rooms were equally intimidating, with matching wallpaper, dark antique furniture, and accompanying tall ceilings.

He wasn't going to leave the foyer until the family knew he was there. Rory most certainly wasn't going to follow Alec Walker upstairs.

"Darling, is that you?" Margaret Walker appeared at the other end of the long foyer. She was dressed for dinner in a dark silky dress and heels. The Walkers always dressed for dinner. Her face lit up when she saw him. "Rory! Thank you so much for fetching my darling husband from the airport!"

Walking over, she squeezed Rory's hands.

"Thank you for having me to dinner," he said. "These are for you."

He thrust the flowers at her.

"For me?"

Suddenly flustered, he wondered if he should have bought two bouquets—one for Isabel and one for her mother.

Had he mis-stepped?

Just then Isabel came bounding down the stairs. Unlike her mother, she wore jeans and a silk shirt. Smiling, she ran up to him and hugged him.

"You brought my mom flowers?" she exclaimed. "You're the sweetest."

Relief filled him.

"I'll let you two catch up while I go check on your father," Margaret Walker said and headed toward the stairs. "Leave the suit-case for Bruce. He can bring it up later."

Of course he would.

As soon as he thought it, Rory forgot about Bruce because Isabel was in front of him.

"I missed you," she said, looking up at him.

"Same," he said and smiled.

It had only been two days, but he'd missed her, too.

Rory had been smitten from the first second he'd laid eyes on Isabel. And the more he came to know her, the more he fell for her. Now, she was his whole world. Isabel was shy and sweet and wicked smart. Easily the prettiest girl he'd ever seen, she was the whole package. With light brown hair that fell in waves to the small of her back, she was tiny and had the biggest blue eyes he'd ever seen. Her voice was soft, and she always smelled like candy.

They had been at a wedding of mutual friends. He had been friends with the groom in college, she had been friends with the bride. It had been a destination wedding and over the course of a long weekend in Aspen, they had fallen in love.

It was only later when they talked about continuing their

romance when they returned to Washington, D.C., that she had told him who her powerful father was. Rory wasn't intimidated. He'd worked as a congressional aide for the past two years. He knew who Alec Walker was. Kind of a blowhard, but also a man who got things done. He had a certain respect for the man.

Because he thought he knew him, Rory wasn't as intimidated as he should've been when Isabel asked him over for dinner to meet her family. That first time, he'd felt a little nervous pulling up to the palatial estate and being greeted by a valet and then a butler at the front door.

Walker had been waiting in his study and the butler directed him there. The two men had a good chat over cigars and that's when Walker had offered him the job as his aide.

"My man just left, you see," Walker had said. "And the reports on you come back satisfactory. I think this will give us a chance to get to know one another."

Rory had opened his mouth to protest when Walker continued.

"You're about to tell me that you have a job. Well, don't worry, I talked to Senator Kellogg, and she understands. She said you can start with me on Monday."

Anger rose up in Rory. He stubbed out his cigar and stood, ready to storm out. But just before he reached the door, Isabel opened it.

"Hi," she said with a shy smile. "Daddy, you've been keeping Rory all to yourself. Did you tell him about the job?"

There was a moment of silence.

She raised an eyebrow. "Did he tell you?" Her face looked so concerned.

He smiled. "Yes," he finally said. "It's a great opportunity."

They sat down in a formal dining room and Rory was introduced to Mrs. Walker. She was as sweet as her daughter. They even looked alike except she had red hair while Isabel had light brown. She immediately hugged Rory when they were introduced.

"I'm a hugger," she had said. "Call me Margaret."

That would never happen. His girlfriend's mother would always be Mrs. Walker.

As they sat down in front of empty place settings, Alec Walker pressed a small button that was positioned on the table near his right hand. Some swinging doors flew open, and a parade of three people came in bearing platters of food, as if they had been waiting on the other side of the door for their cue.

"This is Bruce," Walker said. "He's my manservant. If you ever need to reach me at home, you can call Bruce directly. I will give you his number."

The older, pudgy man in the crisp white shirt gave a wan smile and said formally, "Nice to meet you."

"Likewise," Rory said. *Who has a manservant? And what exactly is a manservant, anyway?*

Now, two years later, Rory and Bruce didn't acknowledge each other in any way. Isabel had said it was because Bruce was jealous of him. Her father now relied more on Rory.

"I think Bruce might be in love with your dad," Rory had once joked.

She shrugged. "Bruce has been with us since I was born."

End of conversation. Now, Bruce was stiff as he set a plate with a serving of roast beef, mashed potatoes, and green beans before Rory.

"How was your flight?" Mrs. Walker asked.

"Awful," Walker said. "I need to fire that jet service. This is the second time I've used them, and both times we had terrible turbulence."

"Daddy," Isabel said, always the diplomat. "The weather was terrible. I bet they did everything they could, but sometimes you can't avoid it."

Giving her a dismissive smile, he said, "Sure, they could've."

When she looked down, anger filled Rory. He would never talk to her that way when she was his wife, and he would never talk that way to their daughter. Walker was an arrogant jerk sometimes.

Her mother noticed Isabel's mood shift and said, "I heard back from the stationers. They will have the prototype for your wedding invitations on Friday."

Isabel looked at Rory. "Do you want to come over and see them?"

"Of course," he said. He couldn't care less about invitations, catering, flowers, etc., but he did want her to be happy, so he was really trying.

After dinner, as they usually did, Walker invited Rory to have a cigar with him in his study.

"The meeting went well?" Walker said as he took a puff of his cigar and then examined the cherry.

Rory froze. It seemed like a loaded question. *Went well? No clue.*

"I guess so. I don't really understand what they were talking about."

He figured that would be the safest route to take. By the smug look on Walker's face, Rory knew he'd given the right answer.

"Some people screwed up. Now they want me to try to fix it."

For some reason, Rory got the feeling his future father-in-law was lying.

11

THIS TIME, TO MAKE SURE HE ACTUALLY LEFT, STELLA walked the detective to the door. She'd just given him the talk. They could have nights like this, but as soon as he wanted something more serious, it was over.

Surprisingly, he'd agreed.

Wrapped in a sheet from her bed, she led him to the door.

As they walked past the dog on the couch, he growled, but stayed laying down, eyes trained on Griffin.

After opening her door, she looked up at the detective.

"You're okay with this arrangement?" she asked, double check-ing. "I can call you up to handle stuff like this?"

"Stuff like this?"

When she didn't smile back, he said, "Yeah. That'll work for me."

"Good," she'd said. "Time to go."

The detective paused in the hall before she could shut the door.

Stella stopped herself from rolling her eyes but tapped her foot impatiently.

"You know, last time I was here..." he began.

"Yes?"

"You were having some pretty messed up dreams."

Stella's breath caught in her throat, and she fought to keep her voice neutral. "Oh yeah?"

"You were moaning and talking in your sleep."

Her heart was pounding so hard she could feel it throbbing in her neck. She stared, waiting for him to finish.

"You kept saying 'Where are they?' You seemed pretty upset."

Searching his eyes, she waited for a beat. He looked as if he were about to say something but didn't. She wasn't going to give him any explanation. Stella LaRosa did not explain herself or her life to anyone.

"Thanks for the bourbon," she said and closed the door.

It looked like he'd been about to say something, but she locked the door and went to bed.

When she woke eight hours later, the sun was out, and the dog was curled up at the foot of her bed. He began wagging his tail at lightning speed when he saw her eyes open.

"Poor baby," she said. "I bet you have to go to the bathroom."

Stella pulled her hair up in a messy bun, threw on some leggings and a hoodie, then slipped on her glasses since she didn't want to waste time putting in contacts. The dog was whining and waiting at the door.

"You're so smart," she said and looked around. She didn't have anything resembling a leash.

He'd stayed by her side last night, but it had been late and there hadn't been any cars or people around. Stella lived on a busy street and didn't want him to rush out into traffic or scare people walking by.

The dog did have a dirty collar. That was half the battle. She scanned her apartment and her eyes fell on a long fabric tie she used to hold back the curtains on one window. She looped it through the dog's collar and headed out.

Outside, the dog peed the second they hit the sidewalk. A woman walking by made a face.

"Sorry, he really had to go," Stella said and shrugged. After he did number two, she realized she didn't have anything to pick it up with. She bought one of her own newspapers from a news rack and used that to scoop up the poop before heading back inside.

That afternoon she walked into the newsroom for her shift with the dog on a leash. He'd been vaccinated, washed, and treated for fleas, ticks, heartworms, and other parasites. Stella felt accomplished.

"Hey!" Garcia said. "Last night was an emergency. You can't have this dog in the newsroom again."

"I have to," Stella said. "If he barks, I'll get evicted."

"Get it out of here. Now. I'm done being the cool editor."

"You were the cool editor?"

"Haha. Now get out!"

"Fine."

Turning on her heel, the dog followed, giving a woeful look back at Garcia.

"Don't worry," she said loudly. "We know when we're not wanted."

Garcia rolled his eyes.

As she was walking to the elevator, a woman she didn't recognize ran after her. The woman had on a knit sweater and huge glasses. She furtively glanced back at the editor's desk and then said in a low voice. "You can have your dog if he's an emotional support animal."

The woman scurried away.

Stella smiled.

Two hours later, she walked in again with the dog. Right as Garcia was about to blow his top, she slammed a letter down on his desk.

"What the hell is this?"

He skimmed it and scowled.

"Enjoy taking that mutt on every assignment."

"I will."

But as soon as Stella said that she frowned. Was he actually her dog, now? That hadn't been the plan.

"Speaking of assignments, I need you to take over that warehouse homicide. Josh was just called off it."

"Why?"

"It came down from the big boss. No clue."

Stella nodded and headed straight to her desk. The dog followed and curled up under her desk at her feet. She'd have to buy a dog bed. Then she realized she was being foolish. How could she own a dog when she couldn't even take care of herself? And it just wouldn't be fair to keep a dog when she had such a crazy schedule at work. Despite her retort to Garcia, he was right. She couldn't take a dog out to crime scenes. Half the time he'd be stuck waiting in her car. It wouldn't be fair to him. Besides, everything she loved died she thought, and her throat began to close up.

At the same time, there was no way in hell she was going to give this dog up unless it was to someone who would love him like he deserved.

Distracting herself, she picked up her phone and dialed Josh's number. She could see his head across the newsroom. It looked like he was typing away furiously. She saw him pause and pick up the phone.

"Why was I given the story?"

"Good question," he said. "It wasn't because I puked, I can tell you that."

"Who made this decision? What big boss?"

"I think it was the publisher or the rep who deigned to speak to us on the publisher's behalf."

"What did he say?"

"She," he said, emphasizing the word, "said she wanted me to cover this quadruple homicide court case because our intern was going back to school."

"That sounds legit."

"It's not. I just talked to the intern. She wasn't planning on going back to school. The publisher *actually* told her that they'd run out of the funding for the internship program early."

"Is that true?" Stella asked.

"I'm digging into it."

"Are you saying we're really investigating our own publisher?"

"Publisher is a generous name. Hedge fund manager would be more appropriate."

Stella bit her lip. Very interesting. "Keep me posted."

"You bet."

Dude had softened up since she made it clear that she didn't think she was too good for him the other night. Good. Stella had enough enemies in the newsroom. All those snarky women from the gym and then Marilyn, the snooty reporter who wanted to make Stella her bitch.

As soon as she hung up, her phone rang, it was Garcia. He was standing up looking at her across the newsroom as he spoke, holding a big bowl of popcorn. Stella could smell the buttery scent and her mouth watered.

"The publisher got a tip that the homicide was a suicide, so I'm calling you off the story for now," he said between bites.

Stella didn't answer.

"Collins?"

"Yeah?"

"You're off the story. You can start digging around on that oil story if you want but run everything you find by me."

She hung up without answering.

For a few seconds she stared at her blank computer screen.

Suicide, huh? How would the publisher know this first? And why was the publisher so interested in micromanaging this story?

She dialed Griffin.

"I was told to back off the warehouse homicide," she said as soon as he answered.

"Is this Stella?"

She was put out, and it was clear in her voice. "Um, yeah. Do other female reporters have your number?"

"Sorry. I'm a little distracted. But I can't tell you anything."

"Can you at least confirm it's a suicide?"

"What?" he sounded surprised. "No. It's not. I just sat through the autopsy."

"Why is my publisher calling me off the story and telling me it's a suicide?"

She heard some voices, and then he mumbled. "Call you back."

Slamming down her phone, and keeping eye contact with Garcia, she headed toward his desk.

"We need to talk."

"Okay?"

"Not here."

There was a whining sound. The dog had followed her, she leaned down and grabbed the leash.

"The dog needs to pee. Come with me."

Glancing around for a second, Garcia shrugged and then nodded.

"Does the dog have a name?" he asked in the elevator.

"No."

"Why not?"

Stella didn't answer, just frowned.

Outside, as the dog sniffed around, Stella came out with it.

"I think the new publisher needs to back off. I just got off the phone with a source who said it's not a suicide. Why would I be called off this story?"

Stella expected to have to argue her case, but instead Garcia paused and looked off into the distance. There was some sort of fundraiser race or something, because about fifty people with paper bibs ran past on the other end of the street.

The dog sat at their feet, looking up at them expectantly.

When Garcia didn't answer for a few seconds, Stella said, "So? Why? It's a good story. It's not a suicide."

"I really don't know," he said. "This whole being owned by a hedge fund stuff is new to me. I'm used to publishers who have integrity and who would never interfere in news coverage, but it might be a new world. I've had my head down doing the job of three editors since they took over a few months ago. I can't believe I didn't see it."

"What do we do?"

He frowned. "I'm not sure. I don't like it, but I also know that they are looking to get rid of people who don't share the same so-called vision as them."

"So you're just going to throw out all your ethics to keep your job? And not fight for your reporters or the news, hell, let's just call it what it is–the truth?"

"I didn't say that."

Stella didn't like that answer. But then she thought about the pictures she'd seen on Garcia's desk. He had a wife and two little kids, and he'd mentioned his wife was pregnant with another child due soon.

"Fine, I'll back off that story, but only if you let me go after the oil story."

"I think that's more of a national news story. Possibly international? I mean we really specialize in local news here, Collins. I know you're used to going after the big fish, but that's not our wheelhouse."

"Drop the jargon Garcia and let me win you a Pulitzer. Come on. There's a huge story here that nobody is going after."

"Because they're afraid."

"But I'm not," she said and looked down. The dog had decided to poop right then and there. On the sidewalk. Stella ignored it for a second.

Garcia made a face.

"It's just poop," she said and crouched down to pick it up with a bag. She'd bought a little dog-bone shaped poop bag holder that attached to the leash.

Shaking his head, still looking at the sidewalk, he said, "You should be afraid."

"The other papers are going after the monopoly angle, how the mergers of these two companies will create the sixth largest economy in the world," she said. "But nobody is even questioning how this unknown Texas billionaire got the rights to that newly discovered oil field, right?"

"The story is he had some overseas connection because of his wife. She's Persian."

"Nah. That's not it. Her family are merchants, not oil barons."

"How do you know? Nobody can find any information on her. I just read about that this weekend."

"I know."

He looked at her and frowned.

"What are you trying to say?"

"I think it's an inside job. I think that someone in the government arranged for him to get the rights, and that whoever that person is, they are going to get paid a lot of money to see this deal go through."

Garcia sighed, throwing his hands in the air. "Fine. Go digging."

"I'm on it."

She was already walking down the street toward her car when he called her name.

"Collins?"

"Yeah?"

"Just don't get us killed."

12

DANVILLE

Stella pulled up to the brightly lit home with mixed feelings. She put her car into park, rolled down the window, and turned off the ignition, keeping her eyes on the house. But she stayed in the car.

The two-story brick structure in San Francisco's East Bay had been home for as long as she could remember. Even though she spent every free second in the city itself and considered that her hometown, the reality was that her childhood was spent in the East Bay. Her parents had even kept her bedroom the same way as it had been when she was a teenager and gone off to live in the city for college.

Reaching into her glove box, she extracted a pack of old cigarettes. Usually, she didn't smoke, but today she needed something to tamp down her nerves. Sunday dinners, once the highlight of her week while she was growing up, had become tricky. Most of the time, instead of enjoying her family's company, she felt like she was navigating a minefield.

It had begun when she returned from overseas a year ago. The first Sunday dinner after she was back, she'd learned that her Uncle Dominic had started having dinner with her parents and siblings after Aunt Coral died. And not only that, he brought his sons, her cousins, Alfredo and Giacomo—Al and Jack.

Stella never liked the two. They'd picked on her since she was little, grabbing and throwing her in the pool if she even walked by them on the patio. Taunting her during cousin hide-and-seek sessions. Scaring her by killing small animals, stuffing them, and then leaving them in her bed. Then, they were only assholes. Now they were dangerous assholes.

Thinking about them, she must've been giving off angry vibes, because the dog in the passenger seat began to whine. Exhaling out the window, she absentmindedly stroked his fur. The breeze brought the smoke back in the car with the slight fragrance of lilacs from the hedges that lined her parent's driveway.

That's when she noticed that the driveway, while filled with cars, didn't hold Dominic's Cadillac. Craning her neck, she saw that Al and Jack's stupid testosterone-fueled cars weren't there, either.

A smile spread across her face.

Now she could enjoy her night without fending off her uncle. He liked to corner her at family dinners and ask what it would take for her to come work for him. Money was not an object he had said.

That had been part of the reason she'd fled the country to go report overseas. He had begun to pressure her at her college graduation party, saying that it was her obligation to the family to help out.

The worst part of all was that her parents wouldn't defend her. Her dad became a little mouse and her mother just laughed. Her big brother could do no wrong. Her mother told Stella that Dominic only wanted to help and provide her with the sort of life she deserved. One with a big house, fancy car and designer clothes.

"I don't want any of that," the twenty-two-year-old Stella had said. "I want to change the world. That's why I studied journalism."

"Oh honey, it's time to grow up. There's no changing anything," her mother had said. "Just enjoy the benefits of being born into this family."

"Benefits?" Stella had raged. She'd seen red the rest of the night and only later had been told what she'd done and said. Screaming about her poor deceased relatives—Uncle Joe and Aunt Kathy—knocking over a bookshelf in the living room, punching and kicking holes in the wall before her brothers and father had restrained her.

They carried her into her room and locked the door. By the time they woke the next morning, she'd already crawled out the second-story bedroom window and hopped on a plane to Paris. Her old journalism professor had been there waiting with the job he'd offered a few months before.

Now, a decade later, her uncle had started in on her again. The first Sunday dinner she'd been back, he'd cornered her and told her the family could really use a journalist with her connections. She could keep her job and still be on the family payroll.

The first time, she'd politely refused. The last time, she'd told him what he could go do to himself.

He'd grabbed her arm, but before she could kick him in the nuts he'd leaned in and whispered. "You treat me with respect, or maybe the newspaper gets a little tip about what your last name really is. Lying on an application could probably get you fired."

Glaring at him, she'd yanked her arm out of his grip.

"Might be worth getting fired," she'd said with gritted teeth and stalked away.

Now, sitting in the driveway she realized she'd been stressed for days about seeing him again. She shouldn't have to be anxious about visiting her parents. Something was going to have to change.

Grabbing the box of cannoli she'd bought in North Beach, she went around to the passenger door and let the dog out. He happily trotted behind her as she made her way to the front door.

Her mother threw open the door before Stella could ring the bell. As often happened after a few days apart, Stella was struck once again by how green her mother's eyes were. Was the woman even Italian? Now those green eyes were dangerously narrowed.

"Stella!" her mother hissed in a whisper. "What were you doing in the car?"

"Sorry, Ma," she said. "I just was—"

"Who is this?" her mother interrupted and stooped to pet the dog who was wiggling madly.

"Isn't he sweet?" Stella said, grateful for the distraction from her mother's question.

Stella looked at her mother, crouched on the ground. The woman was less than five feet tall and still had the same figure she'd had as a high school cheerleader. Besides a few lovely smile lines around her eyes, her mother didn't seem to have aged a bit. She wore stylish sneakers, black Lululemon athletic leggings, and a form-fitting athletic top in fuchsia. Her bleached blonde hair was pulled back in a neat ponytail.

"Mom, you're adorable."

"Oh honey, that's you!" her mother said, but her beaming smile told Stella she was flattered.

The dog was wriggling around, his paws sliding on the slick Italian tile floors. Her father came around the corner with a big smile. He was showing his age a bit more, a little thicker around the middle, but still tall and strong. He wore his black hair short but not too short and had a little goatee that Stella thought was cute and made him look a little like an Italian Javier Bardem.

"Stella! Get over here!"

Feeling like a little kid, Stella ran over and hugged her dad.

He squeezed her and then drew back. "I'm grateful every day that you are back here where you belong."

"Thanks, Dad."

He gave her a look. "I'm serious. Your nana—god bless her— said the rosary every day you were off covering the wars."

"I know, Daddy. Nana was the best."

Stella was grateful she'd returned home before her grandmother died. She would've been heartbroken to miss the funeral. Then her dad frowned. He was looking over her shoulder.

"You got a dog?" he asked.

"Not really."

"Isn't she a sweetheart?" her mother cooed.

"It's a he," Stella said.

"I love him," her mother said, hugging the dog and petting him. Standing up, she gave a small whistle. "I bet he's hungry after the drive. Come on baby, I'll find you something to eat."

Stella laughed as her mom disappeared into the kitchen. She'd known exactly how this was going to go down. Her mother was the biggest animal lover Stella knew, but her father had finally told her no more pets after the last dog died a few years ago.

"How are we going to travel with a dog when we retire?" he'd said.

But Stella knew he'd never retire. Uncle Dominic wouldn't let him. In her family, you were in it until the end. Look at the older uncles. They were in the family business until they died. It was the way it was. Her father was the youngest of the brothers. He would never get out.

After Stella helped her mother bring in a big bowl of leafy green salad, a dish of warm green beans with garlic slices, pasta with red sauce and a plate of fragrant meatballs and sausages, Stella poured everyone some of the wine she'd brought.

"You already brought the cannoli, you didn't need to bring wine, too!" her mother protested, but Stella could see she was pleased.

"Where is everybody?" Stella asked, spearing an Italian sausage off the platter and adding it to her shallow pasta bowl of spaghetti.

"Your brother Christopher is in New York closing some big deal with your uncle and cousins. Laura is watching your cousin Jamie's baby so she can go on a date."

"She's still with that low life?"

"Stella! He's the father of her child!"

"Big deal. He's also a waste of air."

"Stella! He might become part of the family! Watch what you say."

"Heaven help us," Stella said under her breath and speared a forkful of the pasta. "What are they doing out there, anyway?"

"Importing something that is going to set his family up for life, Christopher said."

"Ha," Stella said. "Importing. Sure."

"What does that mean?" her father asked her in a sharp tone as he twirled the spaghetti on his fork and shoved it in his mouth.

"Whatever. I don't want to talk about it."

"And your brother Michael and his family are in Florida visiting his in-laws. I don't know how they can live there. It's so muggy."

"I know, Ma."

"I like the dry heat," she said. "Who wants to walk outside and be soaking wet? Ridiculous. And the bugs!"

"Good thing you live in California," Stella said. She'd learned a long time ago to just agree with whatever her mother said. She broke off a piece of the warm bread and dipped it into some red sauce. "What do we import anyway, Dad?"

She narrowed her eyes.

"Stella." His voice held a warning.

"I was wondering if you could watch the dog for a few days," she said brightly and smiled at him.

"For crying out loud! We don't have any room for another stray in this house."

"We got plenty of room," her mother said. "This whole house is empty. I'm here alone every day and every night. I need a dog. And that's it."

"Baloney!" her father threw down his napkin. "The last thing we need is a dog."

"Then retire and let's travel like you've been promising me."

"Celeste, you know my brother doesn't want me to retire."

"I'll talk to Carmen about it," she said. "You know it's the wives who really control everything," winking at Stella.

"Is it?" Stella said and shook her head.

He rolled his eyes. "I put my foot down on this one, Celeste. No dogs."

"Okay, fine." Her mother said this distractedly because she was leaning down, giving the dog little pieces of Italian sausage.

"You're such a good baby, such a good boy," she cooed. "Maybe we could just make you our grandbaby since your mama isn't going to give us any."

"Ma!" Stella wailed.

"Well, am I right?"

"Stop it right now."

"Your dad says we can't have a dog right now, but maybe we can have sleepovers. Because he is such a sweetie."

"Since when does dad tell you what to do?" Stella said as she began stacking the empty dishes.

"Estella Sofia LaRosa! Have some respect."

Her dad topped off her wine glass and then his own. "Celeste, I'm going to borrow Stella for a minute in the backyard. Business."

Her mother's eyes narrowed. "Business?"

Stella shrugged. But as they walked toward the back door, her mother yelled after them.

"Go ahead! Go ahead and put another nail in your coffin. Once you're dead in the ground, I'm going to fill this house with dogs. I'll have so many dogs they'll call me an Old Dog Lady. But it's your choice. You want to die a terrible death before your time, it's up to you."

Stella followed her father into the back yard through the sliding glass doors. There was a stone path leading through a garden area. The path was lit by small lights. Her father led them out to a stone bench under a tree. It was surrounded by lemon trees and half a dozen lemons had dropped to the ground. He kicked one gently off the path with his foot and lit a cigarette.

"What's up?" she asked, eyes narrowing.

"Your uncle wants to talk to you."

"No." Leaning down, she began to gather the stray lemons. The air smelled so lemony and fresh. She set the fruit on the bench, lining it up carefully and avoiding her father's eyes.

"It's important or he wouldn't ask."

"He knows how I feel about joining the family business."

"Yes, we all know how you feel. This is something different."

"What does he want?"

"He knows you have some, let's say, connections in law enforcement out here."

"How in the hell does he know that?" She was furious. "Is he having me followed?"

"Your uncle knows everybody."

"Then tell him to find his own damn connections, since he knows everyone." Holding the last lemon in her hand, she chucked it deep into the garden. Hearing it hit something in the distance, she was tempted to scoop up all the lemons from the bench and practice her pitching.

"He needs your help."

She stooped down, scooping up two more lemons. She narrowed her eyes and threw those toward the back wall, too. "I'm not going to hear him out. That's absurd. Tell him to back off."

"Stella, if you don't show some respect and hear him out, it's gonna come back on me."

"He can't touch you."

"Have you watched the Godfather?"

"What does that have to do with anything?" She swore and then paused her arm in mid-air with a lemon still in her hand.

"Your language. Truck driver. Nana would roll over in her grave."

Stella let the lemon roll off her fingers and onto the ground at the mention of her beloved grandmother. "I'm sure Nana let loose a cuss word or two raising you hooligans."

That softened her father up. He snickered.

"Listen, Stella, you've got to show respect for Dominic. If not for you and your mother, then for me. I'm disposable."

"What the hell does that mean? Your daughter won't help him, and he whacks you? Dead horse head in the bed? I don't believe it." She reached over and took the cigarette out of his hand. She took a long drag and handed it back.

Her father shot a quick glance over his shoulder at the house. "Your mama will kill me if she sees something like that."

"I'm an adult now, Daddy. I'm responsible for my own actions."

Her father inhaled the last of the cigarette and then dropped it onto the path and stepped on it. "I know. Believe me I know. If I had any control over you, I wouldn't have let you go write about the wars overseas. You're lucky to still be alive."

"Maybe."

"No maybe about it," he said. "I'll text you his number. Just hear him out."

"Tell Mama thanks for dinner."

"Stella!"

But she ignored him and walked away and out the side gate, slamming it behind her. She stomped to her car, trying to tamp down the fury that threatened to explode in her. Was her family ever going to leave her alone?

It was one reason she'd dreaded coming back to America.

But she also hadn't had a choice. If it were up to her, she'd still be covering wars overseas. Now, back in the family fold, her worst fears were being realized. The family was trying to suck her in again, but she was no longer that fresh-faced nineteen-year-old they once knew. She'd seen and done things they never could imagine.

If they thought they would bully or coerce her into doing their will, they were dead wrong. Her stance on the family business was non-negotiable. She'd drawn the line in the sand a long time ago. In fact, all her decisions in life had basically been centered around one goal: avoiding the family business. And it certainly hadn't changed now.

Black Rose

She'd just started the engine when her dad came flying out the back gate waving his hands wildly.

"Hey! Hey! You forgot your damn dog!"

Smiling, she waved her hand cheerily out the window as she drove away.

13

ALTHOUGH HE'D BEEN TOSSING AND TURNING ALL NIGHT long, Alec Walker wasn't disturbing his wife's slumber. She was in the adjoining room. Walker always slept alone in the huge four-poster bed in the master bedroom.

Years ago, he and Margaret had decided to sleep in adjoining bedrooms. Ostensibly, it was done because he snored. But really, they both wanted their own space. He loved his wife, but his desire to have sex with her had dissipated years ago. Occasionally he paid a hooker during his trips away and scratched that itch. Margaret had never complained.

Now he sat up, turned on the lamp on the nightstand and poured himself two fingers of bourbon from the crystal decanter he kept on his nightstand. He downed the golden liquid with shaking hands.

Foolishly he'd thought that the threat would end with Bellamy.

When Headway had been created all those years ago, he hadn't realized what a tight-knit group the operatives would form. But in hindsight, it made sense. He had recruited the best of the best, and part of what made them that way was their utter lack of familial ties. They didn't have a wife and kid at home that an enemy force could threaten. No ailing mother who could be used against them. Everyone, save Stella, was in the world alone. And so, of course, they had formed a family of their own.

They were loyal to the core. And now, it was clear that to be safe Walker had to assume that what one person knew, they all knew.

He thought of Stella LaRosa and the invisible layer of protection around her. He didn't know if the others on the team knew who she really was. He doubted she'd told them, but who knew? She'd become part of the team's family, which is probably what she'd wanted all along when she moved to Europe: to discard her birth family and create her own.

The LaRosa's were powerful.

His father had taught him this at a young age growing up in Cleveland, Ohio. He was fourteen years old when one of his father's best friends was beaten to death outside a bar. That friend was a city council member.

"Son," his father had said after the funeral. "Did you see those men in the black ties at the back of the church?"

He'd nodded. "They were the ones who murdered Henry."

"Why were they at the funeral? Why aren't they in jail?"

"They're Mafia."

"I thought that was only in the movies."

"No, son. They are real. Henry was playing with fire. He didn't want to give them a contract for the garbage service here. Said that was illegal. So, they killed him. Now they have the contract."

He'd frowned. "So why don't the police do something about it?"

"That's why I'm telling you. Your friends with Christopher, right?"

"Yeah." Now he was really confused. "His uncle is one of those guys."

He thought back to the funeral, one of the men in the back nodded at him when he and his father walked by. He'd been stunned and quickly looked away.

"The cops aren't going to do anything because the cops are afraid of them, too," his father said. "You don't have to be afraid, though. They know I'm not going to cause any problems. But if those men come into the store when you're working, don't argue with them and don't mess with them."

His father owned a small grocery store.

"Why would they come in?" he asked.

"They might be putting out feelers because they know me and Henry were friends. But you don't have to worry about it."

The men never did come into the grocery store, but from then on Alec Walker treated his friend, Christopher LaRosa, differently. He gradually made other, closer friends, but always tried to stay on Christopher's good side. Just in case.

Later it had paid off. The LaRosa's had come to him when he first entered the political arena. They had made his life easier and every once in a while, to repay them, he'd made their life a little easier. But Walker had outgrown their manipulations. No longer a council member, he was more powerful than ever and, on his way to even more influence.

The LaRosa's were powerful, but he knew that they wouldn't be able to protect Stella. Not this time around. The stakes were much too high. The players were much too important. All night long, Walker's mind had been racing. He had to come up with some way to ensure that the threat was eliminated.

Finally, at dawn, after having downed three more glasses of bourbon, he got out of bed. He pulled on his robe and padded downstairs to the servant's kitchen. Bruce was already up, of course. He seemed startled when Walker walked in and jumped up.

"Easy, Bruce," Walker said. "Finish your coffee. I'm just going to grab a cup and go into my study. Make sure I'm not disturbed."

"Yes, Alec."

Walker gave a tight smile. He'd once told Bruce it was okay to call him Alec. It had been a weak moment. Even his own goddamn wife didn't call him Alec.

He'd probably been drunk when he said it. He'd immediately regretted the familiarity and had regretted it ever since. Luckily, Bruce only called him this in private, but it always made Walker cringe. It was spoken in a creepy, intimate whisper that repulsed him.

Pouring his coffee, Walker walked out without a word and headed to his study. Once inside the masculine, book-lined space, he locked the door and dialed the familiar number.

"I couldn't get away last night," he said.

"This has gotten way out of hand," the man on the other end said.

"I didn't sign up for this."

"Don't worry. Nothing can be traced or proven."

"How did Bellamy find out about it?" he asked, opening the blinds that overlooked his manicured backyard. The grass hadn't been cut short enough. He'd have to talk to the gardener about that. And the trees needed to be trimmed.

"I'm looking into it."

"I have a bad feeling about this." He closed the blinds back up. The sight of his garden was giving him a headache. He didn't have time to deal with domestic matters. What the hell did his wife do all day anyway?

"Hey. This might cost us a few pennies, but we're going to make sure nobody talks."

"That's the opposite of how this is supposed to work. It shouldn't cost me a dime. I'm not the one putting out the money. Let's just get that straight right now."

"Calm down. It's under control."

"Is it? I talked to my source in San Francisco, and it looks like it's far from under control."

"Do you mean the cop?"

"Hell yes, I mean the cop!" Walker realized he was shouting. He glanced at the thick study door. His wife was still asleep. Damn woman slept until 7 a.m. every day. And Bruce knew better than to eavesdrop.

"It's taken care of."

"It better be!" Walker hissed and disconnected.

Slamming his coffee cup down hard, he sent the hot liquid flying everywhere, splattering the papers on his heavy wood desk, which made him even angrier. This was not going the way it was supposed to go. Not even close.

14

ON MONDAY, STELLA STARTED HER SHIFT BY HEADING straight to the county morgue to request the autopsy for the guy who had his head blown off.

A woman with gray hair in a messy bun was at the front desk. She wore a tie-dyed dress and a purple crystal hung from a black leather cord.

Stella introduced herself and asked what the procedure was to request an autopsy report.

"You got a card?" the woman asked.

"A card?"

"You know, a business card?"

"I'm pretty new. I guess they're ordered."

"Hmm," the woman said.

"Can you please help me? I can show you the newspaper with my stories in it."

The woman shook her head and with a huff said, "When was the deceased brought in?"

"Friday."

"I can't help you."

"Why not?"

"We don't release the autopsy reports until the toxicology reports come back. Usually six to eight weeks."

"I heard this one was fast-tracked," Stella said without skipping a beat.

"I don't know about that. I'm just telling you what's standard procedure."

"Can you at least look?"

The woman gave a long-suffering sigh. "Name?"

"That's the problem. I don't have one. He came in Friday. How many unidentified bodies came in Friday?"

"You'd be surprised."

"Can you please look for me?"

The woman tapped her long pink nails on the keyboard. Then she frowned. "I think I got the one you're asking about, but the case is sealed."

"What exactly does that mean?"

"It means you'll have to do a public information records request to ask for it."

"Okay. Well, thank you for your help." It wasn't the woman's fault. She was just doing her job, and she'd gone out of her way when Stella didn't even have a name. "I'm new to the newspaper. I'm still figuring out how everything around here works."

The woman seemed to soften up a bit. She lowered her voice after looking around. "I just want to warn you. Most of the time, the record they have you look at isn't worth squat. They'll black out everything that means anything."

"They'll give it to me redacted?"

"Yep. And they'll take weeks."

"Is there any other way I can get it?"

"Not that I know of. I can't even access it and I work here."

"Who can access it?" Stella asked.

"The investigators."

Stella smiled again. "Thanks."

As soon as she stepped outside, she texted Griffin.

Why is the autopsy report sealed?

Who is this?

Stella Collins. The San Francisco Tribune.

I don't know how you got this number, but you have to go through our public information office. I told you that the last few times you called. I'm blocking you right now, so don't bother texting or calling again.

Stella stared in disbelief at her phone. What the hell? The bastard.

A few seconds later, another text appeared from an unknown number.

10 p.m. Joe's Place.

It was the bar where she'd met Griffin. She'd have to wait several hours, and the suspense would kill her. Something must have happened. A chill ran across her scalp.

Griffin was spooked. He knew something.

After telling Garcia she was meeting a source, Stella left the newsroom and was at Joe's ten minutes early. The dark bar was long and narrow, with only a handful of booths. An old pinball machine took up a large portion of the area behind the bar. A group of millennials were gathered around it, watching a guy play.

Stella spotted Griffin seated in a booth in the back corner. She didn't recognize him at first. He wore a straw cowboy hat pulled low on his forehead and a flannel shirt.

"What the hell, Griffin?" she demanded as she slid into the booth. "If you're trying to keep a low profile, you've failed miserably."

"Have you ever heard of the Helzer brothers?"

"The who?"

"Two crazy brothers in the East Bay who kidnapped and killed a bunch of people in an attempt to steal their life savings. They had an accomplice, a woman named Dawn. They put a lime green pantsuit and straw cowboy hat on her. She wheeled herself into the bank in a wheelchair to deposit the fraudulent check. When investigators asked what the trio looked like, all the bank tellers could remember was Dawn's cowboy hat, green clothes, and the wheelchair."

"Whatever, I'm still not convinced," Stella said.

The bartender brought over their drinks. Stella eyed the woman in the low-cut top and Daisy Duke shorts. The woman ignored her completely. Not only did most bartenders not deliver drinks to tables, but most didn't look like off-duty fashion models either.

Stella caught the woman winking at Griffin as she set down the drinks.

"A fan?" she asked as the woman walked off.

"Who?" he asked and frowned.

"Never mind."

"I ordered you a Bulleit."

"Damn, Griffin, you're good."

"I was thinking that part of my disguise is that I'm here with my girl."

"Your girl?" Stella said and arched an eyebrow.

"You're making it look like we're having a business meeting. It will be less suspicious if we look like a couple."

Before he was done speaking, Stella had slid over beside him, put her hand on his jaw and kissed him long and hard. Then she pulled back and stayed seated with their thighs touching, leaning over to see his face.

"How's that, cowboy?"

"I made a mistake."

"Do tell?"

"Should've told you to meet me at your place."

Stella laughed. "Too late. What's the scoop? It seemed important."

"I have no idea why I'm risking my entire career to share this with you."

Stella froze. "What?"

"I'm telling you because something isn't right," he said. "My chief whisked this case away from us as soon as the fingerprints were run. Next thing we know there's feds in the precinct. They were in the chief's office for a good hour. When they came out, the chief said the death had been ruled a suicide and that the feds had taken it over."

"That suicide thing again."

"Yup," he said. "No way that guy ate his gun and then the gun disappeared."

"How can they get away with that ruling?" Stella asked.

"You'd be surprised. The sheriff's office runs the morgue, and the sheriff is an elected position."

"That's insane."

"Tell me about it," Griffin said and took a long drag off his drink. "And here's the thing, the chief said we were supposed to forget everything we'd heard and seen about that death."

"But you didn't," Stella said and swirled the amber liquid in her glass.

He shrugged.

"I had printed out a copy of the autopsy report and took it home. Usually I make a murder board on the wall in my home office for every case I investigate. Notes, maps, photos. I like to have the autopsy report stuck up there, too."

"Was there something important in the report? Is that why they're being so secretive?"

"Besides evidence that there is no way the man shot himself, the only other important thing in the report is the name."

Stella sat back. "Who was it? Who is our dead guy? Must be a big deal. How can they cover up the death of someone important? That's crazy."

"Stella, it's not who he is, it's what he was."

"Okay, Sherlock, I'm too tired to figure out your riddle. What are you saying?"

"Stella." He leaned in close to her ear and whispered the rest.

"The prints and DNA came back to a former SEAL Team Six member who has been dead for twelve years."

The blood rushed out of Stella's face. Everything spun. The dim lights began to glow way too bright, and the jukebox was too loud.

Finally, she was able to form the words she'd been thinking in her head and ask the question out loud.

"What was his name?"

15

THE WORDS HUNG IN THE SILENCE.

"Mark Bellamy."

It took all of Stella's concentration to keep her expression neutral.

Griffin kept speaking. "Like I said, former SEAL. KIA in Afghanistan twelve years ago. His family, what was left of them, had a funeral and everything."

He stopped and took a drink.

Stella tried to form words that would make sense in this situation. But inside, all she was thinking was, *Bellamy is dead.*

From what Josh had described seeing, most likely he'd had his head blown off execution style in a seedy warehouse. Bellamy had been assassinated for a reason. And if so, that meant his cover must have been blown. And that meant that the other members of the team were in danger. And so was she.

"As best I can figure it, that's why the feds are involved," Griffin said, continuing his train of thought.

"That would make sense," Stella managed to sound casual as she took a sip of her own drink. She was glad the dim light in the bar hid her flushed cheeks, which felt like they were on fire. Meanwhile, she was scanning the bar under hooded eyes. Thinking back, she realized she'd gotten sloppy. She had no idea if she'd been followed to the bar. She had lost her street sense. More than a year back in the states and she was acting a fool.

There was a guy sitting at the bar who was watching them through the mirror.

Stella stiffened.

"What is it?" Griffin asked.

"Do you think you're in danger meeting me here to discuss this?"

"What?" he said in surprise. "I think the only danger is me losing my job by talking to a reporter."

"What about three o'clock at the bar?" She leaned in to kiss him so nobody would see her lips moving. "He's watching us."

Griffin turned and met her lips with his own before answering. Then he turned away and took a sip from his glass. She saw his gaze trained on the bar.

"He was here when I got here. He wasn't paying any attention to me until you walked in. Looks like he's checking you out, babe."

Babe.

Stella mentally winced. She had rules. She'd made them during her hookup era last year:

No cuddling. No dates outside the bedroom. No spending the night. And definitely *no cute nicknames*.

"I think we both need to tread carefully," Stella said.

"Both? Are you going to follow up on this?"

Crap.

"Maybe."

Turning to see his face, she asked the next question. "Are you?"

He nodded. "I think so. I don't like it when some dude in a suit comes into my town and tells me that a murder is a suicide and I have to back off."

"Yeah. That's not cool. Has that ever happened to you before?"

"Not in twenty years on the force."

Stella smirked. "You're that old?"

He laughed. "Well, I was a baby when I joined the academy, so yes."

Her laugh sounded hollow and fake to her ears, but she hoped he bought it. Her entire body was tense. Downing the remains of her drink, she was planning how to make her exit. She was starting to have a hard time breathing. Bellamy was dead.

What about the others?

Was she next?

She had to get out of there and call Harry.

"You doing okay, scoop?" Griffin was watching her carefully.

Smiling, she hoped it reached her eyes. "Yeah. But I'm beat."

"Want some company?"

She shook her head no.

He frowned. She leaned over, gave him a slow kiss, and then pulled back.

"That was nice," he said and reached for her, but she drew away.

"Just for appearances sake, cowboy. Don't want anyone to suspect you're a cop on the city payroll tipping off a journalist."

"Of course not."

"Are you staying?"

"Unless you change your mind about me coming with you to your place. Otherwise, I'm having another drink."

"Let's catch up later," she said and turned to walk out.

In the night air, she let the shock of what she'd learned hit her. It felt like a punch to her solar plexus.

Bellamy.

Unlocking her car, she sat inside for a minute before starting the engine. A dark swarm of memories surrounded her. Closing her eyes, she surrendered to them. Mark's smiling face was front and center. Once upon a time, he'd been family. But all that had changed in a heartbeat. After Syria, the team had scattered. They knew better than to ever be in touch again.

Everyone had gone deep undercover. Except her. She'd always been the one in the public eye, acting as a journalist, but under-cover the entire time. She'd been easy to find.

The first year back in America, she'd leaped to answer every text and phone call. It had never been any of her teammates. Finally, she'd realized that they weren't going to be in touch.

It had been heartbreaking in some ways. They had been the people she'd trusted most in the world. They'd felt more like family than her own family. But she also knew they had to lie low. If they didn't, they were risking their lives. But she had thought they might at least trust her enough to reach out. And to think that Bellamy had been here in the city all along.

Grabbing her phone, she texted Griffin. *Got an address for the dead guy?*

She cringed, calling Bellamy "dead guy." But she couldn't let Griffin suspect a thing.

Not ten seconds passed before he wrote back. *I'll shoot it over once I get home. It's in the autopsy report.*

Thanks.

You're going to get in trouble snooping around, he wrote.

So are you.

Fair enough.

She began to drive. Once she was satisfied nobody was following her, she dialed the number she had memorized and pressed the phone to her ear.

"Stella."

"Harry."

"Glad to hear you're still alive."

"That's why I'm calling."

"You okay?"

"I am. Bellamy's not." She had tried to keep herself composed, but a sob had escaped with the words.

"What happened?"

"He was murdered. Feds swooped in and said it was a suicide.

But he was assassinated, Harry." There were a few moments of silence.

"Where are you getting all this?"

"I've got a homicide detective source with the San Francisco P.D."

"Does he know what we know?"

"Nope."

"You don't trust him?"

"I trust him. I just don't want him to lose his job."

"He might lose a lot more than his job, Stella."

Laughter and loud conversation filled the other end. "Where are you?"

"I was out having a cigarette, but now I'm back in the bar."

"Isn't it past your bedtime?"

Harry was a good C.I.A. agent. But not a great one, electing to put drinking over spying. Yet, he was as loyal as they come, especially to Stella. She knew he was half in love with her and maybe she was half in love with him. But he was old enough to be her father. The one night they'd spent together had been a mistake.

Pulling onto her street, Stella knew Harry was the only one who might be able to help her now.

"This local cop? Is he going to dig?" Harry asked.

"I think so. But this is way over his head."

"It's over yours, as well."

"Whatever. I want to find out what the hell is going on."

"I thought you were done with all that?" His voice was gentle and kind, but it still made her angry.

"I am. I'm going to find out what happened and publish it in my paper so the whole world knows."

"Good," he said quickly.

They were both silent for a few seconds before he spoke again. "I'm glad you got out of that life, Stell."

"Me too," she said in a soft voice.

"But I'm not sure writing about it is a good idea, either."

"I have to. I have to make them pay in some way."

"It's too big for your paper, too, Stella, and you know it."

Stella bit her lip.

"You need to proceed as if every single person who gets wind of this is as good as dead."

"I know."

"I'll do some digging and get back to you ASAP."

"Thanks, Harry."

"Of course. I've been thinking about you a lot."

She closed her eyes. *No, Harry. Don't go there.*

"Wondering if you'd changed your mind. About us."

"Harry... I wish I could. I really do."

"Me too," he said quietly and hung up.

16

THE NEXT MORNING WHEN SHE WOKE, THE SUN WAS already up and shining into her bedroom. A rare warm and sunny summer day in the city. Reaching over, she checked her phone.

There was a text from Harry.

Traced Bellamy to a hotel in the city. He's using the name Danny Craig.

It listed the hotel address.

She didn't know whether to laugh or cry when she heard that was his alias. He'd always been a James Bond fan.

After she showered, dressed, and downed an espresso, Stella headed to the hotel. She'd thrown on a black blazer over her uniform of jeans, boots, and a tight top so she'd seem at least a tiny bit more professional. Parking up front in the valet spot, Stella walked into the red wallpapered lobby and then headed to the long leather-topped front desk.

She eyed the clerk behind it.

A tall skinny man with cropped hair and a bobbing Adam's apple. His features were sharp, and he had an Ichabod Crane vibe.

He wore an old-fashioned bellhop uniform. When he turned and saw her, a look of slight disdain crossed his face.

A sneer appeared as soon as Stella introduced herself as a reporter. "The Ivy respects the privacy of our guests. We don't share any information."

"I get that, and I respect it," Stella said. "I'm not just a reporter. He was a friend of mine."

Despite herself, her voice broke.

The man's face remained stony.

"Is there a manager I can speak with?" she asked, knowing she was facing a dead-end with this guy.

"I will get the manager, but you should be ashamed of yourself. A man is dead, and you lie about knowing him just to get a story?"

That did it.

"Hey, pal, relax. You're off base."

He huffed away. She watched his shiny loafers cross the Persian carpets as he wove through giant white pillars and then disappeared through a back door. A few minutes later he came out and ignored her as he helped a couple who had just walked in.

Stella walked around the Art Deco lobby, eying the oil paintings on the wall as she waited for the manager to appear. Each of them was eerie, they all depicted dark scenes of violence and death. She was staring at one that showed a mass beheading, when a man appeared at her side. He was shorter than she was and had a long-twirled mustache.

"I just came out to reiterate what Mr. Morton already told you. We don't share information about our guests with the media."

Stella walked out without even acknowledging him. *What a waste of time.*

Instead of going to her car—which hadn't been towed—she circled around to the back of the building and peeked down the alley.

A door was propped open. Within seconds, she was inside. It was the laundry room of the hotel.

A woman looked up, startled, and Stella apologized. "I need your help," she said. "My friend stayed here the other night and something bad happened to him."

Stella held out her phone. It was a very old picture. It was taken in Bangladesh at a hotel bar. Bellamy was hunched over his drink. Nick was beside him. The two were laughing.

"This one." Stella put her finger under Bellamy. Why she had to pick a picture of Bellamy with Nick she'd never know, but she tried hard not to stare at Nick's face.

The woman squinted at the photo and then nodded.

"He was here with a woman."

"He was?"

"She's still here."

"Still here? Right now?"

"No. I just cleaned her room. She went out earlier."

"What does she look like?"

"Red hair. Tall." The woman looked at the other door quickly.

Stella nodded and left.

Walking back around to the front of the hotel, she got into her car and moved it a few spots down where it was less conspicuous as she prepared to stake out the building. Keeping her eye on everyone who came and went, Stella waited to see anyone with red hair.

Thirty minutes later, a taxi pulled up to the front of the hotel. Stella sat up as she saw a redheaded woman in the back. She was about to leap out of her car, when she saw the hotel desk clerk come outside, followed by a bellman with several pieces of luggage. Within five minutes, the luggage was loaded into the trunk and the cab left. Stella followed closely, but she knew where it was going.

The airport.

As they drove through the airport entrance, another cab cut Stella off and then stopped, blocking her way. By the time she caught up, she saw the woman had checked her bags on the sidewalk and was walking inside. Her red hair was pulled into a tight bun, and she wore a beige trench coat, dark sunglasses and matching sky-high heels. She exuded money.

Stella once again parked her Jeep illegally in the loading zone, threw her hazard lights on, and tried to catch up with the woman. She saw a glimpse of her entering the line for security.

Racing over, she got there just in time to see the woman bypass the regular line and glide through the T.S.A. Pre-Check. Now, she was on the other side of security, placing her expensive-looking handbag on the conveyor belt.

Stella followed her path to the Pre-Check line but when she got to the front, the T.S.A. clerk asked for her boarding pass.

"Um?" she kept her gaze trained on the woman who was about to walk through the metal detector.

"Is there a problem, miss?"

Stella knew she only had seconds to act.

"Excuse me? Miss?" Stella shouted. A woman turned, but not the redhead. "Mark Bellamy!" She said loudly. A few people looked. But not the woman.

Of course. He would never have been able to use his real name.

"Danny Craig!"

But the woman had turned a corner. Damn it.

"Security," the T.S.A. agent said into a handheld radio.

"I'm so sorry. I thought that woman left something in my taxicab."

The man just stared at her. A few seconds later, two police officers were at her side.

"Can you help me?" she said. "A woman who went through security left something in my cab. Can I just go in and give it to her?"

"Why don't you give me her name and I'll find her and tell her to come back here," the balding, middle-aged police officer said.

"I don't know her name," Stella said. "She was a passenger in my cab."

"What did she leave?"

Stella knew it was useless.

"Never mind. Thanks anyway."

"We'll walk you out," the slim, graying cop said.

"It's not necessary."

"Even so."

Annoyed, Stella walked back out to the front of the airport terminal in time to see her car being towed. She looked back and saw the two police officers standing in front of the doors with their arms crossed. Heading to the taxi stand, she hailed a cab and gave the driver directions to the tow yard.

17

THE NEXT MORNING, STELLA WENT TO VISIT HER MOTHER IN the morning before her night shift started. Her dad had flown to New York with her uncle the day before, so she knew her mother was all alone in the big house. All alone except for the dog, that is.

When she opened the door to her parents' house, the dog came running out of the living room wagging its tail like mad and then rolled over onto his back.

"Aw, aren't you a sweetheart," she said and crouched down to scratch his belly. She had to admit she missed the dog, but she didn't want to get evicted either.

"Ma?" she yelled, standing. "Where are you?"

"In the kitchen!"

Stella found her mom sitting at the kitchen table with half a pie in front of her.

"Breakfast?"

"I'm just so stressed, honey."

"What's wrong?" Stella said as she grabbed the Moka pot, put water and coffee grounds in it, and placed it on the stove. "Did you name the dog yet?"

"It's your niece, Jamie."

"You named the dog, Jamie?"

"No, your niece. That's the problem. Why I'm stressed."

Stella had heard some rumblings among the women of the family that Jamie, who had a newborn, was having problems with her baby daddy.

"I asked what you named the dog," Stella said, watching the coffee percolate on the stove, the black liquid bubbling. She peeked inside, willing it to be done faster.

"Don't open the lid like that," her mother chided her.

"The dog, Ma? What's his name?"

"*Poplettino*. I call him Tino."

"Little meatball? Might as well have just cut his balls off. Couldn't you have named him something a little more alpha?"

"It's Tino. It's final. He loves his new name! Tino!" The dog came racing in, sliding on the slick floor.

Grabbing a plate of almond biscotti, Stella sat down at the table. "What's going on with Jamie that makes you stress eat an entire pie?"

"Your dad had already eaten half of the pie before he left."

"Jamie," Stella reminded her mother. "What's going on?"

"It's bad, Stella. Real bad. He's beating her now."

Stella's eyes narrowed. "What?"

"Laura went over there, and Jamie wouldn't open the door. She just wanted to see her grandbaby, Keira. Finally, Jamie let her in. She had a black eye and a cut. He beat her. Hit her! What kind of a man does that?"

Stella found that she'd clenched her fists and jaw. The rage that had filled her at the thought of a man beating her sweet niece was overwhelming her.

"Did she tell Chris?"

Christopher was her brother, Jamie's dad, and Laura's husband.

"She's too scared. Christopher will kill him. *Murder.* You know, he will."

The words weren't hyperbole.

Stella nodded.

"Laura tried to get her to leave with her, but Jamie refused. She's got like Stockholm Syndrome or something. I said she could stay here. We've got all this room, empty bedrooms everywhere."

Stella stood.

"Does Jamie still live in that apartment in Martinez?"

"Stella," her mother's voice warned. "Your Uncle Dominic said we've got some federal eyes watching us. They might even be listening to you and me right now. We can't do anything, that's the only reason nobody knows. Your dad and uncle would get in trouble if they did something. We've just got to talk Jamie into leaving him. That's all. We can't do anything else."

Stella shrugged on her jacket.

"What about your coffee?"

Stella grabbed the Moka pot and poured the coffee into a mug. At the last second, she grabbed another almond biscotti off the table. "I'll be back."

"Stella, I'm serious. We've just got to talk her into coming here. That's the only thing you can do. We can't do anything else."

"That's what I'm going to do."

And talk the man out of ever touching her niece again.

The road was empty as she headed toward the Oakland Hills and the Caldecott Tunnel that connected Oakland with the rest of the East Bay. Inside the tunnel, she felt a slight twinge of claustrophobia. She'd overcome most of the phobia—unless she was in a very small, cramped area. The larger spaces, such as tunnels, rarely gave her pause anymore.

But every once in a while, the fear came surging back. She could feel it sneaking in right then. Instead of focusing on the tunnel walls that felt like they were closing in, Stella concentrated on the road in front of her lit up with her headlights.

A fearsome idea snuck in anyway, *what if the tunnel lights went dark at the same time her headlights did?*

Shaking the irrational compulsive thought away, a few seconds passed before she emerged into the daylight on the other side. Ten minutes later, she exited the freeway in Martinez, parked in front of the duplex and eyed the building.

Dude must make a decent living to afford a place like that in this part of town. If he wanted to continue to be able to make any money at all, he'd better listen to what Stella had to say.

Slamming her car door, Stella went around to her trunk and unearthed a tire iron from near the spare tire. Then she was at the front door, ringing the bell. There was no answer, but she saw a curtain open and then fall back at the large living room window.

Pounding on the door, she shouted, "It's your Aunt Stella!"

Nothing.

"Open the door or I'll break in," she screamed and glanced around. Nobody was in sight.

Lifting the tire iron, she gripped it like a baseball bat, positioned her hips and let loose.

With a resounding *crack*, the glass shattered and fell in a few large pieces onto the grass.

Stella leapt through the broken window, rolling and coming upright in a defensive stance. Both legs spread, tire iron held before her, a fierce determination shone in her eyes.

A man came rushing out of the next room armed with a pair of brass knuckles.

"Who the hell are you?" he said.

"Your worst nightmare," she answered through gritted teeth.

Stella had never seen this lowlife before, but he matched with who she'd imagined would beat on her sweet niece. Short and bulky, with a tattooed neck and forehead, he wore a dirty tank top paired with board shorts. Scratch her idea that he had a good job. This guy was 100 percent a drug dealer.

Standing there, he eyed her for a second before he spoke. "You're the one who broke into my house. The law says I can kill you and get away with it."

There was the sound of a baby wailing. The house smelled like feces and sour milk. And there was another sickly sweet smell beneath it, marijuana. The man's irises were red.

"Jamie?" Stella yelled. "Get the baby and a few of your things and go out the front door. Get in my car."

"Stella?" It was her niece's wobbly voice.

"She's not going anywhere," the man said, and clenched his fists. "Don't listen to her. She's crazy. You know you can't take the baby with you. I told you what would happen."

"I know," Jamie said. Stella could hear her crying. "I'm not going anywhere."

Fury swept through Stella.

"Listen Davis, let's just cut to the chase here. Either you're going to let her leave or I'm going to kill you." She said the words flatly.

He scoffed. "You're the one who's already dead. And it will be justified."

But she heard his voice waver.

"You're not going to kill me. You don't want a dead body on your hands because that means cops, and cops mean an investigation and your little stash of whatever drugs you sell will be found. And judging by the tattoos on your face, this isn't your first rodeo in the prison system, so you're probably a three-strikes dude who will go away for a long time. And all that's fine with me because my main goal here is to make sure you never touch Jamie again."

Taking a step closer, he shook his head. They circled one another. Davis lunged, throwing a swift punch at Stella's head. She ducked, avoiding the brass knuckles but lost her grip on the tire iron letting it fall with a loud clatter to the floor.

She backed up and then surged forward with a roundhouse kick. Davis blocked it with his beefy forearms, grunting as Stella's boot connected with his flesh.

Exchanging a flurry of jabs. Stella landed swift punches and kicks in quick succession. Davis wasn't nimble, so he was unable to avoid many of her strikes, but his own punches were powerful. A few times he managed to break through her defenses and land crushing blows that sent Stella reeling.

Stella noted Jamie's screams as furniture was knocked over, and the room became a battlefield. Davis lunged and his fist connected with Stella's abdomen, nearly knocking the wind out of her, but she quickly retaliated, countering with a spinning back kick to his chest that sent him stumbling backward, off balance. Determined to finish the fight, Stella dropped to a crouch and scooped up the tire iron. Then she charged, leading with the heavy piece of metal.

"Stella!" Jamie screamed.

Davis had a gun, pointed directly at her. She froze for a second, but then darted forward without hesitation. Davis fired a shot, missing Stella by inches as she ducked and came up with the tire iron swinging with deadly precision. The heavy piece of metal struck his forearm with a resounding *whack* and knocked the gun out of his hand. Then she lifted the tool and delivered a powerful strike to the side of his neck. He crashed to the ground, unconscious.

Stella stood over him, breathing heavily, sweat dripping from her brow. One bloodied fist still gripped the tire iron.

"Oh no!" Jamie said. "Is he dead?"

Stella looked over for the first time at her niece. The girl was rail thin in a dirty dress and holding a baby against her.

"Jamie, pack your things and load them into my car."

The girl just stared at her.

"Now!" Stella yelled.

Then Jamie nodded and rushed into the other room. Stella looked around and then grabbed some ties for the drapes that were hanging unused on the walls. She hefted Davis into a kitchen chair and bound his ankles and wrists to the chair's arms and legs. His head drooped forward onto his chest.

Jamie came back into the room with the baby in a car seat and a suitcase.

"Is that everything?" Stella asked.

The girl nodded.

"Take the baby and get in my car."

After Jamie walked out, Stella rummaged around the kitchen cupboards until she found a pitcher. She filled it with cold water and dumped it on Davis's head. He made some sounds and then his eyes flew open. They narrowed as soon as they saw her.

"You bitch. You're dead." His words slurred.

Stella chewed on her inner lip for a second, and then walked over and landed a swift but brutal punch to Davis right in the left eye. He reeled back. The chair almost tipped over backward, but Stella grabbed the front of his shirt and pulled him to her.

"Who are you?" he spluttered and then spit out some blood, dribbling down the front of his shirt.

"I already told you. I'm your worst nightmare."

"Are you a cop?"

"Do you think I'm a cop?"

He shook his head.

"This is illegal," he said.

Stella began pulling open drawers until she found what she was looking for—a large butcher knife. "I'm going to spare your life, but only on one condition."

No answer, so she continued. "If you ever even so much as look at Jamie or the baby, I'll hunt you down and feed you your own pepperoncini. Do you understand?"

His face scrunched up. "My own what? Pepper what?"

She walked over and swiftly jabbed his groin with the butt of the knife. He let out a grunt.

"Your joystick, moron."

His eyes grew wide. Then raising her hand, Stella flicked the blade with deadly precision, slicing a thin line down his cheek to his jaw.

He howled in pain. "Maybe every time you look in the mirror you'll remember that I'm serious."

"I get it." he said. She looked into his defiance-filled eyes.

"I don't think you do. You're already planning on how you're going to find me and make me pay for this. But you don't understand who is in charge here. It's not you."

"I'll kill you," he shouted and blood-filled spittle splattered across his chest.

"Maybe I should cut your junk off right now to make sure you understand just how serious I am?"

"You're right," he said, his voice filled with venom. "I am going to find you and make you pay."

"Listen Davis. What you don't understand is that I'm not some drug dealer psycho like you're used to dealing with."

"You're right, you're some stupid broad."

Stella ignored his words. "See the difference between them and me is that I only give one warning."

"I'm not afraid of you."

"Oh...you will be."

Stella walked out of the kitchen. He began to scream, but she was back a few seconds later with a gas can and a lighter. Just then, Jamie poked her head back into the house.

"Get in the car, Jamie! Now!" Stella screamed.

Dumping the gas can over his head, she then sprinkled the rest of the fluid that was left in a circle around him. Then she leaned down and flicked open the Zippo lighter.

"No!" he screamed. "I promise. I won't even look at her again. I'm done. I get it. I knew she had some crazy family, but I didn't know. I won't touch her ever again."

Stella straightened and closed the Zippo.

"I'm going to keep my eye on you, Davis. If I find out you're beating on another woman, I'm going to come for you."

She turned and walked out the door.

18

REPRESENTATIVE ALEC WALKER HAD ALWAYS BELIEVED Carter Barclay looked more like a cowboy than a billionaire. As the limo pulled up the drive of the Texas ranch, Walker spotted the oil man off to the side of the house, deep in discussion with what looked like a farmhand.

Barclay wore jeans and a black button-down shirt even though it had to be near one hundred degrees in this forsaken part of the world. His ruddy face bore deep lines under the shade of a massive black cowboy hat, and his feet were in sturdy scuffed brown work boots.

Nobody could say that Barclay was a dandy, that's for sure.

As they grew closer, Barclay turned to watch the vehicle approach. The driveway to the main house was gravel for some ridiculous reason that Walker couldn't fathom, so their arrival left a huge dust cloud in their wake. The nickname for the house was the Log Cabin Mansion. It was indeed a mansion, and it was, indeed, made of logs. Walker always expected some giant spider to come crawling out from between the logs. The home was centered around a stone fireplace that could fit a football team inside.

Instead of heading toward the porch of the mansion, Barclay, still talking to the farmhand, strode toward an outhouse, also made of logs. The farmhand followed, and the limo driver pointed the vehicle toward them. Walker watched the billionaire as he took off his hat and wiped the sweat off his brow, his face was grim.

For a second, Walker was worried, but dismissed it. The billionaire was not the smiling type. Walker snuck a look in his pocket mirror to smooth his hair, and then took a handkerchief out to mop at the sweat on his own brow. Even with the air conditioner in the car blasting, it was still hot as Hades. He'd never live in Texas. If he could help it, he'd never step foot in the hellhole again, but today he didn't have a choice.

Not only was it miserable in this state, but also very inconvenient for Walker to have to leave Washington on the whim of another man. But the billionaire wanted an in-person meeting, and Walker had learned long ago that Carter Barclay didn't go to anyone. Everyone came to him.

Barclay finished his conversation and the ranch hand left, heading for a large barn behind the main house. Barclay walked over to the car as it stopped. Walker couldn't help but notice the holster with the pistol at his hip.

Just like a real cowboy? Or something else?

Without waiting for the driver, Walker opened the door and unfolded himself. He stuck out his hand, "Carter."

"Walker. Thank you for coming. Why don't you walk the pasture with me? I've got a horse that's giving me some trouble, so I want to keep an eye on her. She's pregnant and acting a little strange."

It astonished Walker that Barclay oversaw his ranch when he could buy the state of Texas if he'd wanted. It was obviously something he loved.

"I'm afraid I am overdressed," Walker said, looking down at his three-piece suit.

"That you are," Barclay said.

He turned to the driver. "Get the golf cart."

The two exchanged pleasantries about their wives and children for a few minutes, until the driver came around the corner of the house in a golf cart.

Barclay hopped into the driver's seat and nodded at Walker. "Let's go." As soon as they were out of earshot of the house, Barclay said. "You've known me a while and you know I'm a reasonable man, right?"

"Yes," Walker said.

"So you know I don't make threats lightly, right?" Barclay spun the wheel and stepped on the gas, heading toward the edge of a pasture. Walker's mouth went dry. He nodded. "This problem with your team? It has the potential to destroy everything I've worked my entire life for."

"I understand."

Walker wondered if he were being taken out to a deserted pasture to be killed. Nobody knew he was in Texas. He'd flown under a fake name on Barclays' orders. The billionaire had sent him the fake passport and made the reservations. He was a dead man.

When Barclay had approached him, he'd been desperate. About to lose his campaign, go into foreclosure on his house, file bankruptcy and possibly land in prison for shady campaign financial practices. Barclay had offered him a lifeline.

"I heard you have some friends in Syria," Barclay had said.

"I know a man."

"There's an oil field there I need."

"He has friends up high."

"That's good, but you're putting the cart ahead of the horse. There are some Syrian citizens who stand in my way."

"I can handle that, too."

"You and your man will be generously thanked."

"He's going to need to thank his friends, as well," Walker had said carefully.

"That's a given."

"Very well."

"Work on that first problem. The oil fields need to be free and clear of any claims before anything else happens.

"I've got the perfect solution," the oil man said. "Look for some campaign contributions from a few companies you've never heard of. Since you're in Virginia, there won't be any limits on them and so you'll see some nice donations to your campaign. My lucky numbers are seventeen and forty-nine. Identify contributions that end in those numbers, and you'll know who they are from."

Walker didn't know what else to say, except to thank the oil man.

"Don't thank me yet."

It had taken a few months, but Walker had made sure there was no claim to the oil fields, had reached out to his man in Syria, and then the sale of the oil fields to Barclay had been approved.

Everyone involved had been happy. Walker was financially stable again. His man in Syria was pleased, and some government officials in that country had new cars and sweet vacations. Nobody was any wiser.

Now, the merger of Barclay's company with a larger oil company needed to pass muster, and all would be well. At least that's what he had thought. Then Mark Bellamy happened.

And now Barclay was threatening him. *What the...?*

Barclay pulled the golf cart off to the side of the path. Walker was prepared to fight for his life, but he knew that even if he managed to kill the billionaire, he'd never get off this ranch alive.

The other man turned to him. "I need to know that you've got this handled, Walker. Need to look into your eyes and see that you realize how serious this situation has gotten. This is going to screw us all. And if I have to, I'm going to make you take the fall. I don't want to do that."

Walker felt his whole body go limp with relief. He wasn't going to be killed, at least not right then. The oil man was threatening to make him the scapegoat, but he was too smart for that. He'd been too careful.

Walker nodded and looked at Barclay's piercing blue eyes.

"I realize how dire this situation has become. I will stop at nothing to make sure we all walk away from this unscathed."

Barclay stared at him for a few seconds and then nodded. He turned and started the golf cart. He did a U-turn and headed back to the main house.

Walker felt a cold shiver run down his limbs despite the oppressive heat.

There had been no talk of a pregnant horse. Only the wide-open pasture with no one else around. Somehow he'd passed the test and was going to be allowed to go home.

19

IN THE ELEVATOR AT THE NEWSPAPER, STELLA NOTICED blood on her black jeans. She rubbed at it, but it'd already dried. Oh well, it sort of looked like oil. She'd dry swallowed some pain killer on the drive over and put pancake makeup on the redness and bruising along her temple and right cheekbone.

After dropping Jamie off at her mother's with the baby, Stella had to leave right away to get to work on time. She'd missed her workout in the newspaper gym, but she'd gotten in some cardio anyway, she thought with a smirk.

She'd just settled into her desk when Garcia yelled her name across the newsroom. Grabbing her notebook, she stood up and headed over. She'd forgotten to stop at his desk to see what was going on. Must be a breaking news story. Stella hadn't heard anything on the police scanners driving in, but that didn't mean there wasn't something.

"Are you still working that suicide—or whatever it was—down by the waterfront?"

Stella froze. She hated to lie, but this was for Garcia's own good. "No. Why?"

"Caitlan Archer cold called me this morning and said she'd heard a rumor you were still asking around about it."

Stella paused before answering. She knew she had to be very careful about what she said.

"Archer?"

"Oh, she's the publisher's rep. The one who called us off the story last week."

Stella had been thinking about that a lot lately. If the publisher had called them off the story, the only reason she could think of was that they somehow knew who Bellamy was. She could trust nobody.

When Garcia mentioned that Stella investigating the oil company story could land them in trouble, he'd never have imagined a simple homicide would be even more dangerous.

She avoided Garcia's eyes as she answered, shifting her gaze to the objects on his desk. "What made her think I was still looking into it?"

"She said you were asking about the autopsy report."

"That was before." Stella started to turn to walk back to her desk, but Garcia wasn't done.

"Listen. I don't like this anymore than you do. I think the publisher should keep her nose out of our business and our jobs. Our integrity is on the line. I thought about it all weekend. I say you should do whatever you want. Keep investigating if you will but keep a low profile. When you uncover a good story, come to me with the facts and we'll go argue our case to the hedge fund board."

As he spoke, Stella stared long and hard at the framed photographs on his desk. He had a wife with an infectious smile and three adorable little kids. The family photo almost made her heart ache with the sweetness. Garcia might be a tough newspaper guy at his core, but he was also a husband and father. But whoever killed Bellamy wouldn't care about that.

Harry's words came back to her: *You need to proceed as if every single person who gets wind of this is as good as dead.*

Garcia continued. "I'm ready to put up a fight over this. Your comment last week got me thinking. I didn't become a journalist to be told what to write and what not to write."

"Me either," Stella said. "But honestly, I don't think anything's there. I think it actually was a suicide."

Opening his mouth to say something, he then shut it. He was examining her face. Stella knew it was as placid as a still lake.

Just then, his phone rang. He turned to get it and she managed to escape back to her desk. Stella started to use the paid search services to try to find out more about Bellamy and his fake name— Danny Craig. There was precious little information about him.

She found a marriage record. He'd married some heiress, and they had lived on a ranch in Montana. This was the redhead. The woman was *newsworthy*. There was a small article about her new husband dying "unexpectedly" and her retreating to her family home. Maybe Stella would have to pay her a visit in Montana. Meanwhile, first she'd try the old-fashioned way.

After finding a cell number for the woman, Stella debated her attack. Either admit she was a reporter, or admit she was an old friend. Before she decided, the woman picked up.

"I'm so sorry to bother you," Stella said. "I'm an old friend of Daniel's and I was hoping to speak to you. I'm so sorry for your loss."

There was a small sniffle, and then a refined voice said, "Thank you."

Stella waited out the silence as the woman continued to sniffle on the other end.

When she seemed to have caught her breath, she said, "What can I help you with?"

"I had lost touch with him. I was hoping to hear more about what happened?"

She held her breath.

The other woman sighed. "I don't really know. The authorities told me that he was basically in the wrong place at the wrong time.

It was a case of mistaken identity. Apparently, a drug dealer confused him with someone else."

"Good Lord!" Stella said, feigning innocence.

"It's been an utter nightmare. We were only in town for two days. He sent me home because I had a migraine. He decided to walk home and..."

"That's when it happened?"

"Yes," she said and sniffled again.

"I know this seems weird to ask, but I just want to know. Was he happy? I haven't heard from him in more than a year and I just want to know what happened in that year. I know it's selfish, but it would help me to know he was happy this last year."

"Did you work with him in Asia on that nonprofit project?"

"Yes!" Stella said quickly. Maybe too quickly.

"I think he mentioned you. He said he had a close group of friends there he lost touch with."

Stella didn't answer. A lump had grown in her throat. It was sticky and hard, and she tried to swallow it down.

"I think he was very happy," the woman finally said in a small voice. "We were deeply in love. We were planning our future together on the ranch. We had big plans. We had even talked about kids."

"I'm so sorry." Stella meant it with her whole heart.

"Thank you."

"I know the police said it was a case of mistaken identity, but I have to ask. Did anything strange happen before he died? Anything that seemed off?"

"Why do you ask that?" The woman seemed alarmed.

"Because during our work in Asia, we did sometimes run into some rough people."

"Danny never told me that." Her voice was clipped.

"Well, he probably wanted to protect you so you wouldn't worry."

"There was nothing weird. Everything was...wonderful."

"Thank you. I won't bother you any longer. Thank you for sharing that."

"Wait," the woman said. "There was one thing."

Stella held her breath.

"He had a meeting scheduled for the next day. Right before we were going to leave. He had arranged for me to get a massage at the hotel during it. He was acting weird about it. Wouldn't tell me who he was meeting or why."

"What do you think that was about?"

"I actually thought he was going to get me another ring for our anniversary. It's next week. I'd told him that one of my favorite jeweler's was in San Francisco, so I assumed it was about that."

"Probably," Stella said, hiding her excitement. "What was the name of the jeweler, if you don't mind?"

"JW Smith."

"Thanks, and I'm sorry again for your loss."

Stella hung up and dialed the number she found for the jeweler.

"Hello, I'm an investigative reporter for the *San Francisco Tribune*, I'm sorry to bother you. I'm looking into a missing person. Retracing his steps, he might have had an appointment with you last Friday. Name is Danny or Daniel Craig."

"Missing person?"

"Yes sir."

"I don't take appointments."

"Okay," Stella said. "Did a man come see you that day?"

"The shop was closed that day. I had a family emergency."

"Thanks for your time."

The man hung up.

20

THE NEXT DAY, STELLA WAS DEEP INTO HER NIGHT SHIFT, writing about a string of takeover bank robberies when her phone rang. The windows of the newsroom were black, reflecting the empty desks and large screen T.V.'s hanging from ceilings and walls. Garcia was at his desk across the room. One of the guys from sports was pounding away at his keyboard, and there were four copy editors in their corner working hard to get the paper ready for bed.

Stella rummaged through her bag and found her cell phone. When she saw the number, she shook her head.

It was Griffin. She was annoyed. Didn't he know how to text? Glancing at the clock, she saw it was almost 11 p.m., when he knew she got off work. If he thought she was the kind of woman who did last minute hookups, the kind of woman who would agree to meet him without any notice, well, he was wrong.

She frowned. Okay, she might meet up with him. Maybe he wasn't wrong, but still.

"When's your next day off?" he asked.

"Tomorrow," she said, already filled with suspicion. "Why?"

"I know a really great Greek restaurant in Oakland. Seven p.m.?"

Damn it, he wanted to go on a date.

"I thought we weren't doing this," she said. "The deal was I call you to handle certain activities that you are very skilled at doing. The emphasis on *me* calling *you*."

He burst into laughter. "It's not a marriage proposal. You need to eat."

She did love Greek food. The inside of her refrigerator was looking grim. Despite being Italian and having a gourmet chef in every single one of her blood relatives, Stella hated to cook. Let's face it, eating out was her thing.

"So?" he prodded. "If you're worried about the drive across the Bay Bridge, we can meet at Union Square and take B.A.R.T. That way, we don't have to deal with rush hour traffic or parking."

"I don't do B.A.R.T."

"You don't do B.A.R.T.?"

"No."

"Too bougie for public transportation?"

"Ha!" she scoffed. "Hardly. I don't get into little tubes that go underground beneath a million tons of ocean water in earthquake country."

"A million tons?"

"Sure. Something like that."

"Are you claustrophobic?" Damn, he saw right through her.

She didn't answer.

"You could take the ferry across? Or let me guess, you get seasick?"

"Hmmm..."

"You are high maintenance, Collins."

"Maybe I am."

"So, what's your major objection? I'll pay. You know I'm delightful company. I'm not hideous and I don't chew with my mouth open. I will open the door for you and pull out your chair. What is it?"

Her major objection was that she didn't go on dates with her friends with benefits. But Griffin was complicated. Plus he was also a source for her. Maybe her rules could be bent. Slightly.

"You shouldn't be seen with a reporter," she said, glancing over at Garcia, who was hunched over his computer monitor. "Especially one who is using you as a source and *one you are sleeping with*."

"I'm not worried."

"You really hate your job don't you?" she replied. "Because it sounds to me like you're itching to get canned."

"I'll wear a fake mustache."

Cute. But no way.

"I still think it's too risky."

"Fine. I'll bring the food to you, and we'll eat hiding in your apartment like fugitives."

"That's not a good idea," she said.

"See you at seven. At your place."

"I won't be there."

"Then I'll leave it in the hall."

Damn, he was persistent. Knowing she could flat out tell him not to come and he would respect that, she didn't.

"Fine. Text me the name of the place. I'll meet you there."

Griffin was a decent guy and, let's face it, she told herself, satisfying in the bedroom. A sliver of guilt filled her thinking this. Stella reassured herself that the feeling was absurd. It was okay to enjoy and want to have sex with another man. It was almost like she had widow's guilt.

Except that she'd never been married to Nick. Even thinking that sent a stab of pain through her.

For a few seconds, sitting at her desk, tired from a long day at work, she had a weak moment and allowed herself to feel the pain of losing him. He'd been everything she'd ever wanted. He was fierce and deadly to others, but sweet and loving to her in private.

A memory overcame her. It was the night she realized she was in love with Nick. The team had been separated in Angola and everyone had made it back to the meet spot but Nick. They waited for a few hours, and then Bellamy and Jordan had gone to find him. They came back to the second-floor hideout, shaking their heads.

"What did you find?" Stella demanded.

"There was a lot of blood," Jordan said. "And this."

She held up the Saint Christopher medal that Nick always wore, its chain was broken. Stella had stared at it in shock. Bellamy swore and punched the wall, his face red with fury.

"It's not for sure," said Matthew. He'd always been the voice of reason.

Jordan rolled her eyes. "I'm going to bed."

She headed toward the corner and propped herself up against some moldy pillows, kicked her feet up on a box and closed her eyes. Watching her, Stella wondered how she could be so cold-hearted, but then she saw tears streaking Jordan's dirty face.

Matthew had grabbed the communal pack of cigarettes and grunted that he was going to stand watch on the roof. Bellamy followed without a word.

That left Stella blinking back tears. Stella had seen death in her life. Lots of it. People she loved, like her grandpa and her Uncle Connor and her friend's dad. But this was different. For the past two years, these people had become her family. In many ways, they'd even grown closer than some families.

Not knowing what to do with herself, she tucked her gun in her back waistband and headed downstairs to the street. Outside, the air was oppressive. It was hard to breathe. And it wasn't because she was holding back sobs.

After crouching down in the doorway for more than thirty minutes, she finally sat, letting her legs splay in front of her. There was a slight lightening to the east. Delirious from lack of sleep and grief, she had to do a double take when she saw a familiar silhouette heading down the sidewalk toward her.

By the time she was able to pull herself to standing, Nick was in front of her. Bloody and bruised and limping, his clothing torn. She reached for him. He grabbed her and kissed her roughly. From that moment on, they'd been inseparable.

And now he was gone.

She'd never get over him.

21

THE STRESS WAS GETTING TO ALEC WALKER, SO HE BEGAN taking nips of his flask in the backseat of the limo that drove him from his office in D.C. to his home. The driver, one of his regulars, met his eyes in the rearview mirror. Walker gave him a steely gaze and purposefully lifted the silver-plated flask to his lips maintaining steady eye contact. The driver looked away first.

By the time dinner was over, Walker had already demolished several pre-dinner bourbons and had half a bottle of cabernet with his roast beef dinner. He was slurring his words when he stumbled to bed. When the phone rang, he was disoriented, thinking he'd woken up late but then realized it was three in the morning. He snatched up the phone and when he saw the number, he answered in a hushed voice, "Give me two seconds," and rushed downstairs to his office.

He couldn't risk Margaret hearing anything even though she was most likely sound asleep in her own room.

In his office, he locked the door and turned on the classical music station to further prevent any possible eavesdropping. He knew it was going to be bad news. The only way someone would overhear is if his phones were tapped, and he had that checked every Tuesday.

"I'm here," he said gruffly.

"This is blowing up," the voice on the other end of the phone said. "Do something or we're both ruined."

"It's under control," Walker said.

"The hell it is."

"What are you talking about?" Walker scratched his head and glanced at the door. *Had the handle just turned, or was he imagining things?*

"We've had to take out some big players. Some important people are asking questions, and this is gonna lead to more questions. Big questions."

"Jeez. What do you mean you had to take out some big players?" Walker walked over and yanked open the door to the hall. It was empty. He closed it and locked it again. Jeez, he was getting paranoid.

"This has gotten out of control," the other man said. "People who should be in line are playing for the other team. They should be on our side."

"What team? English, for Christ sakes."

"The cops. S.F.P.D. Digging around."

"You're kidding? They are all on our payroll. That's impossible."

"There's one rogue detective. Name's Griffin."

Walker tensed. "Don't ever say names over this line again. Do you understand? Ever."

"My apologies."

A rogue cop. This was bad. Really bad. The cops were supposed to be the good guys, and they were supposed to support everything Walker did out of principle. Plus, he paid them well to do so.

"Did you offer them enough money to shut their trap and mind their own business?"

"Money isn't going to work here."

"Money always works. We just need to make a one-time

exception and offer a little more in this case. The other cops should be able to put the pressure on this jerk. It's just one guy, right? And he's a detective, not a lieutenant or commander, right? Pay them to ship him out to the docks to check for illegal importation of those stupid Kinder Egg things that kids were choking on."

The voice on the other end remained silent. Walker's head was starting to hurt. Great. If the alcohol didn't give him a proper hangover, all this nonsense would.

"Hello?" Walker said and reached over and poured a few fingers of bourbon. Hair of the dog that bit him usually worked.

"We need to use brute force."

Walker sighed loudly. He pulled back the drapes facing east to see if the sun was rising yet. He saw a faint gray glow on the horizon. He knew any sleep was over for the night.

"Are you sure?"

"I've explored every other option. It's our only choice."

Walker exhaled loudly and then downed the rest of his drink before he answered.

"Do what you must," Walker said in a resigned voice.

Without waiting for a response, he hung up the phone. He caught his reflection in the dark window. The green light on his office desk cast an eerie shadow, and his eyes had deep dark circles and his cheekbones were hollowed out. He looked ghoulish. Alec Walker quickly looked away.

He paced his office for a long time after that.

How had he gotten to this place? How had he landed in a position in his life where he was ordering the killings of cops?

It didn't sit well with him, but you did what you had to do, he told himself. If the cop wasn't following the rules, he had to go. It was a damn shame. But it was survival of the fittest.

So many things that had happened in his life had been utterly out of his control: His mother's drinking and subsequent uncontrollable anger. His dad's not-so-secret girlfriends on the side. The family friend who took him on a trip in grade school and molested him. His sister's death.

But no more.

He would regain control of this situation no matter what it took.

Glancing at the framed photos in his office documenting his childhood and rise to power, Walker thought, "You've come a long way, baby."

And that meant he wasn't going back, no matter what. When Alec Walker had first gone into politics, he truly had believed he could do good in the world. He would help people by listening to what they wanted and delivering that message in a way that others would listen, and laws would be made and changed.

From a young age, he discovered how screwed up the world really was. Criminals were roaming the streets targeting the innocent. The government was screwing the hard working folks by taxing them for things that lazy people should be able to pay for themselves. Minorities were taking over the country and stealing all the good jobs. He would change things for the better.

In college, studying political science, he'd worked on local, state, and national campaigns and the fervor of idealism had been everything he'd ever hoped and dreamed for in life. He was a natural. Handsome, charming, and hell, let's face it, able to manipulate just about anyone. When he was in third grade, his teacher had called his mother to say that in thirty years of teaching, she'd never had a student who could manipulate her in the way that Alec Walker did.

At that young age, Alec Walker realized it was his superpower. As he grew older, he honed his skills. In middle school, it got him good grades. In high school, it got him laid. In college, it got him money, drugs, and more women. After he graduated, it got him elected. Now it got him power. Power and more money than he had ever dreamed a middle-class kid from Ohio could have in this lifetime.

And now that dream was going to blow up. He'd lose everything.

Because of one stupid slip up.

He could kiss his career goodbye, his house, his cars, his designer clothes, maybe even his wife.

In the back of his mind, he knew there was one other thing he wasn't willing to admit would be taken away: his freedom.

He would do everything in his power to stop that from happening.

Everything and anything.

22

HER HEELED BOOTS ECHOED DOWN THE EMPTY SIDEWALK AS Stella hurried to the door of her apartment building. The street was dark and deserted, and for some reason it made the hairs on the back of her neck stand up. She glanced around as she unlocked the door to the lobby and before opening it, looked both ways. The street was still quiet. Slipping inside, she firmly closed the door behind her before she raced up the stairs to her place.

Stella flung open her apartment door and tossed her messenger bag on the couch. She was running late.

Although she'd had the day off, Garcia had called in the morning and asked if she could cover the closing arguments in a mass shooting trial. The court reporter had called in sick. She'd agreed, telling him that she needed to cut out in the late afternoon, but had ended up staying a little later than that writing up the story. She'd still have time to get over the bridge and to the restaurant.

Now, stripping down and hopping into the shower, Stella realized she had butterflies in her stomach when she thought about meeting up with Griffin. She was nervous like it was a date.

But she didn't date. She was not the dating kind. There were only a few men in the world who knew Stella LaRosa for who and what she was, and they were stone-cold killers. They didn't judge her, and she didn't judge them.

Other men would not understand. Especially a police officer who had sworn a duty to protect lives, not take them. This was not a date, she told herself. She reminded herself of what Griffin had said, it wasn't a marriage proposal, it was just dinner. He'd texted her the name of the restaurant the night before.

Stella didn't know why, but instead of reaching for her trusty black jeans, she tugged a black summer dress off the hanger and slipped it on. She eyed herself in the mirror. Wearing a dress felt so foreign. During her decade overseas, she'd never worn a dress. Not once. A dress got in the way. It made her feel soft right now to wear it, vulnerable. Shuddering, she shook off that thought.

She wasn't in Fallujah or Angola. She was going to a restaurant in Oakland.

Staring at herself, she thought that maybe with a dress she should put on some makeup. She dug into a drawer and in the back unearthed some eyeliner, mascara, and a bright red lipstick. It took a few minutes to apply the makeup, but she was pleased with the results. It had been a while since she had put on a full face of makeup, but she thought it looked good. She brushed out her long hair until it was silky.

Giving herself one last glance, she decided she had pulled it off. It felt strange but also a little exciting.

Driving to the restaurant across the Bay Bridge, she turned up the volume on her radio and sang along to a catchy new pop tune to avoid road raging over the stop-and-go traffic. But she'd given herself plenty of time to get there. She realized she felt happy. This time, she didn't allow the guilt to squash that small sliver of joy.

There was only one brief moment during the drive when she caught a glimpse of a man walking on a sidewalk in Oakland that had thrust her back in time. Something about the man's gait had reminded her of Nick. Quickly, she shook off the unbidden memories.

She pulled up and parked near the front door of the restaurant shortly after seven p.m. Walking up, she peeked inside the large plate glass window. The restaurant was full, but she didn't see Griffin anywhere. She hung around outside for a while. Checking her texts, she saw that this was indeed the restaurant he had mentioned and there was only one place by this name in the city. At seven thirty p.m., she checked her texts one last time and left.

What a creep. He ghosted her.

Even if there had been a homicide he was called out on, he still could've taken the time to text her, so she didn't sit around for a half hour waiting. Back in her car she sped back across the Bay and whipped into the parking lot of a liquor store near her apartment. She bought a bottle of Bulleit, grabbed a bag of ice, and threw money down on the counter.

A few minutes later, she stormed into her apartment and flung the booze and ice on the counter. Slamming into her bedroom, she ripped off the dress and tossed it toward her bathroom's trash can. Then, in the bathroom, she angrily swiped the red lipstick off and scrubbed her face hard to remove all the makeup.

Throwing on an old Giants sweatshirt and shorts, she poured herself a drink and curled up on her couch to watch a movie. But as she scrolled through titles, she became increasingly upset.

She flipped the T.V. off and took her refreshed glass of bourbon and ice to the roof. There was a small garden up there and a few rickety chairs. She was happy to see it was empty.

Standing on the edge of the waist-high wall surrounding the roof, she watched the fog roll into the city from the ocean. It was a bit unsettling to watch the fog swallow the stars and the lights as it grew closer.

A deep sense of melancholy overcame her. It had been a foolish idea to think that she could be happy. Nick was dead. Now, Bellamy was dead. When was she going to face the fact that she had no right to be happy when the others were dead? Griffin had some strange effect on her, but it was like a faint weak signal she recognized. It wasn't what she had with Nick. Nobody could ever replace Nick or what they shared.

Why had she ever agreed to dinner? If she had been smart, she would've kept it to what worked: Quick sex. No emotions. No relationship. Just a purely physical arrangement. But she'd let herself catch feelings—just a little—and when Griffin had invited her to dinner she'd imagined something more than sex. Something that would never work. Never. That's what happened when she let her guard down.

She would be sure to never do it again.

23

STELLA SPENT THE NEXT DAY COVERING A MISSING person's story. A young woman had been drinking at a bar the night before and walked out without her coat. She never made it home that night, her roommates told police. Witnesses said she'd left the bar intoxicated and alone. Nobody at the bar left after her for at least another hour, so she wasn't followed from there. Her car keys were found in an alley a few blocks away. Nowhere near where her car was still parked. Stella knew this story was unlikely to have a happy ending. But she put the woman's name and picture out there anyway, saying the authorities were asking for the public's help in finding this woman.

But it was unlikely she had stumbled over to a friend's house and was sleeping off her drunken night. This was not going to end well.

As she was writing the story, her cell phone dinged. She looked down. It was a text from her mother asking Stella to call her. Ignoring it, Stella looked again at the last message from Griffin. Along with the name of the restaurant, he'd written, *Can't wait!*

With an exclamation point and a star-eyed emoji. She'd laughed at the emoji at the time.

Now, her finger hovered above the phone. She wanted to text him and ask, *What the?*

Her style was to let men chase her. She normally would never ask someone who stood her up what had happened. Normally, she would just move on.

But Griffin didn't seem like the type to flake or ghost. Plus, she'd end up seeing him at crime scenes, so she couldn't very well ignore him forever.

Knowing she was going to regret it, she sent a quick text, "Didn't think you were the type to flake without a text."

Then hit send. She waited. No. He wasn't the type to flake. It didn't make sense.

After she turned in the missing person story, Stella submitted Freedom of Information records requests for campaign contribution information for Congressman Walker. In addition, she dug around trying to find financial information for both the oil companies. Despite herself, she found herself checking her phone every so often, hoping that Griffin had texted back. But nothing.

Stella was checking her email when Josh stopped by her desk on his way out.

"I was wondering if you could follow up on a story I was working on. My kid's got a soccer game tonight. The story's written, but if you get any new info, can you do a write through?"

"What's up?" She knew she sounded impatient. She was eager to get back to the oil story.

"Homicide detective is in a coma. He was assaulted last night. We only need an update if he ends up croaking."

Stella could feel the blood drain from her face and her hearing went bonkers for a second.

Josh stared at her. "You good?"

"What's his name?" she managed to ask.

"Robert Griffin."

Stella grabbed her bag and shoved her things into it, and then stood.

"What hospital is he at?"

"General."

* * *

Stella stepped out of the elevator onto the Intensive Care Unit floor with trepidation. Two uniformed police officers sat outside a room on the left side of the hall. At first, when she checked in at the nurse's desk, the woman behind the desk said Griffin couldn't have any visitors.

Stella thought fast, letting a false tear roll down her face. "I'm his girlfriend. Please?"

"Family only."

"We were supposed to get married this weekend," Stella said smoothly.

The woman gave an exasperated sigh. "ID?"

Thinking fast, not wanting to be connected to the newspaper, Stella handed over her real ID. It showed her real name, Stella LaRosa.

The woman glanced up. "You Dominic's kid?"

"Dominic's my uncle."

"I'll clear you for visits. But you're his sister, not his girlfriend, okay?"

"Thanks."

Stella walked over to Griffin's room. The two cops glanced at her. She had a sticker badge on her shoulder.

"You got clearance?" one asked.

"Yes," she said pointing to the sticker.

The cop, a young, freckled-faced kid, glanced at the other one who shrugged. She opened the door. The room was dim. Griffin was in a hospital bed in the middle, surrounded by a bank of machines which were whirring and buzzing with various lights and beeping sounds.

He was restrained. Grabbing a chair, she pulled it over to his right side.

"Griffin? It's Stella."

There was no response.

His face was an unnatural color. Or maybe it was just the lights. His hair was goopy with something. Blood? Ointment? Glue?

"I'm sorry I got mad at you and thought you flaked." She watched his face carefully, but it remained placid.

"Who did this?" She found her voice was laced with anger. "Who did this to you?" she asked again.

She sat there for a while before a nurse entered.

"Hi," Stella said. "How's he doing?"

"And you are?" the nurse asked, his scrubs patterned with SpongeBob.

Stella was about to say girlfriend when the nurse said, "Only family is allowed."

"His sister."

The nurse began adjusting Griffin's IV. "You're not his sister."

"Fine. It was the only way I could get in here. Are you going to kick me out?"

"You the one who put him here?"

"Excuse me?" Stella said.

"No?" the nurse said. "Then you can stay. He could use the company."

"Has anyone else been here to visit?"

The nurse shook his head. "Not a soul."

"No other cops?"

"Just the ones guarding him outside."

"That's heartbreaking."

The nurse nodded and exhaled before saying in a low voice. "Step outside with me for a second."

Stella followed him. Leading her away from the two armed cops sitting by the door and said in a low voice, "His only emergency contact was an ex-wife. When they called her to tell her, she said she hopes he dies and rots in hell."

"Wow," Stella responded.

"He can hear us, so be careful what you say inside there," the nurse warned.

Stella nodded and turned to walk back into the room. Taking a seat by his head, she reached for his hand to rub his palm and fingers.

"Griffin, you gotta wake up and tell me who did this to you."

There was no response. The room was silent except for the beeping of the bank of machines.

Stella sat there for three hours, occasionally rubbing his hand, and speaking encouraging words. Finally, when she caught herself falling asleep for the third time, she stood to leave.

Before she left, she turned one last time to look at Griffin. He looked so helpless. And so alone.

24

HE DUCKED BACK INTO THE SHADOWS OUTSIDE THE hospital. She was so close he could almost smell her on the ocean breeze that flowed down the street. He watched as she quickly glanced from side to side before she crossed the street. She entered a parking garage, and he lost sight of her. He took a step forward and then checked himself.

The area was filled with people—groups of young people who had arrived shortly after an ambulance had pulled up with lights and sirens to the Emergency Room entrance. The young people had poured out of their vehicles and were pacing, trying to get a glimpse as a young man was unloaded on a gurney and rushed into the E.R. Some of the women were wailing loudly. Some of the men were shouting, raging about how they would make someone pay. Several squad cars arrived with lights on and parked with the officers not getting out of their vehicles, but making their presence felt.

In a way, he was grateful the street outside the hospital was so busy. Otherwise, he might have been tempted to approach her. But it was too soon. He needed to stick to his plan. Seeing Stella LaRosa in person had done something to him. Something he didn't like. It had reminded him that he was more than just a killing machine.

He balled his hands into tight fists. Some killing machine, the cop was still alive.

A crowd of drunk millennials had come around the corner and one of them had screamed bloody murder. He'd been forced to leave without getting the job done.

It was the first time in his life he hadn't completed an assignment.

He'd lurked in the shadows waiting for his chance but police cars had arrived within moments. After slipping into the hospital he'd seen the detective's room was heavily guarded.

When he reached out to his contact, he was told that killing the cop in the hospital would have brought too much attention. The death had to have happened during his first attack where it could be mistaken as a robbery gone bad. The man in charge told him that if the cop ever regained consciousness then that would be the time to take him out. Right now, he was incapacitated and that would be enough. For now.

Leaving the cop alive made him feel restless. It wasn't just about finishing what he started, it was also something else. Examining the feeling, he realized he felt unsatisfied.

The satisfaction of killing fulfilled a deep-seated need in him. He knew that much. But he also wasn't willing to explore where it came from. That would mean digging deeper into what made him who he was today. Any psychologist would blindly point to a child-hood riddled with abuse, but it was more than that.

As soon as he'd been recruited as a killing machine, he had found his true purpose in life. It was the only thing that scratched the itch that kept him up at night. The power he felt in taking a life was a rush like no other drug had ever succeeded in giving him. He realized he was jonesing. That leaving the cop alive had left that yearning inside him unfulfilled.

Since his flight didn't leave for a few more hours, he would satisfy that itch and leave town with nobody any wiser. He knew just where to go. Skid row, or what passed for it in San Francisco. The Tenderloin District didn't have as many homeless people as it had years ago when he'd been here. All those second-generation hippies in San Francisco had tried to find housing for the vagrants, but there were still enough of them to fill a church.

The church opened its doors to the homeless every night, which he found utterly repulsive. Even imagining going to church and sitting in a pew where a disgusting homeless person had drooled and farted and snored, made him want to vomit. Well, the church would have one less occupant tonight.

He waited around the corner, picking his prey among a stream of homeless people headed for the church. Eying them as they turned onto the street, he saw him. A man about his age.

It would have to be fast, so none of that filth and grime rubbed off on him.

Ducking back into the entrance to the alley, he poked his head out once the man got close enough, then he held out a crisp twenty-dollar bill. "Psst...I got something for you."

The man's rheumy eyes narrowed, and he hesitated. "I don't do that stuff," the man said.

"No, man, I just want some information."

"Yeah?"

"Yeah. You see things, right?"

The man nodded.

"Well, I got this and another one if you tell me what you saw today."

"I just gotta tell you what I saw? What if I didn't see what you wanted me to see?"

"Still get the money."

The man looked both directions and then turned back toward him with a sigh.

"Back here, where nobody can see us."

The homeless man followed, shuffling his feet. When they had reached the middle of the alley, the first punch was thrown. The man reeled back but surprisingly stayed on his feet. He was strong and managed to retaliate with a powerful right hook that cut through the air but missed its mark.

He stood there panting, blood streaming down his face. His eyes widened as he saw his opponent in the light of the streetlamp.

"Come on, you want that money don't you, you disgusting excuse for a human being!"

The words were punctuated by a bout of flying fists.

But the homeless man stayed on his feet, swaying and holding up his arms to defend his face but catching the well-aimed strikes in his ribs and abdomen.

He moaned and cried, but within seconds his legs were swept out from under him. Landing hard on his back with a thud, the man began to scream as the other man stomped on his abdomen, legs, arms, and head. Looking around to make sure nobody had heard the screams, the man took the last of his fury and landed a powerful, bone-crunching kick to the man's face.

After that, the homeless man didn't move again. He backed up, stumbling and panting, looking down at the man. Then he wiped his hands off on his pants and turned to leave.

25

THE SUN WAS POURING THROUGH THE TREES, WARMING THE frost off the grapevines dotting the rolling green hills as Stella drove the winding roads of Danville.

A low mist hung on the horizon obscuring the base of Mt. Diablo, which loomed in the distance. The mountain wasn't large by mountain standards, not even four thousand feet high, but to Stella Mt. Diablo was the backdrop to most of her life. When she was in high school, it was a favorite spot for her and her boyfriend to go and make out with its stupendous views in all directions. To the west, you could see the Farallon Islands that lay past the Golden Gate Bridge, and to the north, you could sometimes get a glimpse of the snowy peak of Mt. Lassen some four hours and 240 miles north. A bittersweet feeling overcame Stella as she remembered how innocent she had been and how those days would never return.

Without thinking, she stomped on the accelerator and the box of cannoli on the passenger seat slid as she took corners a little bit too fast, the warmth of the sun beating down on her from her open-top Jeep. She reached over and turned up the volume on her stereo. She was listening to a playlist she'd made when she was drunk twenty-four-seven and had really been into female hip hop artists. They were angry. She was angry.

She'd stopped by the hospital this morning to visit Griffin. There had been no change, and the nurse told her she was still the only visitor. It broke her heart. How could she be the only person he had when she had just met him?

To shake off her despair, she blared her music and tried to blot out thoughts of the pale-faced cop hooked up to way too many machines. Then, too soon, the driveway to her parents' place appeared. She turned off the music and slowed down as she pulled up to the house. The driveway was packed with cars.

After standing at the door for a little too long, she finally turned the door handle and walked into her parent's house with trepidation. When she opened the front door, the dog came running to see her, wiggling. Leaning down, she hugged him hard and whispered, "Tino, give me the strength to deal with these creeps."

Uncle Dominic and his jerk sons were back in town.

She could smell the garlic and onion aroma from the pasta sauce and her mouth watered. She also got a whiff of fresh bread. Seeing her mom and dad and eating delicious food would be worth showing up today. When she walked into the foyer a bit further, she heard loud voices and weeping.

What now?

Stella shed her jacket and juggling the cardboard container of cannoli and a bottle of wine tucked under her arm, she headed for the dining room. Her mother had recently painted the walls of the windowless dining room a deep burgundy and reupholstered the chairs in black velvet, so the space felt more like a mortuary to Stella than the cheery, yellow wallpapered space she'd grown up eating in. And right now, it especially felt like she had walked into a wake when she saw the scene waiting for her.

All the women were gathered around Jamie, who sat in a black velvet chair. Eyes red and puffy, tears streamed down her face.

Quickly Stella scanned the room for the baby and then sighed with relief when she saw the child in her sister-in-law's arms.

Stella opened her mouth to ask what was wrong but before she could her mother was at her side, pinching her arm hard.

"Ow," she said. "What the hell, mom?"

"Don't you dare curse around me," her mother hissed in her ear in a loud whisper. "Come with me into the kitchen and help me with the lasagna."

"Okay?" Stella said and shrugged when her cousin Bonnie met her eye and raised an eyebrow.

They passed the patio door on the way to the kitchen. All the men were outside smoking.

In the kitchen, her mother cornered her. "Stella, I told you not to hurt Davis."

"I only hurt him a little."

"A little?" Her mother's voice rose in a shriek. "A little? Did you think he was going to escape that fire? He's dead, Stella. Dead. Only a little!"

Oh no.

"Ma, I didn't set a fire. I thought about it, but I didn't."

"Then how did he burn to death hours after you brought Jamie here?" she said, her voice a low hiss. "The police showed up asking questions. Your dad and Dominic are trying to do damage control, so you don't get arrested for murder!"

"Well, they can't arrest me for something I didn't do!" But inside, she knew they could. She was there. She beat him up. Jamie even saw her with the gas can. Damn it.

Stella shoved the box of cannoli across the counter, thrust the wine bottle into her mother's arms and stormed outside.

The men stopped talking when she opened the door. They all looked at Dominic. He jutted his chin, and they all filed past her into the house. Even her father.

"Daddy?" she asked as he passed.

"I'll be right inside, honey," he said and leaned over to kiss her cheek.

She was furious. *For once in his life, could her father stand up to her Uncle Dominic? Just once? For his daughter?*

"What the hell's going on?" she said to her uncle, crossing her arms and glaring.

He didn't speak, just lifted the cigar to his fat lips, inhaled and then exhaled. She was about to turn around and leave when he sighed. "You don't want to be in the family business and yet you do something like this?"

"You and I both know I didn't kill him," she said through gritted teeth.

"Heh? That doesn't matter. What matters is the police have eyewitnesses showing you go to his place to get Jamie. Then they have your prints on some tire iron found near his body. It's not good, Stella."

"I didn't set the fire. When I left, he was alive."

"Don't worry. I've got a connection. But my point is that if I'm going to dig you out of situations like this, you're going to have to return the favor."

Stella felt a fury tear through her and knew she was about to say something she'd regret. Instead of speaking, she turned and walked into the house.

"My generosity could stop at any second," he yelled after her. "Don't you forget it."

26

RORY MURPHY STEPPED INTO THE ELEVATOR AMID A GROUP of men his age all in black suits. He suddenly felt like a hick in his gray jacket and black pants. It didn't help that conversation ground to a halt as soon as he stepped inside.

Then one man with a Superman-style jawline and matching black hair that swept back on his forehead cleared his throat. "What say you, gents? Drinks at Barmini, and then we head to the party at George's place?"

Rory knew they meant George Stephanopoulos, the once political aide, now celebrity news anchor.

"Sounds good," another guy answered. "Tom Brady and Kate Hudson are going to be there."

"Brady's not bringing his wife?"

"Ex-wife, dummy."

"That's why I was asking."

Rory tried to tune out their bragging, but then one of them nudged him.

"Hey, Murphy, you going to the party tonight?"

On the surface it seemed like an innocent question, but the

laughter that followed it confirmed otherwise. These men, supposedly Rory's peers, had always made him feel awkward and less than. He'd thought that would change when he began working for Walker, but it seemed like it had only grown worse.

Now, in the elevator, one of the men in the back coughed out the word "nepo." The word was thinly disguised by his cough. Rory wasn't completely clueless. He knew that the word was slang for children who were granted jobs or status based on their parents.

For a second, he thought about correcting the guy and telling him that, in fact, Walker wasn't his father, so it would be more like a "nepo son-in-law." But only after he married Isabel. He quickly shut down that idea. Even though they were all adult professionals, something about this group screamed jerk frat boys and he wouldn't put it past them to throw a punch or two if he got snarky.

"I'm going to take that as a no," one of the men said. "That's too bad. Lots of hot women there. You do like women, right, Rory?"

"He's dating Walker's daughter, you dummy," another guy said. They were speaking as if he wasn't even there.

"That's why I asked."

Rory felt his face grow hot. He clenched his hands into fists and turned around to find the man speaking when the elevator door opened with a loud bell. He heard the crowd outside the elevator waiting to come in. Before he could move or speak, the other men in the elevator began to rush out, pushing him with them. By the time he was turned around and oriented again, they were at the front doors, leaving.

He wanted to *kill* them. Putting up with their Ivy League bull didn't bother him. He'd been shunned by good old boys his entire life. But for them to dare speak badly about Isabel made his blood boil.

He stormed out into the cool night at a fast march, stomping down the sidewalk on the way to the Thai food restaurant where he was retrieving Walker's dinner.

By the time he entered the restaurant, Rory had cooled down.

Those idiots would never find anyone that could hold a candle to Isabel. She loved him. Would never have even given those types of men the time of day. She saw right past their arrogance to the insecure little boys they really were. Rory knew he may not have their looks or charisma, but he had more loyalty and integrity in his little finger than they had in their whole bodies.

"Hi, Rory!"

It was the sweet older woman who worked behind the counter. He had been lost in his thoughts. He smiled at her. She handed him a large paper bag neatly folded on the top.

"Are you sure I can't throw in some pad Thai for you? You need to eat, too, sweetie."

Smiling, he said, "I had a big lunch Mrs. Li, but I'll be in on Friday."

"See you then," she said. "Have a good night!"

"Thanks, you too. Don't work too hard."

Walker had an account with the restaurant and shortly after Rory had begun working for him, had taken his young protege there. It was now Rory's favorite. But he could only afford to eat out once a week, so he tried to frequent the place on Fridays when he had time.

Back in the building, he was relieved to see that most people had left for the night.

Rory Murphy was about to enter Walker's office when he stopped. The Congressman was speaking on the phone in low, angry tones. The words *civilians* and *Syria* and *murdered* could clearly be heard.

It was after hours. There was nobody else left in the office and possibly the building, so Rory leaned in, straining to listen.

"This is going to blow up my entire life," Walker said. "You got what you wanted. Those Syrians are dead. He got the oil fields. We got the money. The merger is going to be approved. But all of our work is going to be destroyed if one of the team members opens their big traps. The girl came to my office. *My. Office.* In Washington, D.C. She was asking questions. This is way too close. It needs to end now. Yesterday! I want every single one of them dead. *Every. Single. One.*"

Rory drew back.

What?

This was bad.

He heard the phone being slammed down hard and took it as his cue to enter.

"Excuse me?"

Walker looked up with glassy eyes, and it seemed like he didn't recognize Rory for a few seconds.

"Yes, son?"

Rory held up the takeout Thai food he'd been ordered to pick up.

"Oh, yes. Set it right there," Walker said in a distracted voice, and pointed to a side table. "You can go home now. I'm going to finish up some more work and then I'll just call my regular driver."

"Yes, sir."

Rory set the food down, hoping that the congressman didn't see how badly his hands were shaking. Then he smiled and backed out. He quickly walked to his car. It wasn't until he was on the freeway headed toward home that he felt like he could breathe again.

27

As it happened so often lately, Stella had been working late at the newspaper and didn't even realize it had grown dark outside. She'd been busy researching and digging for a possible connection between Congressman Walker and Bellamy.

There was nothing.

After her shift, she was going to go visit Griffin at the hospital again. When she'd called the nursing supervisor earlier, she'd been told his condition hadn't improved. She called and visited every day. They said it would be hard to tell if he had brain damage until—or if—he awoke from the coma.

She'd just packed up her things when her cell phone rang.

It was Harry.

His voice was ragged.

"They got Jordan."

No. No. No.

For a second Stella's throat felt like it was closing up. She stared in horror at the empty newsroom around her. Even though Garcia and the copy editors had left for the day, she held back the scream of rage she wanted to let loose.

"Now we know for sure," Harry said. "They're going after the team."

Stella stood. Her whole body was shaking. She reached over and before she knew it, she'd plucked a large dictionary off her desk and hurled it across the room. It struck a nearby wall and fell to the ground.

"Stella?"

"I'm sorry. I'm just stunned. It's too much, Harry."

"Where was she?"

"They broke into her apartment in Cleveland. Made it look like a burglary gone bad. But I talked to her neighbor, the guy heard the killer say something about Bellamy."

"No!"

"I know."

"Listen, Stell, I've got to run. But before I do, remember, you've left that life behind."

"What are you talking about?" she gritted the words out. How had he sensed her murderous rage over the phone?

"I know you. I know you sometimes better than you know yourself."

"Whatever."

"Let me handle this. It's not worth getting involved."

"I'm not going to sit back and let them get away with this. But don't worry. I'm not going to kill anyone."

She meant it. If she could go the rest of her days without taking another life, it still wouldn't make up for her past. But it would be a start.

"Good," Harry said. He sounded distracted. "I've got a lead on something. I think I know why you guys are being targeted. I'm meeting a source later. I'll be in touch."

Before Stella could press him for information, he'd hung up.

"Be careful, Harry," she said, but it was too late. The call had disconnected.

For a few seconds, in the empty newsroom with the windows

black with night, Stella put her arms on her desk and then leaned down, burying her face in her hands as she wept for Jordan. Those bastards. Bellamy, and now Jordan. She needed to warn Matthew.

Finally, after she allowed herself to cry, she lifted her head, wiped her tears, and stood.

This was war.

Whoever was killing her friends was going down if it was the last thing she did. Meanwhile, she still had some responsibilities. To Matthew. She needed to find him and warn him. And she realized Griffin was in a coma because she hadn't warned him of how grave a danger he was in.

Packing up her things, she headed to the hospital. By now, the cops stationed outside greeted her with half-friendly nods. She knew she was the only visitor Griffin got. That was another reason she took time to visit so she could hold his hand and speak to him softly and encourage him to wake up and help her hunt down the person who had done that to him.

Tonight, for a reason she couldn't explain, she leaned down and kissed his forehead when she said goodbye.

Damn it, Stella, she told herself. *You've become such a softie.* Something about the detective not having a soul in the world visit him had hit her hard.

She was just leaving the hospital when she got a text. Harry. He was going to be in town the next night and wanted to meet her for dinner.

"8 p.m. The Lounge. Ritz Carlton."

"I'll be there," she texted back. He knew something. Something important enough to fly to California and tell her in person.

* * *

Stella walked into The Lounge at the Ritz Carlton at 8:05 p.m.

Pausing in the doorway, she was glad she'd dressed up. It had been years since she'd been to the restaurant, but she knew it wasn't a place where she would fit in with her black jeans and motorcycle boots. And she knew if she was meeting Harry, she needed to blend in.

Unfortunately, she might have picked the wrong dress for that. She wore a form fitting black leather dress that grazed her knees. While it showed very little skin, it hugged all the curves she usually had hiding under her jeans. She'd paired the dress with her highest Manolo Blahnik stiletto heels and ruby red lipstick. As she glided through the sumptuous space, heads turned in admiration.

She was uncomfortable with the attention. Not because she was unused to the male gaze, but more that she didn't want anyone to remember her meeting Harry. But just like Griffin's story of the pink cowboy hat, she would rather they stare at her body in the black leather dress than remember her face and that of Harry's. Thinking of Griffin sent a pang of guilt through her. The attack on him was her fault. She was certain of it.

Now, the maître d' who had been leading her stopped in front of a table in a dark corner, curtains to the side that could be pulled closed for privacy. Harry's face broke into a broad grin, and he stood and kissed her cheek. Stella hugged Harry tight. It was like hugging a beloved teddy bear. He wasn't overweight, but he definitely had a small paunch and some softness about him now.

Drawing back, she held onto his forearms, and examined him. His black hair was now flecked with silver and his mustache was completely white. There were crinkles around his chocolate brown eyes when he smiled, but they still contained the same warm and caring gaze. When Harry looked at Stella, she always felt safe. She cherished that.

Squeezing his arms, she pulled away, and they both settled into the booth. He plucked a bottle of Champagne out of an ice bucket and poured her a glass. An array of cheeses and olives were spread on a tray before them.

"What's the celebration, Harry?" Stella asked, taking her glass from him.

He held his glass up to hers and clinked it. "Seeing you again in person."

Stella gave a small smile.

She'd made it clear to Harry long ago that they would never be more than friends. Sleeping with him that long ago night had been sweet, but ultimately a mistake. Unfortunately, Harry didn't see it that way.

She sipped from her glass and set it down.

"I do have news, of course," he said.

"Worth flying out to San Francisco for?" she asked and winked.

"I'm not going to lie, Stella. I coulda told you over the phone. I wanted to see if you'd give me another chance."

"Harry." She looked away as she said it. He was such a good guy. But not the one for her.

When she looked over at him again, he was looking down. But he quickly rallied and smiled, drumming his fingers on the tabletop.

"Bellamy's murder was connected to Syria."

Her breath left her body. She stared at Harry for a few seconds before she answered.

"The compromised op?"

"Yes."

"Did the terrorists who set us up decide that taking Nick's life wasn't enough? They got what they wanted. Innocents dead. America blamed. Headway disbanded. My leg is full of uranium."

"Maybe," Harry said.

"Whatever," Stella snapped.

The sudden rush of rage and grief threatened to overwhelm her. Heads turned at her raised voice. Looking around at the faces watching her, Stella took some deep breaths. After a few seconds she regained her composure, meeting Harry's eyes.

He exhaled loudly before he spoke.

"Stella, I don't think it's the terrorists."

Harry left the sentence there for her to contemplate.

153

Stella began to nod slowly, at first, and then faster. "That's the only thing that makes sense, but I still can't figure out why. What did we see or know that makes someone want us dead?"

"Tell me about that op again, Stell?"

"It was a total disaster. Worse than a disaster—it was a nightmare. We had a source, Nick's source, actually, that led us to believe a group of terrorists were in this hall having a meeting." Her forehead creasing as she recounted that day. "I was sent in to do my job, early re-conn. I said I was a journalist doing a story about the history of the historic site. The manager let me in. When I walked in, it was a party, Harry. A kid's party. Little kids running around. Cake. Balloons."

"For crying out loud. How come I never heard this?"

"Who would want this out?" Stella asked. "It was bad enough that the media got a hold of the fact that we had bombed a gathering that included children."

"They tried to keep your names out of it. I don't think any of you were named."

Stella ignored this. It didn't matter.

"That's why you got out," he said. "That's why you are so adamant about leaving that life behind."

Nodding, she continued her story.

"I rushed back out to tell the others to abort, but as I did, I heard the planes coming." Stella closed her eyes. A few tears squeezed out. She clenched her fists. She'd never recounted that day out loud before.

"Go on, Stell," Harry said. Leaning over, he wrapped a strong arm around her shoulders. "Go on and let it all out."

Harry handed her a thick black napkin that she buried her face in. After a few seconds, the tears stopped.

Harry squeezed her hand as she continued. "I ran outside to tell the team it was a mistake. We'd been set up. That it was a goddamn kid's birthday party. Nick looked at me—I'll never forget the look on his face—he looked at me and ran inside. A few seconds later, the hall exploded from the bombs."

"I'm so sorry."

"He ran in to save the kids Harry," Stella said, her voice catching. "I tried to stop him but Jordan, she tackled me. She tackled me. She saved me, Harry."

There was a long silence.

Then Harry said, "We're going to get them. We're going to make them pay, Stella. Okay?"

"Yes," she said, and her eyes became steely. "We will. We have to."

"I might have a lead. I'm still putting the pieces together, but I think that the dates line up between the op and the purchase of that oil field that's been in the news. That merger that they are looking into."

Stella sat up in her seat and her eyes widened. "What are you talking about? There's a connection with the op? The one in Syria? The last one?"

"I'm pretty sure there's a connection, I just need to find out what it is."

"You think that's why Bellamy and Jordan are dead?"

Harry nodded. "Maybe."

"Why?"

"I think they knew about the connection. What I suspect is that whoever killed them has reason to believe that all of you have the same information. You guys were such a tight-knit group, that theory holds water."

"Oh no, this is bad," Stella said.

"It's definitely not good."

"The detective I told you about, he's in the hospital. In a coma. They said it was a random attack, but obviously he was getting too close to something. We need to warn the others." As soon as she said it, she realized there was only one team member left: Matthew. There were no "others."

Harry must have noticed the emotions flashing across her face because he grimaced. "I'm already on it," he said and took a long drink.

"Thanks, Harry. You're the best."

When he reached over and took her hand in his, his hand was soft. He wasn't a field guy. Not really. He worked mostly at a desk.

"Do you think so?" His words were slurred. He'd started drinking a while ago, she realized.

She gently pulled her hand away from him and said in a gentle voice, "Do you have far to go to get back to your hotel?"

"Oh, I'm staying here darling."

"Good. I don't think you should drive."

He nodded morosely. "I won't."

She downed her drink and stood to leave.

"That's it?" he asked in a sad voice. "You don't want to go up with me, do you?"

"I don't think so, Harry."

She felt sad. He was a really good guy. She loved him. But not in the way he wanted.

"You didn't even have any cheese," he said in a dejected voice, and gestured to the plate on the table.

Leaning over, she gave him a kiss on his cheek. It was rough and scratched her face. She didn't care.

"Is it because you still love him?"

Stella looked at him a long time before, saying "Take care, Harry," and walking away.

He smiled back, but his smile was even sadder.

Outside waiting for the valet to bring her car, Stella looked up at the windows of the hotel wondering which one Harry was staying in that night. She felt guilty. Maybe she should have offered to drive him to the airport the next day or even meet him for breakfast. But encouraging him was the cruelest thing to do.

28

THE SUN WAS ALREADY STREAMING THROUGH THE WINDOWS of Stella's apartment when the phone rang, waking her. Her first thought was joy that it would be a sunny morning in the sometimes gloomy, fog-shrouded San Francisco, but then irritation set in that someone would dare call this early.

Don't people know about texting?

After a few failed attempts to find the phone, she unearthed it from under a clump of her duvet. It was Garcia.

"It's seven a.m. Garcia."

"Yeah, I know. I'm calling because I'm going to need you to work a double today. I'll make it worth your while. Josh is busy with a kid in the hospital."

"Oh no, what happened?" Stella asked.

"Nothing serious. Needs a few stitches, but you know how the children's hospital E.R. is—he could be there for eight hours, and I need a reporter working ASAP."

Stella didn't actually know how the children's E.R. *was*, but she didn't remind Garcia of that fact.

Sitting up, she rubbed her eyes. The apartment was a disaster.

There were clothes strewn across every possible surface—even the stove in the kitchen. She'd planned on doing laundry and cleaning this morning, but that clearly wasn't going to happen.

She couldn't care less about overtime or Garcia "making it worth" her while. But she was curious what was going down. That would get her out of bed.

"What's up?"

"There was a homicide last night that I want you to chase," Garcia said.

"Of course." A homicide would be worth getting out of bed for. That was her forte, covering terrible things, she thought wryly.

"This one is a little different."

Stella sat up. "Oh yeah?"

"This vic is a C.I.A. agent. The feds are swarming all over this and trying to lock us out..."

Everything Garcia said after *C.I.A. agent* was a jumble of words she couldn't comprehend. It was like a swarm of hornets was buzzing inside Stella's head. Her heart felt like it was going to leap out of her chest.

"Collins? Collins?"

Distantly, she heard Garcia saying her name.

"Okay, I'm on it," she managed to choke out before disconnecting.

Then, she curled into a small ball and stared at the wall. After a few seconds, the tears came. At first they were silent tears, then they turned into wails. She flailed, kicking and punching her bed. Burying her face in her pillow, she screamed and beat at the bed covers with her fists.

They got Harry.

Lying in bed, her face streaked with tears, head throbbing and her heart aching, Stella wished with her entire being that she had stayed the night at the hotel with Harry. If she had, he'd still be alive.

Harry's loss wasn't as devastating as losing Nick, but it was still one of the worst things that had ever happened to her. She knew she'd never get over it. Harry had always been there for her for as long as she could remember. They had met when she first joined Headway. He'd been stationed in Morocco, and they'd become fast friends.

Nick had never liked him. Not really. Later, she realized it was because Nick had always sensed that Harry was in love with her. Stella hadn't known that at the time. Not until she'd lost Nick.

It was Harry who came to pick her up when she was released from Walter Reed. She'd been given a cane to use for a few months. He took one look at her and shook his head. He took her to the bar in the hotel where she was staying until her flight back to California the next morning.

"They fix you up okay?" he asked, taking a sip of his tequila.

She shrugged.

"What is it?"

"It's going to take some time to get my round kick back up to speed," she said lightly.

"You got this."

Noticing the look on her face, he said, "Any other long-term damage? To the nerves or something?"

"Hard to say. They did say they think there is a decent chance the shrapnel contained uranium."

"Oh, Stella."

Stella looked away, unable to bear the look of concern in his eyes. She didn't know why she'd told him that small but terrifying detail. Sure as hell she wasn't going to tell anyone else that, especially her mother, but Harry had that way about him. She trusted him.

Instead of talking more about it, they kept drinking and shut down the hotel bar. He'd escorted her to her fourth-floor hotel room. At the door, she'd looked up at him and then grabbed his hand, pulling him into her room and then her bed.

In the morning, he'd been gone. He let her calls go to voicemail. Finally sick of it, she'd called him in the middle of the night.

His voice sounded groggy when he picked up.

"It's me," she said.

"Stella," he said. "I can't."

"Can't what?"

"I can't just be friends."

"Oh come on, we've been friends for years." She knew deep inside she sounded heartless, but she resolved to stand firm.

"I'm not like you," he said. "It won't be enough."

"I don't want to lose you," she said. And she meant it, she had a soft spot for Harry. He was the salt of the earth. He was one of the few truly decent men she knew. That's why in the middle of her soul crushing grief over Nick, she'd let her guard down in her grief and let him in for one night.

"Stella, you know I'll always be here for you if you need me, but it can't go back to how it used to be."

They'd been great friends. He'd always respected her relationship with Nick. She'd never once suspected his true feelings for her.

"When you were with Nick," he hesitated after saying the name, but then continued. "I never allowed myself to think of you that way. I knew where your heart was. And now I realize it will always be there. Even though he's gone."

She'd chewed on that for a few seconds before answering. "I can't help it Harry."

"I know," he said. "Stella, I can't compete with a ghost. Nobody can."

He was right.

Now, unable to stop the weeping that had soaked the pillow beneath her head, Stella realized that now Harry was also a ghost.

All bets were off. She hadn't wanted to be a killer again, but they would make her go back to that life. Because someone was going to pay for Harry's death.

29

STELLA STORMED INTO THE POLICE STATION WEARING HUGE dark sunglasses to hide how red and swollen her eyes were from crying. She'd thrown on leggings and a giant black hoodie along with combat boots. She knew she looked a little shady, but she didn't care.

The clerk looked up at her in surprise.

"I need to speak to Tommy Mazzoli. Is he working today?"

The woman slowly nodded. "Yeah, Mazzy's on today. What's this about?"

"It's personal."

The woman raised one eyebrow.

Stella stood her ground.

"Who shall I tell him is here?"

"Stella not from Sicily."

"Alrighty then." The woman picked up her phone. "Hey, Olivia, can you radio Mazzy and tell him someone is here to see him in the lobby at the precinct? Tell him it's—and I'm quoting here—Stella not from Sicily." The woman hung up. "They'll let him know."

"Thank you."

Stella turned and began to pace the small precinct lobby. When she leaned over to pick up a magazine off a table and then threw it back down, she realized she was shaking. She was filled with a mixture of fury and grief. Harry was a good guy. He hadn't deserved this.

Standing in front of the glass doors, she watched the cars pulling into the parking lot across the street. She wondered if Mazzoli would park there, park somewhere in the back and come in through the station, or if he would just pull his squad up front.

Thinking about stupid stuff like this, she realized, was keeping her from screaming as she waited.

Two silver sedans pulled into the lot. Idly, she watched them park side by side, as far away from the precinct door as you could park. Stepping closer to the windows, she wasn't surprised to see six men in suits get out of the vehicles. They stood around in a cluster, talking.

The feds who were called in to deal with Harry's murder, she thought bitterly. The ones that were going to make sure nothing about his death ever saw the light of day.

Just then, a squad car pulled up front. She recognized the driver. Mazzoli. As she walked down the steps, she kept her eyes trained on the men. One of them noticed her and must've said something because instantly all the heads turned to look at Stella.

They'd clocked her. They knew exactly who she was. She walked right past Mazzoli's open window.

"Hey, Stella not from Sicily!"

Without turning, she said, "We're being watched. Meet me at the Blue Moon coffee shop in twenty minutes." She continued to her car without waiting for an answer.

If those men were behind Harry's murder, she'd be putting the cop in danger by speaking to him in front of them. Pulling away, she headed in the opposite direction from the coffee shop. She drove slow and sure enough before she'd gone two blocks, she spotted one of the silver sedans three cars behind her.

While cursing the lack of get-up-and-go of her old Honda, Stella sped up and squealed around a corner, lifting her emergency brake to slow the car for the turn. Then, almost as quickly, she made another left and then zoomed at full speed down the narrow street in time to see a silver sedan shoot past in front of her. She waited a few seconds at the corner and then crept onto the road, keeping five cars between them. If they were good, they would immediately spot her, but she would still give it a shot. It was difficult to track the car from that far back, but she would try for as long as she could.

Stella tailed the car down side streets, and then down the Embarcadero where she got stuck in traffic. Eventually she lost the sedan when it was one of the last cars through a yellow light. Turning around, she still had time to make it back to the coffee shop and find a seat in the back before her meeting with Mazzoli.

He walked in, looked right at her, and then jutted his chin back toward the street before turning around and walking out. She looked around. Nobody seemed to notice. Gathering her things, she walked outside. His squad car was empty. She looked around and saw him in front of a market. Mazzoli made eye contact and walked into the store.

She followed him inside the crowded and massive Chinese market. He was near the front, pushing a cart and heading down an aisle. Stella scooped up a basket and followed him. When he stopped to examine some spices, she finally caught up.

Without looking at her, he said. "Something's going on I don't like. You want to know about the C.I.A. guy, right?"

"Yep," Stella said with her back to him, looking at an assortment of dried noodles. "He was one of my best friends. They took him out because he was onto something big. The feds can't be trusted on this one."

"I know who you are," the cop said.

Stella's heart thudded in her throat. Before she could respond, he continued.

"I also know you don't do any of that stuff that your family does. That's why I'm gonna help you."

Walking a little further down the aisle, pushing his cart, he threw some candy packets in the cart. "These are my niece's favorites."

"I'm just warning you that everyone who pokes around in this ends up dead or hurt," she said, reaching for some green tea boxes. "Including cops."

Mazzoli was silent for a few seconds. "You're talking about Griffin."

"Yes," she said.

"My family goes way back in this city." He turned the corner with her following a ways behind. "My great grandfather was police chief. We've had a Mazzoli on the force for generations."

"Not sure that's going to help you."

"What I'm trying to say is that I don't like crooked cops."

"Are you saying Griffin is crooked?" Maybe she'd had it all wrong. Or maybe this guy was off base.

"No, but some others are. That's why the investigation into his assault has been shelved."

"This goes way beyond San Francisco." Stella plopped two more boxes of tea into her basket.

Mazzoli looked at her. "What kind of Italian drinks tea instead of coffee?"

"One who is trying to get healthy. It's either this or put a shot of moonshine in my coffee right now."

"*Mamma mia*," he said under his breath. "Coffee is healthy. It has antioxidants for crying out loud."

"Hey, you asked."

"What do you need from me?"

He walked a little ways down the aisle after someone passed the end cap and glanced at them.

"Names of the feds who swooped into town. Anything that they let slip about the investigation into Harry's death."

"Harry's his name?"

"Harry Krazinski. That man was salt of the earth," Stella said, and her voice broke.

Hearing someone say the name made a lump rise in her throat and tears pricked at the corners of her eyes. She clenched her jaw. She could cry later, after she found out who killed Harry.

"What's your number?" Mazzoli said.

"This is not something that can ever be discussed that way."

Mazzoli nodded and then said, "Never mind. Follow me."

Walking down another aisle with electronics, he grabbed two phones.

"I'm going to set these up, and then I'm going to leave one in the bathroom behind the toilet at the coffee shop. Go get another drink, maybe be normal, and get coffee this time. I'll come in after you. After you see me go to the bathroom, be the next person in. We only talk this way."

Setting the basket down, she walked out, heading back to the coffee shop. She grabbed a coffee even though inwardly she was rolling her eyes, and planted herself at a seat where she could see the bathroom door.

Ten minutes later, Mazzoli walked in and headed straight to the bathroom. Five minutes passed before he walked back out. In the bathroom she found the burner phone wrapped in a plastic bag behind the toilet. She opened it up and turned it on. There was one number programmed into it.

She texted it. "Got it."

There was a reply right away. "I'll be in touch."

30

STELLA DROVE HOME IN A FOG, STILL NOT BELIEVING THAT Harry was gone. It was a nightmare. It brought back a flood of memories. There were so many things she had locked up deep inside. Maybe, now that Harry was gone, it was time to face some of them.

After she got home, Stella unearthed a box from the back of her closet. Grabbing a kitchen knife, she slit the heavy packing tape that sealed it. Then she sat there staring at it.

It sat in the middle of her living room, seemingly innocuous: a plain cardboard box. Beige. Four sides. A little beat up.

But it held her demons.

She backed up and eyed it. Someone had gone to the team's cramped apartment in Syria and sorted through their things, somehow figuring out what belonged to whom. They'd boxed it up and shipped it to Walter Reed. Harry had picked it up for her when she checked out.

"What's that?" she'd asked him.

He looked pained and grimaced as he said, "Your belongings from Syria."

"Oh."

Oh Harry. So sweet and thoughtful.

Tears streamed down her face as she stared at the dented cardboard box. It had been carted across the country and crammed in the back of the closet, hidden not forgotten.

Now it was time.

Stepping into her galley kitchen, Stella grabbed a crystal tumbler and filled it with ice before she reached for the bottle of Bulleit. She poured a generous amount, downed it, and then poured more.

Carrying the glass, she circled the box like it was her prey. But she knew that what was in that box was really the predator. Finally, she kneeled down on her wooden floor and leaned over, gently lifting one side of the cardboard and then the other. Then she leaned forward with trepidation and peered inside the box.

The first thing she saw was her extra flak jacket resting on top. She picked it up and tossed it aside where it landed heavily on the floor. Underneath lay a large shoe box. It had once contained steel-toed boots. Now it contained mementos of her life overseas. She reached for it warily, as if it were burning hot. Lifting it, Stella pivoted and set it on the coffee table beside her without opening it.

The next thing in the box was her old laptop. A special issue Headway encrypted computer with a bullet proof casing that could be dropped from a four-story building and survive. At least that's what she'd been told. It could also be submerged up to fifteen feet and still function after it dried out. She'd never had to test either one of those features. The laptop had always been with her overseas. It had become like another limb. It had always been on her back inside the knapsack she wore during her missions.

It was Stella's lifeline to civilization. Connecting directly to satellites even in the deepest jungles, it was often the way the team kept in touch. It provided information at her fingertips in the most precarious situations. The battery lasted for four days. The box also contained a battery pack that could be attached to the laptop, prolonging its life another three days.

All messages that came to the laptop were heavily encrypted, making it the ideal way for those who ran Headway to communicate with team members, but also a way for the team to communicate with their sources. And each other.

After she and Nick had fallen in love, it had also been a way for them to communicate while they were apart. Even if they were apart in the same city, assigned to different details. They had so much to say to each other. Nick wasn't like her. He'd known from a young age that he was meant to serve his country. He didn't like to talk about it, but he'd hinted that he'd had a rough childhood. From what Stella understood, he'd been in and out of foster homes, and then had been taken in by a special forces guy who basically ran a boot camp for foster kids in trouble.

Nick said the man was like a father and got him and four other boys on the right track to avoid prison and instead become highly trained deadly soldiers who worked for justice and peace. While Nick was basically a lethal weapon in human form, he almost immediately showed Stella his soft underbelly, as she liked to think about it. He told her a story about how he'd tried to save a boy during one of his missions, but the boy had died in his arms. He hadn't actually wept, but his eyes had grown glassy, and he'd swiped at them a few times. His voice had choked up, and he'd let her hold him for a long time. Her heart had broken right then.

Nick was the toughest of the tough, but he would do anything for anyone. He'd proven that over and over during their missions. So during the times he'd grown distant and cold, Stella hadn't taken it personally. She knew he had seen and experienced a lot of dark things in his life, and every once in a while needed time to process them.

Right before he died though, he'd told her that he couldn't imagine a life without her in it. He'd hesitated for a second and she'd known he was about to ask her to marry him, but then the others came in. It was time to go. Within hours, he was dead.

The laptop held so many of their intimate conversations.

Gingerly lifting it out of the box, she set it on the coffee table behind her. Deep in the larger box, under some more clothing items and a flashlight and set of knives, she found the charging cord for the laptop. She stood, brushing her hands off, and put the laptop and its charger in her backpack. She threw in some clothes and toiletries on top of them. Grabbing her phone, she pulled up the airline ticketing information.

Her heart was racing, and her face felt flushed. The shoebox sitting on the coffee table felt like an accusation. She picked it up and shoved it behind her couch. She'd deal with those demons on another day.

31

Unable to sleep during her cross-country flight, Stella went over everything she knew about Bellamy's and Harry's murders trying desperately to find a connection between them, the team itself, and underhanded dealings in Washington, D.C. But she kept coming up short. She needed more information. She needed what Harry was going to tell her.

At one point, somewhere over Texas, she remembered she had another job and texted Garcia. "Family emergency. I'm so sorry. I'll be back in the newsroom in a few days."

He replied immediately. "Good luck."

Stella was surprised. Most editors were such dicks. Garcia was a rare one.

Knowing she'd have to talk her way into the congressman's office, Stella had dressed the part. She wore a navy pencil skirt, high-heeled pumps, a white blouse, and a blazer. She pulled her hair back into a low bun and wore huge, albeit fake, black plastic glasses. She looked like a lobbyist. She'd fit into D.C. just fine. She even carried a briefcase for good measure.

The cab dropped her off right in front of his office building.

Flashing her old Associated Press badge at the security guards, Stella handed over her briefcase to go through the x-ray machine. It housed a few old notebooks and pens and nothing else. She hoped it didn't still contain some leftover gunpowder residue, but she didn't think the machine could detect that. It couldn't be that advanced.

Once through security, she headed straight for the second floor, where Congressman Walker's office was located. A secretary posted outside his immediate office tried to stop her, but she deftly swept past saying she had an appointment.

Stella flung open the heavy oak door and walked in. A young man in a gray suit and an older man in a navy suit sat sprawled in chairs in front of the congressman's desk. Walker, who was behind his desk, stood abruptly and reached for the phone.

Stella held up her palm. "I'm just here to talk."

"Who are you?"

"Stella LaRosa."

The congressman's eyes narrowed, and he sunk back into his seat. "I don't take kindly to surprise visits," he said.

"What the hell have you gotten yourself into, Walker, having a LaRosa family member visit you in the middle of the day?" the elderly man with the silver-hair said.

"Nothing at all," Walker said evenly, keeping his eyes on Stella.

They stared at each other in silence for a few seconds until Stella spoke. "Harry Krazinski was my friend."

"Why are you telling me this?" Walker said.

"I don't know what kind of game you're playing," she said and let her glance fall on the other two men for a second before turning back to Walker. "But this is a warning. I am going to find out who killed him and I'm going to hold them accountable."

She gritted out the words.

"Is that a threat?" Walker said, reaching for a cell phone on his desk. "Because the minute you walked in I started recording. Not to mention I have two witnesses sitting here. A member of an organized crime family storms into my office and threatens me? In front of other people? And I have it recorded? This is my lucky day. Honey, you just sealed my re-election because I'm taking your family down."

When he finished speaking, Stella laughed. He couldn't hide the surprise that flashed across his face.

"What the hell is all this about?" the elderly man said with a scowl.

"It is a threat," she said. "I'm threatening to find out what happened to Harry Krazinski—and Mark Bellamy and Jordan Jones. And when I do I'll put every single detail in my newspaper for the world to read. What happens after that will be up to the authorities. But I have a feeling it's not going to be pretty."

"Listen, I want you to know that I support every effort to find out who murdered one of our government employees," he said. "I would never stand in the way of that. So, I'm not quite sure what this visit is about?"

"It's a warning. And a message," Stella said. "At this moment, I can't yet prove that you were behind those murders, not to mention an assault on a San Francisco police officer. But I will. I guarantee that."

"This is libel!" the silver-haired man said, standing abruptly.

"Let me refresh your memory of libel law," Stella said with a tight smile. "It's only libel if it's not true."

"Get out of my office," Walker's voice was low and deadly. "Now! Before I call security and have you thrown out and arrested for trespassing."

"And for threats and libel!" the silver-haired man said with a huff.

Stella looked over at the younger man. His cheeks were bright pink. When she met his eyes, he looked down. Interesting.

"I'll leave, but remember that I'm coming for you, Congressman. If another member of my team dies, it's going to be even worse for you."

Stella turned and yanked the door open. When she did, there were two security guards standing there.

She turned back to Walker. "Your move."

"Let her go," he said with a glower. "She's leaving on her own."

Stella's heart was pounding as she walked down a long hallway to the alcove for the elevators where she punched the down button. She was fuming. She'd been right. Harry had been right. Walker hadn't denied a damn thing. Now she just needed to prove it.

The elevator door was about to close when she heard someone yell. "Wait!"

When she held the doors the younger redheaded man who had been in Walker's office put one foot inside the elevator stopping it from closing as he looked behind him.

"Are you going to make sure I leave?" she said in a snippy voice.

"No," he said and again looked behind him furtively. "You need to text me. From a secure email server that can't be traced."

He rattled off an email address. Stella quickly wrote it in the notes on her phone, saving it.

But then she said, "I'm warning you. Me having your number could be your death warrant. You don't want to get involved. Everyone who does ends up dead."

He stepped out of the elevator and right before the door closed said, "He won't touch me," he said. "I'm his future son-in-law."

32

HE STARED AT HIMSELF IN THE MIRRORS OF THE GYM AS HE hefted the sixty pound dumbbell rhythmically up from his side and to his chest. Although he had laser focus on his workout, he was also hyper aware of everything else in the gym. Every person that walked in, every move they made was clocked.

For instance, there was a guy that caught his eye. The man had perfect dreads falling to his shoulders, and a chiseled face. He wore designer gym clothes. Although he was probably five feet ten inches, the guy walked into the gym like he owned the place, and his eyes surveyed the entire space surreptitiously.

Their eyes met, and for a second there was the briefest acknowledgement of one another. They were two of a kind. He searched his mind. A series of images flashed before him. He knew this guy. For sure. Not someone he'd met in person, however.

Then it came to him.

The guy was an ex-C.I.A. covert operative spy who had operated around the globe. The guy now had his own podcast about being a spy, exposing tips, tricks, and secrets, but also giving motivational advice. Just because he was officially out of the spy business didn't mean he was out *out*.

That meant that the dude was also searching his memory. Time to leave. He'd had his escape route planned from day one.

As soon as the dude turned his back to add more weight to a bar for deadlifts, he dumped the dumbbell at his feet and made for the exit door, keeping his eyes on the CIA guy. For a split second, the man's eyes met his as he slipped through the exit door. He didn't wait to see if the guy would pursue him down the street, instead heading up the stairs. Moving stealthily and silently, he listened for the door below to creak open. When he'd first scoped out the gym as an option, he'd cased it carefully and planned his escape route. He'd tightened down the screws on the door so the point of the screw would scrape along the steel plate and make a screeching noise.

The gym was the only place he'd shown his face in public. All his groceries were delivered to his tiny hole in the wall apartment, and he only slipped out to do his job wearing a hoodie pulled up over his head. But he needed to travel light and while he had an effective workout routine he could do in the apartment; he needed the weightlifting. *Needed* it.

He was pissed that he'd have to ditch this gym for the remainder of his assignment. He'd have to find a new place or do a modified workout.

When he got to the top of the stairs, he paused for a second and listened. He heard a faint sound below him. You've got to be kidding, he thought. The dude was good. Really good.

Opening the door to the roof, he slipped out, then closed it behind him. It made a faint groaning sound. But because he'd stuck a piece of rubber at the bottom it swung open lightly. Then he quickly ducked behind a door to his left. He'd used WD40 to eliminate the squeaking on this door. He closed it behind him, locked it, and waited in the dark. He'd stashed a knife inside the small closet, but he didn't think he'd need it. He knew he could take the guy with brute strength, but couldn't afford the public scrutiny. Another dead body would be bad enough, but the death of a semi-famous ex-spy? Nope. It would jeopardize the entire operation.

He had to keep his eye on the prize. Instead, he would do the unexpected. He would hide. The dude wouldn't know that the door to the closet he was in had been unlocked a few minutes ago. He would assume flight instead of concealment.

So, he waited and listened, his ear pressed to the door. Then he heard it on the other side of the door. Breathing. Just the slightest exhalation. Then the sound of the door to the roof opening. He'd chosen this escape route because the roof had a very visible and large fire escape ladder that descended nearly to the ground.

He heard footsteps on the roof. He couldn't count on the dude to walk all the way over to the edge of the roof and peer down. So he waited longer. Then the footsteps returned. He listened as the C.I.A. dude loudly walked back down the stairs. Then, for good measure, he waited another twenty minutes before he cracked the door.

He was patient. He'd learned to be over the years. Brute force was good, but psychological warfare would always prevail. It was why he was so good at what he did. Why he was working for the most powerful people in the world now.

Quietly, he went down one floor and then picked the lock of an apartment he knew was vacant. From there he slipped out the window and took that fire escape down into an alley keeping his eyes open for the C.I.A. operative—just in case he was that good.

He walked home pissed off at the CIA guy. He had needed that weightlifting session, if only to release the rage that had been building against the woman. He hated how much emotion she made him feel. The sooner she was dead the better, but he still would save her for last. It would be the most satisfying. And he got off on making himself delay pleasure.

An hour later, he paced the empty room of his apartment, fueled by even more rage. While he was barely controlling the urge to punch holes in the empty four walls, his boss was on the other end of the phone, spewing fury.

He listened silently, glad that the man couldn't see him. If his boss had been able to see his eyes, he'd see death inside them. His fists clenched and his teeth gritted as his boss went on with his tirade.

"She walked right into Walker's office. She knows something."

He marveled at that. Girl had balls. He imagined her walking into the congressman's office and couldn't help but wonder what she said, how she looked up close.

Did the horrors she'd seen and the grief she'd felt register on her face now? He hoped so. Just the thought of her made him sick. He was saving her for last despite what the rich man wanted.

"Get rid of her," the man hissed into his ear.

"She has to be last."

"You don't tell me what to do!" the man shouted. "I'm the one paying you. You *have* to do every goddamn thing I tell you."

"No." He said the word in nearly a whisper. But the boss man had heard.

"What did you just say?"

"We're partners," he said in a low voice. "We're in this together. One of us goes down, both of us go down."

"Are you threatening me?" The man's outrage made him chuckle.

Damn right he was threatening him.

"I've had every meeting photographed. I've had every call recorded. Every interaction is documented. If something happens to me, it all goes public. If I get arrested, it goes public. Do you understand?"

The man sputtered something unintelligible before managing to say, "If you don't get rid of her, I will. And look at the file I just sent you. That's your next assignment."

And then the rich man abruptly disconnected the call.

It was an empty threat. The rich man wouldn't dare get his

hands dirty. He would also be too scared to hire another assassin on his own. He'd needed help to do it once, he wouldn't be able to do it on his own.

There was no threat to his plan. Stella would be saved for last. But she would definitely be sent a warning. Something that would remind her to keep her mouth shut.

Clicking on the secure link, his breath caught in his throat. It was footage from the hallway outside the congressman's office. He watched Stella walk to the elevator. Her movements were tense. She was pissed. But she was undeniably attractive. He hated that he found her so appealing. A second later, another figure entered the screen. It was Walker's aide, the son-in-law. He watched as they spoke. Stella typed something into her phone and then the aide turned and left.

Picking up his phone, he dialed Walker.

"Your boy followed her into the hall. She took his phone number."

"Holy smokes," Walker said and let out a long exhale. "Dumb kid. He caved that fast? His loyalty lasted a day? What in the hell am I supposed to do now? Isabel is going to be heartbroken."

"I've been ordered to take care of him from our friend."

Walker shook his head. It was beyond his control.

"Get it done," he said and hung up.

33

FROM THE SKY, KEY WEST LOOKED LIKE A LITTLE SLICE OF heaven on earth. The varying shades of turquoise water, the pristine beaches, the white houses...it all added up. It was the perfect hideaway for Matthew.

Matthew was the team's surfer boy. He'd grown up in San Diego, in the waves from the time he could walk. He'd talked about retiring to New Zealand where he could surf all day long, but those plans had most likely been scrapped when the op was compromised. He'd said it enough times, that trying to go into hiding there would have been impossible. Even so, it had been the first place Stella had looked for him just in case he was trying to hide in plain sight.

But Key West made sense. As her plane landed, Stella smiled thinking of seeing Matthew in person. Even though the circumstances would be less than ideal—her warning him that his life was in danger—she was excited to see him.

Every op they had, every country they went to, every bar or restaurant they walked in, all eyes were on Matthew. He looked like every gorgeous movie star who had ever played a surfer: longish blonde hair, blue eyes, tanned skin, a perfect physique and able to charm the socks off a nun.

Stella, of course, personally thought Nick was the most attractive member of the team, but she was biased. Nick wasn't conventionally attractive. It was almost as if his good looks snuck up on you as you got to know his personality. Because when Stella first met him, he looked like a thousand other military men she had met. His looks were so generic that he could easily blend into any crowd. When people were asked to describe him, there were no distinguishing features to remember.

Average build. Average height. Average weight. Average features. Brown hair. Brown eyes. But Stella thought he was anything but average, and she knew every scar and mark on his body. When he smiled at her, she thought he was the most beautiful man she'd ever seen.

She was actually glad that all the women gawked at Matthew instead of Nick. Everywhere they went, women fell in love with Matthew, and he loved them back—to a certain extent. He had a different woman in bed every night. They teased him about it. He said he was always honest with the women and told them he wasn't looking for anything serious.

Despite this brutal honesty, he left broken hearts behind in every city. Every single woman he was with thought she could be the one to tame him. He was like George Clooney before the actor found his match in Amal.

Stella remembered one night when they were leaving Amsterdam. They'd been there for two months on a mission. They'd thought they were staying a third month when they'd received word they were leaving the next day.

When Matthew had heard, he'd asked Stella to come with him to his favorite haunts so he could tell all the different women he'd been seeing goodbye. He was considerate like that. He didn't want any woman to think he'd ghosted her. Stella knew it would have been easier, but he wasn't like that.

"Why me?"

"If you're there, they won't try to get me to sleep with them 'one last time,'" he'd said and blushed.

Stella had burst into laughter. "I bet they still will."

She'd been right.

The first bar they'd gone into, Priscilla was already waiting. She scowled when she saw Stella. Matthew introduced her as his colleague and the other woman barely acknowledged her. He told Priscilla his company had called him back to the states, and he was leaving the next morning.

The other woman, a gorgeous brunette with a regal nose, green eyes, and a bombshell body, had burst into tears and thrown herself at him. He consoled her, looking over the woman's shoulder at Stella who was shaking her head.

When he got up to leave, the woman grabbed both of his hands, "Please come stay the night with me? One last night? Please, Derek."

Stella raised her eyebrow at the fake name.

"I really wish I could. I have an early start. I wish you all the best. You are an amazing, extraordinary woman, Priscilla. I'm so glad we met."

Then they walked out. He said the same thing to three other women before they returned home.

And the thing was, he truly meant it. He did find them all incredible women. Which is probably why, Stella thought, he could never pick just one.

She was still smiling about this when she checked into her hotel. As soon as she got in the room, she put her backpack on the bed and took out her old Headway laptop to check her emails.

During her flight, she had texted the congressional aide from a secret, secure IP and email address. He hadn't responded yet. The laptop had special software installed that would help her search for information on Matthew. He wouldn't be using his name, of course. For a second, she thought of searching for Derek, but that was too vague. Instead, she pulled up a program that allowed her to upload a photo of his face and search. It wasn't as high tech as, say, Harry would have been able to use as a C.I.A. agent. But it wasn't bad.

The problem was that unlike an ordinary citizen who threw their pictures up online constantly for no reason other than they bought a coffee, Matthew would be smarter than that. He would know that any image of him that was put online could lead someone to him. And it wouldn't be a friend.

But Stella knew how to do something that others with the program didn't. Harry had given her a supplemental program that allowed her to search surveillance footage in a particular area. It wasn't powerful enough to search nationally, but it could home in on a particular area.

She plugged in Matthew's picture and narrowed her search parameters to Key West. The program began to run. The images flashed by on her laptop. Stella began to zone out and realized she hadn't eaten since early that morning. Her stomach grumbled, and she was imagining digging into a plate of seafood pasta at the restaurant downstairs when the program stopped on a photo.

She sat up straighter in her chair and leaned forward.

"I'll be damned."

It was Matthew.

He was sitting at the end of a dimly lit bar, hunched over with a ball cap pulled low. But he'd made the mistake of looking up and he was laughing. Stella wondered if the camera was near the T.V. screen because everyone at the bar was looking in that direction.

She zoomed in on a napkin. Boom.

The Salty Pelican.

Slamming her laptop shut, she stuffed it in her backpack, searched the room for any other personal belongings, and left. The GPS on her phone directed her to the bar, which was only about a mile south of her hotel. Parking out front, she scanned the other cars.

Black Rose

It was Sunday afternoon and football season. If she was ever going to find Matthew seated at the bar, it would most likely be then. He had always been a fan. During her layover at the D.C. airport, she'd changed into a summery dress and fluffed her hair out. With the addition of some designer sunglasses and red lipstick, Matthew would never recognize her. The Stella he knew dressed in black cargo pants, black T-shirts, and combat boots with her hair slicked back from her face in a ponytail. And she never wore makeup.

Tucking her backpack into the backseat of her rental, she got out of the car.

Entering the bar, she first looked at the end where he'd been sitting in the photo. The spot was empty. Then she scanned the rest of the bar. No Matthew. Disappointment filled her. When she turned to head toward the bartender, something caught her eye. She whirled in time to see a man with sunglasses and a hat come out of the bathroom at the other end of the room. He froze and then turned and sprinted, slamming through a door at the end of a hallway.

Stella bolted after him, shouting, "Matthew!"

She raced outside, slamming the door open and then pausing when she got outside, realizing there was no place for the man to have gone. The door led to a small, enclosed patio surrounded by a six-foot fence. Then she spotted a table near the fence—he'd probably used it to leap over the fence.

Darting forward, she sprang onto the table and scaled the fence. She landed hard on a small sandy trail with the ocean on one side and thick brush on the other. Sprinting, she screamed, "Matthew! It's Stella!"

The path left the beachfront and dove into the woods. Stella ran full bore but never saw anyone in front of her. Finally, the trail opened up into a small shopping center. Pausing as she emerged from the woods, she panted and tried to catch her breath as her eyes scanned the parking lot and the stores.

Matthew was nowhere to be found. He'd had too much of a head start.

In her mind's eye, Stella tried to recall what she had seen in the bar. It had been really dark, and she hadn't been able to really see the man's shape and definitely not his face. But it had to be Matthew. Why else would he have run?

Making her way back to the bar, she walked around and entered through the front door again.

"You catch up?" the bartender asked.

Stella shook her head.

"You a bounty hunter?"

"Nah," she said. "Can I have a bourbon on the rocks?"

She didn't want to press the bartender too soon. Plus, he was the one asking questions, which was the better position to be in.

"Who was he?"

Stella took out her phone. "I didn't think he would run away from me," she said. "He's my baby daddy. But he doesn't know it. I wanted to let him know we had a kid together. I knew he didn't want me for a girlfriend, but to run away?"

She slid her phone over to the bartender, who was caught up in her story. Watching his face carefully, she saw his eyes slide over to the empty spot at the end of the bar. *Bingo.*

"That guy who ran. That wasn't this guy."

He turned to dry a glass with a towel.

"You sure?"

"Yup. The guy in this photo. He was here every day for the past two years. Landon. He left a week ago. Said he was heading to South America on his boat. Said he was tired of dry land."

"You know the name of his boat?"

"Yeah, he loved that baby. He named her Jordan."

"Well, I'll be damned," Stella said and swore softly.

"What is it? Your name?"

She smiled. "No. A friend of ours. I didn't know he was in love with her."

Then her face fell. Jordan was dead.

"Sorry to hear that," the bartender said and reached to refill her bourbon. "Was he stepping out on you with your friend, this woman named Jordan?"

"No. No, they belonged together. Me and him were no good. But I needed to get in touch with him about our baby," she said, remembering her cover story.

The bartender nodded. He'd obviously heard it all before, and then some.

Downing her drink, she left a twenty.

Who was it that had run away from her? The killer? Or someone who was in trouble with the law? Maybe the guy had thought she was a bounty hunter, or a baby mama?

Over at the marina, she asked about the Jordan. It had indeed left a week before. Damn it. Matthew could be anywhere.

He'd probably heard about the murders somehow. Maybe the same person who had reached out to her on the encrypted laptop had been able to find Matthew and warned him too. Stella shook her head. Matthew had a thing for Jordan? She'd never suspected it for a second. If he'd heard about Jordan's murder, he'd have been crushed. He was either hitting the seas to drown his grief or was on the hunt for the killer the same as her.

The more she thought about it, the more Stella realized that it was good he had fled. If she couldn't find him, neither could the killer.

Stella headed toward the airport. If Matthew had been spooked or warned, there was no reason to stick around Florida any longer. In an airport bar, she ordered a drink and unearthed the laptop. When the screen on the laptop flickered to life, she clicked on her messages and saw a new one. The congressional aide?

The subject line was: Urgent. They are coming for you. With trepidation, she clicked on the message.

I can't reveal who this is without putting my own life in danger, but you must know that there is a killer hunting down everyone who was ever involved in Headway. I think you're next. If you know anything, anything at all, you need to tell me now.

Stella read the message again and again.

Who could it be from? It seemed strange that the aide was fishing for information.

She typed back.

How do I know I can trust you?

I'm nobody.

Is this the man I met recently and gave the email address to?

You tell me. Tell me who you gave it to?

Stella didn't like that answer. At all.

What if it wasn't the congressional aide? Then she was throwing him under the bus?

How do I know I can trust you?

Harry was right. There is a connection between the Syrian op and what's going on.

Stella sat back. Whoever this was knew things that nobody should know. And they were still alive.

Tell me something else, she wrote. *Something to help me.*

Think back to that day in Syria. The answer is right there.

I don't understand.

Powerful people want you dead. If you know anything you have to tell me now. I have connections as you know. I can help you.

Does Walker want me dead?

She pressed send and waited. There was no reply. She wondered if no response was a yes, or if she had spooked the aide by mentioning his boss—if it was even the aide writing to her.

She waited another thirty minutes until it was time to board her flight. Nothing.

34

She'd only been home a few hours when her mother called and said Sunday dinner was going to be at her Uncle Dominic's house. Stella didn't like being summoned to her uncle's ranch in Marin County. But the day was gloriously sunny and warm, so she took the top off her Jeep, made a double espresso, and hit the road.

As she navigated the rural roads leading to the ranch, Stella was lost in childhood memories. During the summer, Sunday dinners sometimes shifted from her parent's house in the Danville hills to Dominic's sprawling ranch. Growing up, she and her brothers had always been excited when they woke and were told Sunday dinner was there. It meant riding horses, running in the fields with the dogs, playing hide and seek with cousins, and even, as they got older, shooting beer bottles out of the sky out in the fields with the rifles her cousins used to hunt the pheasants and rabbits on the sprawling ranch.

Stella had first learned to shoot on Dominic's ranch. She remembered all the older men one day coming out to watch her.

She refused to hunt animals, so they set up some hay bales with targets. She was a deadeye shot.

On her eighteenth birthday, Dominic's present for her was a Tiffany Blue Glock 43.

"To match your necklace," he'd said, looking at the Tiffany necklace her mother had just given her.

She stared at him in astonishment. "I don't understand," she'd said.

Taking her outside, he explained the gun was for her to keep as personal protection.

"I don't need protection." she said.

"Everyone needs protection. Besides, that's only half the present."

"What's the other half?"

"Come join us in the family business. You get paid a quarter million a year to be my assistant."

Stunned at the amount of money, she asked, "What exactly do we import?"

He'd eyed her warily before saying, "If you want the job, we talk."

"I don't want it," she said. "Or your stupid gun."

She'd handed the piece of gleaming blue metal back to him. Later, she found it on her dresser in her bedroom. After an internal debate, she stuck it in the back of a dresser drawer. It was a nice gun.

In fact, she had it with her right now, locked in the glove box of her Jeep. She was lucky the tow yard hadn't broken into the compartment and found it. Stella turned down the long driveway. The large two-story white ranch-style house was up on a ridge overlooking the rest of the property. Now, she knew it was up there for a reason. Protection.

The low fence surrounding the ranch was electric, and security cameras dotted the length of it. After her namesake, Aunt Stella was murdered fifteen years ago in her East Bay home, every member of the family had installed major upgraded security systems. For a few years, Stella and her siblings even had bodyguards trailing them to school.

She eyed the house perched above the rest of the land. She could still turn around and go back to the city.

Although her uncle Dominic had couched the invite as a formal Sunday dinner to celebrate her father's birthday, Stella knew that it was a summons mainly intended for her. Her uncle and cousins had been blowing up her phone for the past week, and she'd done a good job of ignoring it. So, he got sneaky.

Her mother had called the day before. *Oh, and by the way, we're going to Dominic's to celebrate your dad's birthday on Sunday.* And that was that. Skipping out of a Sunday dinner would be bad enough, but skipping her dad's large family birthday celebration? He'd be crushed.

As soon as she pulled in the driveway, crowding her Jeep in a spot between two other cars, Stella's mom rushed out of the house, wrapping Stella in a warm hug.

"I love you, honey! I feel like I haven't seen you in ages."

"The newspaper is keeping me busy." Stella didn't argue that she'd seen her earlier that same week. She'd learned a long time ago to just agree with her mother's hyperbole. With trepidation, Stella nodded at the door. "Let's go. I got Daddy a new shirt and a bottle of bourbon."

"He'll love it."

* * *

After a supper that lasted three hours, Stella realized she'd had much more to drink than planned. Which would have been fine except that as she was helping clear the table, Dominic cornered her.

"Let the others do that. I need to speak to you in my office."

Her arms were full of dirty dishes, and he nodded at the couch. "Set them down there."

She scoffed and said, "I'll see you in ten minutes."

Stella didn't wait for his response before continuing on to the kitchen, but she knew he was pissed. People did what Dominic wanted when he wanted, but not Stella.

Fifteen minutes later she headed to his office. Her uncle's consigliere, a tall thin man with slicked back silver hair and more fashion sense than any man had a right to, was waiting outside the closed door. He stubbed out an English cigarette and stood. "Stella, you shouldn't keep your uncle waiting."

Ignoring him, she pushed past him, opening the heavy oak door. Inside the masculine office, the heavy drapes, massive furniture, and dark colors were oppressive after the light, airy day just beyond those closed windows. Every upholstered chair was taken by men—her cousins and uncles and her father. She met her father's eyes, but instead of smiling he gave a small shake, *no*. A warning.

"We need your help," Dominic started. "The F.B.I. has been nosing around asking questions about the family. They're using the word *extortion* in relation to some of our business dealings. You can probably help with that, right? You've got some of those kinds of contacts, right? F.B.I.? We got the local cops as friends, but not so much on the fed level, you know what I mean?"

Stella nearly rolled her eyes. Dominic had ambushed her. He thought asking in front of the whole family would make her change her mind. "I can't help you," she said. "It's unethical."

Glances were exchanged at her words. She looked to her father for support, but he was frowning and looking down.

Once again, it broke her heart. If only her father would just for once stand up for her. Just *once*. She looked at Christopher and Michael. Her brother's faces were expressionless. They didn't dare stand up to Dominic.

Standing, she headed toward the door and reached for the handle.

"Stella, this involves the welfare of the entire family. Your parents. Your cousins. Your nieces and nephews. Everyone," her father said.

"I'm sorry," she said and left.

Without even saying goodbye to her mother, she raced toward her Jeep. She peeled out of the driveway, instantly regretting it when she saw the tread marks she'd left. Her parents would be mortified at her disrespect and this childish display.

Instantly ashamed, she sent a voice text to her mom.

"Sorry, Mama, there was a breaking story, so I had to leave. I love you. Tell Daddy sorry and I love him. I'll bring him his favorite chocolate molten dessert one day this week."

There was no response. Hopefully, her mother was too busy having fun.

Just onto the Golden Gate Bridge, she saw the flashing lights behind her. Pulling over on the bridge seemed dangerous, so she slowed, put her signal on, and moved to the right lane to show she knew she needed to stop and would as soon as she got off the bridge.

The squad car behind her obviously didn't get the message because the driver kept flashing his lights and chirping his siren. She slowed more and was hugging the right-hand shoulder of the bridge.

The cop now had his brights on.

Suddenly, a loudspeaker blared, "Pull over now!"

She was almost to the end of the bridge, so she stuck her hand out the window in an "OK" sign.

Driving slowly, she kept glancing in the rearview mirror but was blinded by the spotlight. Finally, she was off the bridge and pulled over with her window down. There was a cacophony of sirens, and two other squads came to a skidding halt behind the first one. They blocked traffic on the bridge.

Damn it. They were doing a felony stop because she hadn't pulled over on the bridge.

"Get out of the car with your hands up!"

Stella carefully kicked open the door to her Jeep and then got out with her hands held high. She'd covered too many bad, trigger-happy cop crime stories to not feel fear race across her scalp as she did so. She was ordered to face the front of her car. As soon as she turned, she was tackled from behind. Her face hit the hood of her car. Hard.

"Stop!" she screamed. "I'm not resisting. I was too scared to pull over on the bridge!"

Twisting, adrenaline coursing through her veins, she was met by a sneering, burly cop. She managed to duck as he swung his fist in a swift arc aiming for her face. But he wasn't done, he launched himself at her with a powerful left hook that she managed to block with her forearm even though the impact sent her staggering backward toward the back of her Jeep.

Out of the corner of her eye, she saw other officers gather around.

Oh brother. They were watching this like she was in the boxing ring with this crooked cop. He grinned and wiped his mouth as the two squared off. Stella's eyes narrowed. When he charged, she feinted with a left jab and then followed up with a lightning-fast spinning back kick that landed with a thud on his torso. He didn't even stagger back.

Wild-eyed now, Stella began to worry this was a fight to the death. She was his plaything, and he was going to kill her, and then claim she'd resisted arrest.

"I don't want to fight," she said, panting. "If you are going to arrest me, then arrest me." She glanced at the other officers. There were two of them staring at her stone-faced.

"I'm not resisting arrest," she tried again.

"Oh, really?" the cop said. "That's exactly what you're doing. That's why I have to subdue you. Right fellas?"

"That's right. She is a little wild cat."

"Would be a shame if she hit her pretty head on that pavement when she was resisting arrest," the other cop said.

Suddenly, Stella was afraid. They might beat her to death. On purpose or by accident. She had to overcome this cop and run. He outweighed her by probably seventy-five pounds. She'd disable him and run for her life.

Taking a deep breath, Stella sprinted forward, her feet and fists striking in rapid-fire succession as she pummeled his torso, his face, his neck and his groin.

The rules were gone.

He bent over, gasping in pain. She turned to run away but ran smack into the chest of one of the other cops. Then she was face down on the pavement, as a boot repeatedly crunched into her abdomen making her gasp in pain and struggle for breath. She couldn't defend her stomach since she had instinctively thrown her hands over her head, trying to protect it.

In the distance she heard sirens. If she could just hold on a little longer until some other police officers arrived, then these three would be forced to stop. Her arms were yanked down from her head and cuffed behind her back as she squirmed to face away from the blows.

Then, Stella heard the high-pitched voice of an angel. "Stop beating her! She's not resisting arrest. I'm recording this!"

The cops were distracted long enough for her to roll and avoid the black boot she'd seen aiming for her teeth. There was the sound of sirens and skidding tires on the pavement, then shouting. "Officer! Contain yourself!"

"Yes, Sarge."

The first voice was familiar. Stella had turned her head to look when someone yanked her to her feet by her handcuffs. The metal cut into her wrists and she scowled. She was face-to-face with Mazzoli.

Relief filled her, but his face was stern.

"Stella LaRosa you are under arrest for the murder of Davis

Thompson. You have the right to remain silent and refuse to answer questions. If you give up the right to remain silent..."

The rest of the Miranda warning sounded like gibberish to her ears.

This was *insane*.

Only one person would want her arrested for this murder. Only one man knew she was leaving his house in Marin County at this time of night and would be traveling across the Golden Gate Bridge.

Dominic.

35

It didn't surprise Stella that immediately after she was booked and strip searched, she was told to dress in an orange jumpsuit and taken to a visitors room. Of course, her Uncle Dominic was already sitting there. Now she was more certain than ever that he was the one who had called the cops on her. Stella pulled out a chair and straddled it, facing him.

"Orange isn't your color."

"Bite me," she said through gritted teeth.

"They beat you in here?" he said, eyeing her face.

"No. My face fell into the cop's fists as they arrested me."

He frowned, but she didn't care. It was his fault, after all. Dominic still thought she was the timid middle school girl who let his sons beat up on her and was afraid to speak up. But the Stella sitting in front of him was a trained killer. She'd killed men, not as many times as the other assassins on her team, but she'd had to fight for her life a few times. It was them or her.

Nick had made her his protegee, and he had been the best of the best. It was why, after she came out of her drunken, grief-stricken

195

stupor, she took up her training again. Harder than ever. Muay Thai five days a week. The gym six days.

The girl he had known was dead. Although he didn't know that. Not yet.

"I had to leave your dad's birthday party early to bail you out. The whole family is worried. I told them it must be a mistake. I said that I would fix it."

"So, you get to be the hero? When all this is your doing?" she scoffed.

"I don't know what you're talking about," he said smugly.

Crossing her arms, she glared at him. He looked unruffled, which pissed her off even more.

"You happy?" she finally said. "Or are you surprised to see me alive?"

"You are *famiglia*. Even if you don't acknowledge that, you are my goddaughter. I would never wish you dead."

"I don't believe you." Stella raised an eyebrow.

"It takes one call to get you out of here," he said. "One call and your word that you'll help."

She glared at him.

"Stella," he said and gave a long sigh. "Don't do this. I don't know what you have against the family business. It got you that nice house you grew up in. Your college education. All the nicer things in life."

"Your business is repulsive," she growled through gritted teeth. "Just like you. Your business is why your brother Joe is dead."

Dominic's face grew purple. For a second, Stella thought he might be having a heart attack. But he stood without a word and walked away. She didn't stand until he'd left the room. As soon as she did, the cuffs were put back on and she was led back to her cell.

Flopping on the bunk, she tried to stop the tears trying to squeeze out of her closed eyes. The memories came flooding back —the day her idyllic childhood had ended. When she thought back to it, it was as if it had happened to another little girl. When she allowed herself to remember that day, it was as if it were a story she had once read.

With her eyes closed in the jail cell, Stella couldn't stop the story from playing like a horror film in her mind. She tossed and turned on the bunk and moaned, but still it wouldn't stop.

"No!" she said, clenching the thin jail blanket in her fist. Please no.

But then she was back to that day, witnessing what that other little girl, little Stella, had gone through. Heart pounding, the ten-year-old nudged the door with the toe of her sneaker. It stopped after only opening a crack.

She glanced down at the slice of floor on the other side. The door was wedged against a shoe. A man's black dress shoe. The little girl nudged the door a bit more, this time pushing with her palm using a bit more strength. The door budged a little more, pushing the shoe and revealing that it was attached to a foot. And a leg. An ankle with a sock on it.

Stella recognized the sock. It was green and had the silhouette of a golfer on it. She knew the soles read; *I'd rather be golfing.*

It was her uncle's sock.

Her head started to feel funny, and she grabbed the wall for support. She could hear a whooshing noise and wondered if it was the sound of her own blood racing through her head. Her face felt hot. Something fuzzy and lumpy was stuck in her throat. When she swallowed, it didn't go away.

Gripping the wall, she closed her eyes for what felt like a century, but knew it was probably only a second. When her eyes flew open again, she looked down and saw the foot was still there. Her mind would not let her believe what she was seeing. Quickly, explanations raced through her head. Stella clung to one. The one that seemed plausible.

Uncle Joe was drunk. He fell asleep on the floor by the bed. That was it.

But that didn't explain the front door. When she had arrived, the door to her aunt and uncle's house was wide open. And the living room, normally neat and tidy, was a mess.

The small bar cart had been overturned. Bottles of alcohol were shattered, their amber contents soaking the white living room carpet. The fancy glasses, the ones her aunt said were real crystal and expensive, now in broken pieces. The cherished painting of the Virgin Mary surrounded by pink roses, now hung crooked above the couch. One of the couch cushions had a strange stain on it.

In a daze, she saw a small trail of rust-colored dots that led to the stairs. Before heading up them, she'd called out to her aunt and uncle. Stella's voice echoed in the silent house. She was almost relieved when they didn't answer. Maybe they weren't home. But they were supposed to be home. They were supposed to be waiting for her since her mom and dad were out of town.

Casting one last glance back at the sunny day just beyond the open front door, she took a deep breath and started up. Now, about to enter her aunt and uncle's bedroom, she choked back a sob. It took all of her courage to speak.

At first, nothing but an incoherent rasp came out. She tried again. "Aunt Kathy?" Stella was weeping now, snot streaming down her face mingling with her tears. Her voice was nearly unintelligible. "Uncle Joe?"

Silence.

Terror trickled through her. She knew for certain there was a monster on the other side of the door, but she also knew she had to go inside that bedroom. Taking a deep breath, she placed her palm on the door and shoved. The foot was pushed out of the way by her efforts. Now the door was open a little over a foot.

Leaning in, Stella stared inside the room without turning her head. First, she focused on the nightstand by the bed. There was a small lamp with a pink shade. A pair of reading glasses rested on top of a book. An ashtray nearby.

She only saw a tiny slice of the bed from her vantage point. The pink and white floral bedspread she knew so well.

"Aunt Kathy?" she called again, but this time very softly, still sobbing.

Out of the corner of her eye, she saw what she didn't want to face.

The bodies.

Slowly, she swiveled her head to take it in, icy fear crawling across her scalp as she anticipated that someone—or something—awful would jump out at her any second.

However, when little Stella turned her head, the room was empty. Except for the bodies.

Her aunt's body was splayed face down across the floral bedspread. Even from across the room, she could see the back of her aunt's head was a smooshy mess. Her blonde hair now dark and gooey. Her uncle was also face down, a huge crimson stain on the carpet around him.

Then Stella was running down the stairs, out of the house, and racing into the middle of the street. A car heading her way slammed on its brakes to avoid hitting her.

A man jumped out. "What's wrong? Are you hurt? What's wrong?"

With hot tears streaming down her face, she tried to speak, but there was no air left. She looked up at the clouds, hoping to breathe again. Her entire body was shaking. Lifting her arm, Stella pointed to her aunt and uncle's house.

The man looked past her toward the house but didn't understand. "Is someone hurt?"

She nodded.

He grabbed his phone. "I'm calling 911."

A crowd gathered. She looked, wide-eyed with horror at the people staring at her.

A woman came over, "That's Joseph and Kathy LaRosa's niece."

It was that one nosy neighbor. The one the girl hated. The one who would ignore greetings, who would close her curtains if Stella walked by her house. The woman's words were received with a sudden murmuring of the crowd. Their voices were sprinkled with words that felt like slaps across her face.

Criminals.

Mafia. Wops.

The girl clamped her palms over her ears, but still one last comment made it through to her: *Had it coming.*

Rage filled Stella. She dropped her hands into fists at her side and focused her glare on finding the person in the crowd who had uttered those words. Her face grew hot, and her body was shaking as she opened her mouth. When she did, a sound finally emerged from her throat. But it wasn't language. It was a bloodcurdling scream that went on and on and kept on going on until the first squad car arrived a few minutes later.

As soon as the police officer crouched before her, Stella's mouth clamped shut. She didn't speak again for six months.

36

STELLA WOKE THE NEXT DAY FEELING EXHAUSTED, AS IF she'd fought a battle in her dreams that left her with sore muscles and a headache. Then she remembered she was on a janky jail cot, and her aches and pains were from being beaten by the cops. It was all her Uncle Dominic's fault. Such a bastard.

And she meant every word she'd spit at him the day before. He was the murderer. He was the one responsible for his own brother's horrific murder. And he was the one responsible for the murder she'd been arrested for.

The night before, after she'd remembered her uncle and aunt's deaths, she'd cried herself to sleep. At one point, someone else in another cell had asked if she was okay.

"Yes. Thank you."

"No problem. It will get better."

"Thanks."

She'd then put the pillow over her head and tried to sleep. Eventually, she'd fallen into a deep sleep.

Now, the sun was bright through the window, and someone had set a tray of food on the floor. It looked like mush. One corner of brown mush. One corner of orange mush. And some yellow mush. It smelled like old meat.

Even so, some guard had decided to have mercy on her and not make her go eat with the other inmates. Stella was touched by this kind gesture from a stranger.

A female guard appeared and began to unlock the jail cell.

Stella sat up, startled. "Did someone pay my bail?"

The woman just stared at her. The first thing Stella thought was that the woman's eyes were dead.

"Did you bring my breakfast?"

The woman gave a snort. A sliver of apprehension raced down her spine. Stella wasn't sure why. The cell door was now open.

The woman jutted her chin and Stella began to walk that way. Quickly realizing that she was walking away from the jail entrance, she heard another door open and turned to see the lobby. All the other cells were empty. Of course, everyone was at the mess hall eating breakfast.

"Where are you taking me?"

"You want to use the can, right?"

Stella nodded. She did have to use the bathroom, but this was something else. Tensing, her eyes shifted, looking for trouble.

"Keep going that way," the woman said. "First door on the right."

Stella opened the door and saw that the room was empty except for a woman staring at her with clenched fists. Here it was. She turned, but a door made of bars had slammed shut behind her. The guard was on the other side.

Stella whirled to face the other woman, immediately searching to see if the woman held a shank or some other type of weapon.

"Just me and you. Fair fight," the woman said.

Adrenaline coursed through Stella's blood as she clenched her fists and eyed the other woman. Built heavy, she was easily twice Stella's size. Her biceps bulged. Her hair was pulled back tightly from her face and her nose looked like it had been broken a time or two. A long scar ran down one cheek, and she had a tear tattooed under one eye signifying that she had killed someone.

Stella launched the first blow without hesitating, aiming for the other woman's neck. But her strike fell short, and the woman easily stepped back and dodged the strike.

The other woman countered with a left jab that connected solidly with Stella's ribs, making her stagger backward. After she regained her balance, Stella charged and swung her right fist in a lightning-fast arc aimed for the other woman's ribs.

The other woman again easily blocked the blow with a beefy forearm. Stella was prepared for that, and immediately followed up with a swift roundhouse kick aimed to the chest.

The kick landed hard, and the woman let out the slightest hiss of a groan. But then she lunged forward and in a flurry of blows punched Stella's head and face. For a few seconds, all Stella could do was put up her fists and arms to defend herself, but then she saw her chance. With the inmate that close to her, Stella reached up and grabbed the woman's head, lacing and then locking her fingers behind the woman's neck. With all her strength, she yanked the woman's head down hard where it met Stella's lightning-fast knee strike. The woman's nose broke with a loud crunching sound. Stella released her grip, and the woman fell to the ground unconscious.

Turning, she saw the guard was gone.

Stella began to scream. "Medics! This woman needs medical attention."

She heard the pounding of rapid footsteps as someone ran down the hall, their shoes echoing.

A woman, a different guard than the first, appeared and without hesitating, unlocked the barred door. "What the hell is going on here?"

She was an older, heavyset woman with kind, concerned, eyes.

"They locked me in with this woman. She was trying to kill me. I knocked her out," Stella said.

The first guard appeared behind the other woman. "They

started fighting," she said. "I couldn't break it up, so I just locked the door and went to get help. I couldn't find you."

"Didn't look like you were going anywhere," the older guard said. "You didn't follow protocol for an inmate fight."

"I lost my whistle."

The older woman shook her head. "You stay here with Olivia until the medics come. Then you come see me in my office."

Her attention turned then. "And as for you," the guard paused. Stella held her breath, waiting. "I know what goes on around here. They lock the newbies in with Olivia. Looks like they underestimated you, Miss LaRosa. I was just coming to get you."

Stella raised an eyebrow. The guard knew her name.

The woman turned and began to walk away, but then glanced back. "You coming? Someone's here to see you."

Stella brushed past the first guard intentionally knocking into her. "If it's my uncle I'm not interested."

"I don't know who it is, just come with me."

Stella's face was still bloody when she walked into the visitor's room. Her uncle sat there with a smug look on his face.

When she turned to walk out Dominic yelled. "What the hell happened to you now?"

Turning to walk away, she said over her shoulder, "One of the other inmates just tried to kill me and that's all you have to say?"

"Fine!" Dominic said. "See if I care if you rot in prison for murder, I need a snitch in there anyway!"

He yelled those words. Stella felt heads swivel as other inmates looked at her. Fury filled her body.

Back in the hall, she practically march walked back to her cell.

"You'd rather be in jail?" the older guard asked.

"Hell yes. That man is a monster."

"Most men are," she said and closed the door of the cell behind her.

Stella flopped onto the bed. This was it.

It was over.

Staring up at the stained ceiling, Stella told herself it was time to face reality. She was going to prison for murder. It was what her uncle wanted. And Dominic LaRosa always got what he wanted.

He wanted Stella to be his bitch. Well, she'd probably been the only person in the world to refuse him, and so now she was going to rot away behind bars. It was just the final nail in her coffin.

It had begun when she lost her aunt and uncle. Then there were a few good years. Years where she had got to experience what love was. But then Nick was taken from her as well. Now, one by one, everyone else she cared about was being taken away.

Bellamy. Jordan. Probably Matthew.

She'd started to catch feelings for that damn detective. So he's probably going to die now, too.

Harry. Damn it. She'd loved the man. Not as a romantic partner, but she still loved him. Gone. One by one they were being killed.

It was over. She'd probably be better off in prison because it seemed that everyone she had anything to do with was murdered. It would be safer for everyone involved if she spent the rest of her life locked up.

To her surprise, Stella found tears streaming down her face. They dripped onto the disgusting cot beneath her. She cried even more. Pretty soon, her wails echoed in the hallway. She let out all the grief she'd tried to choke back since Nick's death.

"You okay, white girl?" a neighborly inmate asked.

She couldn't even catch her breath to respond. Instead, she wailed louder. Then, hearing herself, she started laughing and crying in tandem for a few seconds.

Exhausted, and nearly every part of her body sore and aching, she fell asleep.

* * *

A sound woke her. She sat up, disoriented. She had no idea if it was night or day. Through her blurry eyes, Stella saw that the kind-eyed, older guard was unlocking her cell.

"You've been sprung, my dear. Let's go."

She stared for a few seconds as it sank in. Dominic must have posted bail so he could torture her at home until she went on trial for murder.

With a heavy heart, she changed back into her own clothes and was given her few belongings. Stella walked into the lobby and saw her cousin, Al, standing there.

Yep. Dominic was going to give her a glimpse of freedom and hope she'd change her mind. She wouldn't.

Her cousin was dangling his car keys. "You look like crap."

She glared at him and followed him out to his ridiculous car. A turquoise corvette, of all things. It could not be more obnoxious, she thought.

Until he started the engine and she heard how loud it was. Climbing in, she rolled down the window and stuck her head out, grateful for the breeze as he drove away from the jail.

"You owe us now, princess."

"Over my dead body."

She crossed her arms and glared out the window.

"You smell."

"Good. I hope it sinks into your car and your next whore asks why your car smells like a stinky woman."

"You're a bitch."

Stella smiled.

37

ALEC WALKER STARED AT THE PICTURE OF ISABEL AS A toddler standing between her father and mother, smiling. She was grinning up at her dad.

They had taken her to Tavern on the Green for the first time. She'd been dressed up in a fancy pink dress with a tutu and a real white fur coat in a toddler size. Real silk ribbons tied in her hair. Nothing was too expensive for his baby.

And Margaret had agreed, Isabel was the light of their lives. Even though both her parents doted on her equally, she'd always been a daddy's girl. Sometimes Walker looked at her, all grown up and so poised and good-hearted, and he couldn't believe she was his kid.

Margaret and he had tried for years to have children. They'd spent a small fortune on fertility treatments and attempts to conceive. It was only when they'd completely given up that Margaret got pregnant. They said it happened like that sometimes.

Isabel was the best thing that had ever happened to Walker. And if he were being honest, he never for one second thought Rory Murphy was good enough for her. But he let it slide. He knew better than to express his disapproval. That's how he'd landed Margaret. Her dad had forbidden her to see him when they were in high school. As soon as they graduated, they eloped. Forbidden fruit and all.

He figured that he'd go along for show and support the Murphy kid's career to make Isabel happy, but that ultimately, she'd tire of him. She'd realize she was meant for more. He'd take her to Europe for the summer and introduce her to some real men, some wealthy successful powerhouse men. Compared to the nerdy Murphy, she wouldn't resist. Couldn't.

The kid was a good guy, he just wasn't good enough for Isabel.

He'd hoped the relationship would end on its own by Isabel's initiative. Never in a million years would Rory break up with her, so he never had to worry about her getting her heart broken. Until now.

Walker had to make a lot of tough decisions in his career, and this was just going to be another one. Sitting behind his desk, he took a deep breath in, held it, and then exhaled loudly. He had his orders.

Carter Barclay had made it clear.

Rory Murphy had chased after Stella LaRosa and given her his phone number. Walker had seen the video footage himself. It was incriminating. It had to go away. And so did the kid.

Unearthing his burner cell phone from a locked drawer in his desk, he dialed the number.

"It's time to take care of the kid."

"Didn't we already discuss this?" the killer on the other end of the phone said in annoyance.

"I'm just making sure. I need it soon."

"How soon?"

"Before dawn, if possible."

"Will do."

"Make it look like an accident," Walker instructed. He found that he choked on his words a little bit.

The killer was silent for a moment. "It will be more money to make it look like an accident."

"Whatever," Walker said, scowling. "Just do it."

He hung up the phone and looked around furtively. If his office was tapped, he'd have been arrested a long time ago. But maybe something new had been installed. Nah. He was just being paranoid.

Everyone else had cleared out hours ago, including Rory Murphy.

In addition to everything else, including consoling his distraught daughter and attending the funeral of a man who had basically committed treason against him, Walker would also have to find a new aide. Damn it. How had all of this gotten so out of control?

He still hadn't figured out how Bellamy found out about it. Walker paced his office.

Needing to leave immediately, so he had an alibi, he had to figure out some place very public to go. Nobody would ever suspect him, but it didn't hurt to cover his tracks in case everything went to hell.

He called up an old friend. "I'm at the office. Can you meet me in ten minutes at the White Horse bar?"

The White Horse was the sort of place where Walker's presence would be noticed. He usually didn't slum it like that, but it also wouldn't hurt his reputation. Occasionally he visited the bar just to prove he wasn't above the people who voted for him. Many of his less successful colleagues would be there, and they would all gather around him to garner his attention and favor.

His friend agreed, and he hung up. It would only take him a few minutes to walk to the bar, which was nearly across the street from his building.

He looked over at the window to see the city below him. However, the windows of his office were dark with night, so the only thing he could see was his own reflection in them. Not what he wanted to look at right then.

It was not a proud moment for Alec Walker. To save his own skin, he was going to have to break his baby's heart even though he thought it was for her own good.

He remembered that in reality Rory Murphy was an okay kid, but Isabel could do better. She really should marry someone above her station. An older man who was already rich and successful. Murphy would never be either of those things.

So in reality, he was doing his daughter a favor, but he cringed thinking of how she would hurt. He'd never wanted her to suffer a broken heart. In fact, from the moment she was born, he'd tried to stop that from ever happening. Now he had no choice.

All for the greater good, Walker.

Not to mention, Isabel would be even more heartbroken if her father were in prison and her inheritance was confiscated by the authorities.

38

RORY STOOD IN THE FAR CORNER OF THE GYM AND WAITED for the leg machine to become free. He whistled a little under his breath, but then quickly clammed up when a guy using free weights shot him a look.

Going to the gym was a necessary evil.

Unlike most of the men here, Rory didn't lift weights to get muscles or bulk up. He did it because it was the healthy thing to do. Even though he was young, he knew that maintaining his muscles would serve him well as he aged.

He wanted to be the type of father who could play at the park with his children and eventually grandchildren. He didn't want to be like his dad who didn't take care of himself, and therefore spent much of Rory's childhood planted in a scratchy old recliner watching sitcom reruns. He didn't have a bad childhood, he just had one where he felt invisible.

If he asked his parents a question, they responded, but for the most part he just did his thing, and they did theirs. His mother was often in bed with migraines and so he learned from an early age how to cook and care for himself. It wasn't so bad. They weren't bad people. They just didn't know any better.

Would he have said his dad was a good dad? No. But Rory was determined to be a good, hands-on father. No, Rory was *going* to be a good father. It's all he really ever wanted—to marry a good woman and have a son. He could imagine tossing baseballs to his son and even teaching him how to play chess.

"Yo!" Rory was startled out of his thoughts by a meathead guy. "You using that?"

Rory looked around confused for a second, and realized he was leaning against a piece of equipment. He hurriedly pushed himself off. "No, sorry."

"It's cool," the other guy said with a smile.

Rory gave an awkward grimace and then noticed the leg machine was free.

Thirty minutes and five more machines later, Rory finished up his workout and was debating whether to shower there, at the gym, or walk the few blocks to his place where he could take a longer shower and use all of his own hair products in privacy. Sometimes it was so sticky out that it wasn't even worth taking a shower at the gym, because after his walk home, he felt disgusting and ready for another shower.

Besides, Isabel was busy tonight. She was going wedding dress shopping with her mother. Just thinking of her in a wedding dress made Rory's heart feel so full. What had he ever done to deserve the love of that woman? She was his queen. He would devote his whole life to making her happy. Hell, he would devote his whole life to just seeing her smile.

Isabel was an angel on earth.

He decided to skip the shower at the gym and walk home. He'd shower there, and then work on a poem he'd been fiddling with to give to Isabel on the morning of their wedding. After he'd met Isabel, he'd gone back to his high school poetry obsession. Something about her had brought it out of him. All he wanted to do was write her love poems.

The other night he'd begun one and was unexpectedly stumped by one part. What he had written just didn't sum up the enormity of his feelings for her—he knew he could do better.

As he walked out of the locker room, he absentmindedly bumped into another man. The man had a strange expression on his face.

"Sorry, man. I wasn't paying attention."

The man looked like he was about to punch him. Rory shrank back. Just then, a group of men in wet swimsuits walked into the gym talking and laughing loudly. The other man turned and walked the other way.

Lordie! Rory had actually felt fear there for a moment.

Stepping out into the night air, Rory hesitated on the sidewalk. He didn't know why but he stopped and took out his phone.

He typed quickly. "Isabel, you are the love of my life." Then he hit send. He wasn't sure why, but it had felt like the right thing to do.

Smiling, he began the walk home, thinking about how blessed he was. Life was incredible. He was going to marry the woman of his dreams. He had a really good job and a great shot of moving up through the ranks with or without Walker. But Walker had mentioned presidential aspirations the other day and taking Rory along with him for the ride. Rory imagined a future where he was Secretary of State or something even more amazing.

He turned from the busy street onto a stretch of warehouses. He never liked this deserted stretch of his walk home, but it was short, and he'd soon be back in a busy residential area. He hurried along though, still a little shaken by the weird encounter in the gym.

At first, Rory thought he was imagining things, but he quickly realized someone was following him down the dark street. Whirling, he saw a dark figure running. He turned and ran, instinctively dropping his gym bag. Fear spiked his adrenaline, and he ran faster than he ever had in his life, his heart pounding in his throat.

He was nearly to the end of the road and could hear people talking when he felt several pricks on his back. It felt like the time he'd been stung by half a dozen bees. He began to scream when he felt an excruciating pain in his side.

It brought him to his knees. He looked up to see a man holding a huge knife that gleamed in the night as it caught a beam of light from somewhere.

Rory immediately recognized the man standing above him.

"You're the guy from the gym," he groaned. "Why?"

The man was hovering above him when there was the sharp sound of people laughing and talking. A door had opened nearby, and people began pouring out. It was an exit for a theater. The man turned and ran.

Rory tried to scream for help, but before his mouth opened, all went black.

39

THE MEN IN CHARGE HAD PROVIDED HIM WITH A SECURITY clearance that meant when he showed up at Ronald Reagan Airport he could walk swiftly past the long lines for ticketing and security and cut right to the front. The agent checking his ID and boarding pass glanced up at him for a second but didn't ask him to remove his dark sunglasses.

Along with his sunglasses, he wore a black beanie and enough scruff on his face so he didn't have any really prominent features. His hoodie was bunched up along his neck and was a bit oversized, so his bulky, muscled frame was also concealed. He wore steel-toed boots, but his clearance level allowed him to bypass the metal detector.

A few of the T.S.A. workers shot sideways glances at him as he strode past. He knew they wondered who he was. Most likely they assumed he was one of them—maybe a T.S.A. federal air marshal who was boarding his flight for his job–to keep passengers safe.

His clearance allowed him to carry his Glock 26, tucked inside his waistband, pressing firmly against the small of his back. Always prepared for the unforeseeable, his ankle holster held a

SIG-Sauer P229. An expandable baton and set of handcuffs were snug on his hip. Rounding out his concealed kit was a folding knife and zip ties. You never knew when those would come in handy.

The chef's knife he'd used on the kid was in the Potomac River. He'd worn a realistic silicone mask designed by a Hollywood FX artist when he'd bought the knife at the Williams and Sonoma in Arlington earlier that day. He'd not needed any of those weapons to deal with the kid.

As he strode past the different gates headed toward his red-eye flight back to California, a woman caught his eye. For a second, he'd thought it was Stella—the Black Rose.

This woman had the same black eyes and dark, silky hair. She was wearing something Stella never would–black dress pants, high-heeled pumps and a silk blouse tied at the neck. It was much too conservative and WASPy for Stella.

He took that back. Stella might wear something like that in disguise on assignment, but never by choice. The Stella he'd studied would wear black leather pants with high-heeled boots and a silky blouse unbuttoned to there. She exuded sexuality, which made her even more dangerous when he thought about it.

But still, this woman was staring. He could feel her eyes boring through his back as he stood in line to grab a coffee at a kiosk. He felt her beside him before he actually saw her.

"That's going to keep you up all night," she said lightly.

"It is indeed," he said and flashed her a smile.

That was all it took—his low, husky voice and killer smile—her cheeks turned red.

"Where are you headed sweetheart?"

"San Francisco."

"Must be my lucky day."

More blushing.

"Or mine," she said lightly.

Boom.

"Just so happens the seat beside me in first class is vacant. Maybe you should join me?"

"How do you know I'm not already in first class?" she said archly.

He grinned. He liked her sass.

But, he didn't say he knew she wasn't in first class because he'd clocked that her handbag was Michael Kors and not Balenciaga, or most likely in her case, Fendi.

"Well, darling."—he plucked his coffee from the clerk—"Be sure to stop by my row and visit after you board."

"I'll think about it." She walked away.

He grinned. Now he had plans for the next morning and a way to release some of the tension that had been building. If the light was dim, he would be able to imagine this woman was the Black Rose, the last member of the black ops team left on Earth.

* * *

The sun was just rising as he looked around his California apartment for the last time.

Glancing into the room as he stood in the doorway, he made sure that all that remained was the stacked cardboard boxes that had been his bed and a few spare water jugs that had served as his sustenance. The trunk that had held his weapons had been loaded into the car he'd bought for cash that morning. He'd thrown his extra set of clothes in the backpack he wore.

He traveled light, and that's the way he liked it.

With his gloved hand on the doorknob, he pulled the door shut so it locked. Once he got outside, he'd throw away the gloves. He'd made sure to wipe down every surface—windows, door, floor, and walls—in the room. It was a habit. He'd filed off his fingerprints long ago.

He knew he should strangle the dumb bitch with the cage at the end of the hall so she couldn't describe him. However, when he knocked on the door, there had been no answer. He'd picked the lock and found the apartment empty. Good.

Luck was with her. She'd live another day. But only because he'd satisfied his urges earlier with the Stella lookalike. He'd frightened her enough that she'd never report him to authorities. He'd convinced her that he was a terrorist and said if she opened her big mouth, he'd kill that cute little nephew whose picture was on her refrigerator in her pathetic little studio apartment.

Now, driving toward the Bay Bridge that would take him into San Francisco, he felt a strange surge of exhilaration course through him. There was only one more thing to do before he left this broken country at long last.

It was time.

The anticipation had built to a crescendo. The morning's activities had been the aperitif to whet his appetite. He couldn't put it off any longer. He didn't want to put it off any longer. He'd made excuses to those in charge, and they had humored him up until now.

He knew it was because they were afraid of him. He was more powerful than them and he was a killer. They thought they were tough, but they paid others to get their hands dirty. And even if they paid someone else to take him out, it wouldn't happen. There were only a handful of people in the world as good as he was at what he did.

If a hit was taken out on him, he'd find out about it. He had enough contacts on the dark web. Nobody would be sneaking up on him and taking him out. He had no doubt that he was the one with all the power now. Soon, he'd show them who was really in charge.

He'd made the last deposit into his Swiss bank account. The last piece was in place. Once it was done, he could disappear forever. The only thing that remained was a dark-haired devil.

Stella LaRosa. The Black Rose.

40

IT WAS NEARLY IMPOSSIBLE TO BELIEVE BUT NOBODY—NOT her mom or dad or her editor–knew Stella had been arrested for murder.

Al had dropped her off at her parent's house. "Tell them you were mugged, and I picked you up from the hospital. Say that you didn't tell them because you didn't want them to worry. Dominic will be in touch."

Stella stood there for a few seconds, watching his car drive away. What was going on?

Instead of going inside, she called an Uber and walked back down the long driveway to the street to wait. Her mother would lose her mind if she saw Stella's bruised and bloodied face and body right now.

Two hours later, Stella walked into the newsroom. It had taken nearly thirty minutes in the shower before the water in the bottom of the tub stopped pooling in pink swirls. After it ran clear, she finally turned off the taps with pruny, wrinkled fingers.

She'd dialed Garcia's number on the way in. "I don't want to scare you when I walk in, but I look a little rough. I was mugged last night."

"Oh no! Are you okay?"

She thought about it for a few seconds and then answered truthfully. "Yeah, I'm good. Just a little sore."

"I was going to call you," he said.

Stella winced. He knew she'd been arrested for murder, and he probably knew she was lying about the mugging.

"I need to meet with you when you get in. Big conference room."

"Am I getting canned?"

"What? No," he said. "Just heard from the publisher and we're going to go in a different direction."

"Damn it."

"Just come see me as soon as you get in."

She was there within the hour.

Garcia stood when he saw her walk in. She followed him to the conference room.

"What is it?" she said, slamming the door behind her.

"I got a call that you might have, let's describe it as 'burst' into Congressman Alec Walker's office the other day and accused him of all sorts of things. "

"I simply spoke the truth."

"Collins, I'd rather tell you to back off than have to tell you to go get them, but this made me look bad."

"How so?" Stella frowned.

"I might have denied it was you because you never told me you were going there."

"Oh, no."

"Yeah."

"I'm sorry. I just didn't want to involve you." It had slipped out.

Garcia frowned. "What the hell does that mean?"

Stella exhaled loudly and shook her head. "It's complicated."

"Spill it."

"I don't want your family to be in danger."

"It's that bad?"

"Yeah."

"Is that why you look like you got hit by a Mack truck?"

"Pretty much."

Garcia clamped his lips together and shook his head. Stella stared at him for a few seconds, trying to will him to drop it. *Just let it go,* she kept repeating in her head.

"I don't need you to protect me."

"Well...we're going to have to agree to disagree on that, respectfully."

Garcia folded his hands together. "I think it's time we both come clean."

Stella squirmed and shot a glance at the window, searching the busy newsroom for salvation.

"Nothing out there is going to save you."

"I can't."

"Then I'll start," he said. "I know who you are. Your turn."

Stella scowled. "What does that mean?" She knew exactly what it meant.

"I'm a newspaperman. My father and his father were newspapermen. The first thing I do when a resume crosses my desk is dig. And dig deep. Homeland Security has nothing on me."

Shaking her head, Stella asked warily, "What did you find?"

"Headway." He whispered the word.

Stella closed her eyes and shook her head for a second, then she opened them, meeting his eyes. "It's too dangerous for you to even say that word right now."

"What do you mean?"

"Everyone on that team is dead except me. They've been picked off one by one, starting with the warehouse murder. And everyone who has tried to dig deep, as you say, has ended up dead. Cops. C.I.A. agents."

Garcia let out a low whistle. "And congressional aides."

"What?" Stella said.

"Walker's aide. He was killed last night. Stabbed to death in a robbery that was interrupted by a group coming out of a show."

"No!"

"I'm afraid so."

"Unbelievable."

"You need to drop this. You need to back off on the oil story because somehow, it's all connected."

Stella stared at him for a long moment. "If you know that much, then you do understand the gravity of this situation."

"Yes, I do."

"So how can we back off? Isn't it our responsibility?"

"It is. But we need to wait for the heat to cool down a little," he said. "Can you at least do that?"

"I don't know."

"Hopefully, it will make them think you've given up, or that you are listening to me telling you to back off. They don't know I know. I convinced them that you would listen to me."

"But it's a ruse, right?" Stella asked. "We back off for a while, but then we go after them, right?"

"Exactly."

She nodded. "You got yourself a deal."

"Now go cover something boring, like the arrest of a bank robber who was actually the C.E.O. of a San Jose start up."

"Fine."

Later that night, after she'd filed a few short stories, Stella checked her email one last time before logging off. There was an email from that AP reporter she'd met at the press conference for Bellamy's homicide, Wade Swierczy.

Hey, I need to talk to you about that murder we both covered. There's something you need to know.

Stella's heart raced. He knew something about Bellamy's murder. Her excitement was mixed with concern. Did he know what he was getting into?

Quickly, she wrote back.

Don't tell anyone a single word. This is very dangerous territory. Call me on this number.

Then she hit send.

Keeping her cell close in case the reporter called, Stella walked out of the newsroom and into the dark night. Feeling morose and lonely, she decided to skip the hospital visit and swing by the liquor store instead.

The nursing supervisor who answered the phone knew Stella's voice by now, so when Stella said hello, the supervisor said, "I'm sorry honey, no change."

"Thanks," Stella replied. "I'm not going to make it by tonight."

"Okay. I'll call you if anything changes. Give me your number."

Stella reeled off her number and then expressed her gratitude.

"Being a caretaker is exhausting, I know," the nurse said. "Take the night off and do something nice for yourself."

"Thank you." Stella hung up. She wasn't a caretaker. She was a friend with benefits who felt guilty about it.

After grabbing a six pack of beer instead of her usual bourbon, Stella wrapped herself in a blanket from her bed and took the stairs up to the roof of her apartment building. She drank from each bottle one at a time under the full moon.

"Another dead soldier!" she screamed to the empty night and threw the bottle across the roof. It shattered when it hit the concrete stairwell wall. "Damn it!"

She knew she'd have to come up here in the daylight and clean up the mess. *What an idiot.*

Staring at the moon, Stella remembered a time when she and Nick had crawled to the top of a roof in Fallujah and drank beer under a full moon. Is that why she'd bought beer and come to the roof instead of visiting Griffin? Even her subconscious was against her.

For a few seconds, she allowed herself to feel the pain of losing

Nick. He'd been everything she'd ever wanted. He was fierce and deadly to others, but sweet and loving to her in private.

The clouds had rolled in from the bay, smothering the moon and plunging her into darkness. Tears streamed down her cheek. They were all gone now. Nick had been the love of her life.

And she knew she'd never get over him.

41

STILL DRUNK, STELLA STUMBLED DOWN TO HER APARTMENT and checked her cell phone. The AP reporter had not gotten back to her yet.

Feeling helpless, she unearthed her Headway laptop. Maybe the congressional aide had sent one last message that might reveal who his killer was. She owed him at least that much before she "pretended" to let the story go.

Logging on, she did a double take when she saw that a message had come in an hour ago. She stared at it for a long time before she opened it.

Clicking it, she was stunned by what she read.

How many more people have to die, you are wondering? I can answer that. Only one. Guess who?

It had been the killer the whole time. She'd assumed it was the aide.

She wrote three words in reply: *Who are you?*

Even though she was starting to see double from fatigue and alcohol, she stared at the screen, willing the killer to email her back. The alcohol was hitting hard, and Stella was sleepy, so she was having a hard time keeping her eyes open. She jerked awake, realizing that she'd dozed off. There was a new message.

We meet tomorrow. Check your email at 11 p.m.

The next morning, she woke at six, slightly hung over but on a mission. She'd had a dark dream about Nick.

In her dream, a disemboweled Nick had led her through the streets of Syria. Every time she thought she had caught up to him, he ducked behind another building. Finally, barely able to catch her breath from chasing after him, Stella rounded a corner and was met with a dead-end alley. All three sides were lined with windowless and doorless tall buildings. At the end of the alley was a small school desk with a laptop on it. She walked toward it with trepidation. When she got to it, she touched the mouse, and the screen flicked to life. It opened up to the facial recognition software she'd used to track Matthew.

But then on the screen was a picture of Walker and the Oil Man.

That's when she had woken up with a start—that was the answer. She would input their two faces and set the search terms so if there was anybody the two had in common, that face would appear.

Even though her head was beginning to throb with the makings of a serious hangover, Stella jumped out of bed and retrieved her Headway laptop. After about a half hour, she was able to figure out how to get the search program to run and look for someone—or several someones—that the two men had in common or had been seen with.

She'd just made a cup of coffee and downed some ibuprofen when the results came back. There were several photos to sift through. Squinting, realizing that her hangover was so bad that simple sunlight was painful. Stella sorted through the results. Then she found it.

Sitting back, she smiled. "Got you."

When her phone dinged, she looked down; it was a text from the AP reporter. She read it and her eyes widened. It explained so much and it would round out her story. She sat down and began to write. After spending another four hours writing a story that knit together her theory, she printed out several copies.

Before Stella showered, she put one of the stories in an envelope and ran down to the corner mailbox in her nightgown and bare feet with her hair giving Medusa a run for the money. Then she headed to the roof and raced back down. When that was done, she finally allowed herself to sit back and breathe. Now, no matter what, she'd covered her tracks. Catching a glance of herself in the mirror in her entryway she cackled. She looked as insane as she felt.

Her eyes were smudged with black from the remainder of yesterday's makeup. Face was still black and blue from her beatings. Her body was sore and tight. It was not an ideal time to meet with a deadly killer. She wasn't in her top fighting form, but she didn't have a choice.

Rummaging in her bag, she unearthed the burner phone Mazzoli had given her. He'd called her the night before when she was on the roof.

She called back.

"I wanted to check in," he said. "I heard that you got out."

"No thanks to you."

"I have to toe the line if I'm going to help you on this. Nobody can know I'm helping you. What am I supposed to do? Not enforce the arrest warrant? Just let you walk away? Your niece said she saw you with the gas can."

"Doesn't mean I killed him."

"It looks pretty bad, but the good news is the charges were dropped. Your uncle has some powerful connections in this goddamn corrupt city."

Stella sighed loudly.

"Listen, I'm on your team."

"Are you?"

"Hell yes. I was calling to make sure you were okay."

"You're the one who arrested me, so you know I'm not okay.

227

They beat me up, and then someone else decided I should have my butt kicked again."

There were a few seconds of silence, and then Mazzoli cleared his throat.

"Stella not from Sicily you and me both know I was doing my job."

"Whatever."

"I've taken care of those cops. They won't be on the streets again for a long time. And yeah, I heard they let Olivia at you. I knocked some heads together over that. I can see that she's punished if you want."

"It's fine," Stella said. "No hard feelings on my part. She's still there. I'm not. I hope I didn't hurt her too badly."

"She's got mad respect for you, I heard."

"Good."

"I got good news, too."

"Oh, yeah?" Stella asked.

"Griffin. He's awake."

Relief filled her. "That is good news."

"But there's still bad news, isn't there? This thing doesn't end. I was watching the news. I saw that congressional aide was taken out."

Stella felt a lump in her throat, something that made it hard to swallow. She finally managed to mutter, "Yes."

"From what I can tell, this whole thing leads back to that oil merger that's been in the news."

Stella shook her head. "Damn, Mazzoli, why aren't you a detective? They're wasting your talent as a patrol sergeant."

"Don't I know it."

"How in the hell did you find all that without ending up tied to bricks in the bay?"

"Day's not over yet," he said. "I made some connections."

"Oh yeah?"

"This politician? He's in cahoots with the oil guy who got the rights to the Syrian oil fields."

"That's what I'm thinking," Stella said.

"What I can't figure out is what the congressman did for the oil dude."

"I can't figure that out either," Stella said. "There are a few Syrian government officials who now are driving nicer cars, taking luxury vacations, even sending their kids away to fancy boarding schools. All within a three-month period. And they all oversaw the approval of the sale to the oil guy, Carson Barclay."

"They got paid off by the oil guy?"

"Looks like it," Stella said. "I do have a theory..."

"Let's hear it."

"There's a guy, a Syrian guy, who has appeared with all three parties."

"Appeared?"

"I found photos of this guy, Basheer el-Mirza, in the background of photos shot of all three of those Syrian government officials. At family gatherings. At official functions. At fundraisers. He knows all of them."

"Keep talking."

"Found the same dude in a picture with Walker three years ago at a Washington, D.C. gala, and—"

Mazzoli interrupted. "Please just tell me you have a photo of him with Big Bad Oil Man."

"Boom!" Stella said. "Two months ago, right before the sale, they both visited the governor's compound in Florida the same weekend. They were seen on the same yacht with some other important Syrians. I don't think it's a coincidence."

"Hell no, it's not."

Both of them sat silent for a few seconds.

"Well, the problem is how do we prove this, share it? I can do more investigating, but since this goes so high up, I have a feeling anything I come up with and try to tell people about will be shut down. Smackdown style."

"Yup," Stella said. "They won't hesitate to kill you to shut you up. We both know that. But while they can kill me, they can't kill a newspaper story."

"Nobody's killing anyone."

"I have the story mostly written. I'm just trying to bolster it with a few more facts. I need access to some Swiss bank accounts, and I don't know how I'm going to do that. I want the story to be rock solid before it goes to print."

Mazzoli was quiet for a moment.

"What is it?" she asked.

"I was just thinking about your C.I.A. friend. I think he was following the money. From what I heard, someone was saying he was poking around asking about some offshore accounts."

Stella shook her head, of course Harry had been a step ahead of them.

"Can you spell it out in plain English?" he asked.

"Walker introduced the oil guy, Carter Barclay, to a fixer in Syria —Basheer el-Mirza. This fixer was paid a lot of money to talk to the Syrian government officials and smooth over the sale of the oil fields to Barclay. Now that Barclay owns them, he embarked on this crazy oil merger. Meanwhile, Walker must have been paid handsomely for his role in the introduction."

"How does that figure with your killer?"

"Mark Bellamy somehow found out about all this and was going to tell everyone. He had a meeting with an AP reporter the day after his murder. He was going to go public with what he knew."

"Still don't know why everyone else on your team was getting whacked."

"I thought about that," Stella said. "We were tight knit. Super tight. The killer must have assumed Bellamy had told all of us what was going on since we all had that special connection with Syria. It was the last op we did, and I don't know how, but Harry told me before he was killed that all of this was connected to that last horrible mission."

"You need to let the world know about this. Now. Before they get to you. Before they try to stop it."

"Tommy?" It was the first time she'd called him by his first name, but she wanted him to remember what she was about to say. "I printed out copies of the draft of my story. I mailed one to my mother's house. I also stashed another copy in my apartment. If you lift up the Virgin Mary statue in the corner by the fern, you'll find it."

"I didn't know you were Catholic."

"I'm not." Not anymore.

"Why are you telling me this?"

"If you don't hear from me tomorrow at noon, you need to get that article and get it in my editor's hands. His name is Garcia. Don't trust anyone else."

"What in the hell do you have planned? Can't you just publish it right now?"

"I just have one more thing to check out," Stella said and hung up.

42

STELLA WAS EMOTIONALLY, PHYSICALLY, AND MENTALLY spent.

Wandering around her apartment in a daze, she felt like there was more she needed to do, but she knew she'd done it all—and then some.

She eyed her surroundings and belongings as if she might be seeing them for the last time. And she knew she just might. She wondered what her mother would say walking into the apartment. The stacks of books. The sexual lubricant in the nightstand drawer. The prescription drugs in the medicine cabinet. The clothes strewn everywhere, including the lacy red bra and matching panties. The shoebox with ammo on the top shelf of her closet. The empty refrigerator. The vodka in the freezer. The pristine, unused stovetop. They were all clues to just who Stella was—a person her mother barely knew.

The worst would be the box she'd unearthed from overseas. Stella grabbed it and her Headway laptop and stuffed them in the cupboard under the sink, behind the trash can. Her family would find it anyway, but at least not right away.

Despite her growing fatigue, she stretched and knocked out some pushups and sit-ups. It felt like she was preparing for a mission in the old days. In many ways it was identical. But it was also much worse and far more serious.

She had put her life on the line before, so that wasn't new, but this was something else entirely. This was fighting for her life. The only thing left now was to bide her time. And to make sure she was as physically prepared as she could be before her meeting with the killer that night.

A nap was in order. She'd trained herself, like any good soldier worth his or her salt, to nap on command. It was a survival skill in the field. Sleep deprivation dulled senses and reflex times, and sometimes that split second where a judgment call was made, or a weapon was dodged could mean the difference between winning or losing—life or death.

Besides, some sleep would most likely stomp out the throbbing in her head. The headache from her hangover and the beatings she'd been taking was starting to come back, so she downed more ibuprofen and yanked shut the blackout curtains in her bedroom.

As she lay there, willing herself to sleep, an unbidden memory of another splitting headache came to mind. On that day, she'd woken to an excruciating headache. The pain seemed to throb in time to the bone-thudding whomping of a helicopter's rotor blades.

Blinking her eyes open, the first thing she saw was a metal ceiling. As she struggled to sit up, Stella realized she couldn't move. She was tied down. For a split second, she was confused. The last thing she remembered was a blast. Before that, she couldn't put the pieces together, but something evil and wicked had happened. Her thinking had been so fuzzy and her attempt to sit up had made it worse.

Think, she'd told herself.

Taking some deep breaths, an image came to mind. She'd been in Syria. On assignment. And then the blast. Now she was a prisoner. But it didn't make sense, why would the al-Nusra Front keep her alive and then fly her somewhere?

That's when she noticed she had an IV in her left arm. On the metal wall across from her, she saw a painting on the interior of the chopper: a U.S. flag. Then it clicked. She was in an AH-1Z Viper. An attack helicopter operated by the U.S. Marine Corps. She'd been rescued.

Lying in the helicopter, some memories flooded back. A scream that was a mixture of a wail and a sob came out of her. The ceiling of the chopper was replaced by three faces looking down on her. Three men. They wore helmets, camouflage uniforms, and flak vests, and carried M27 Infantry Automatic Rifles.

U.S. Marines.

"Hey, Lois Lane. Did you get the scoop?" one of the Marines in the helicopter said. He was hovering above her, looking down with a sneer. His voice was filled with derision.

She glared at him.

"Sorry we couldn't find your little notebook among all the dead bodies," another one said and walked away.

"Go to hell," she said.

Blinking, Stella tried to clear her head. As she did, more memories started coming back to her. The gunfire. The bloodshed. The screams. The explosion. Horror shot through her.

"Where am I? Where is this bird headed?" she asked and struggled to sit up again.

Only one Marine remained hovering above her, he hadn't spoken yet. "We're over the Black Sea en route to Landstuhl."

Landstuhl was the U.S. military hospital in Germany.

"Where is everybody? Where are the others?" *Where is Nick?* Stella tasted blood in her mouth as she spoke.

"We're still some ways out!" He shouted above the sounds of the helicopter. "We're going to get you into surgery A.S.A.P. You caught some shrapnel in your leg."

"I don't give a damn about my leg!" She shouted back. "Where is everybody else?"

Hating the way her voice hitched on a sob at the end of the question, she arched her neck, trying to see past him to look for the others who she prayed were onboard. "Is this the only rescue helicopter? Are there others?"

The Marine just stared at her. Again, she struggled to sit up. That's when she realized: her arms were bound to the stretcher. She had straps on her wrists, ankles, thighs, waist, and chest. Overkill.

"We had to restrain you.," the Marine yelled. "You were trying to choke the nurse. And you gave Corporal Dawson a black eye. You've got a mean left hook." Chuckling, he jutted his chin at another Marine out of her line of sight.

"Let me up now!" Stella screamed in a high-pitched voice.

She turned her head, scanning the rest of the inside of the helicopter. The three Marines stared back at her. The two men in the cockpit area didn't turn around.

She gritted her teeth. "I'm going to ask you one more time," she said, her voice filled with a mixture of fury and terror. "Where is the rest of my team?"

When he didn't answer, she began to scream and flail, straining against the restraints. She bucked wildly and the portable IV stand next to her overturned.

The last thing she saw was one of the Marine's sticking a syringe into a port that led to her IV. Then all went black.

43

HER ALARM WOKE HER AT TEN P.M. SHE STILL HAD another hour before the killer had said he'd email.

Stripping naked, she stepped into the shower. After about fifteen minutes under the hot water, she turned the dial until ice cold shards pelted her body.

Stella lifted her face toward the shower head and with eyes closed, forced herself to imagine the ice raining down on her face felt amazing and not horrific. After a few more minutes of this, she turned off the taps. Her entire body was alive and energized.

Vigorously she toweled off and then pulled on some thick leggings and a sports bra. Stepping into her living room, she ran through a series of stretches and then some light martial arts warm up moves: she jogged in place. She threw imaginary jabs and hooks facing her mirrored wall. Then she did sit-ups, pushups, and pullups. Finally, she folded herself onto the floor and meditated before a short round of yoga.

When she stood and glanced at the clock, it was time. Pulling on a thick sweater, she made her way over to her Headway laptop on the kitchen table.

She opened it at 10:59. A few seconds later, the clock turned to eleven p.m. and a new message appeared.

Larson House. 11:30 p.m. Alone.

He was already there. He wanted to make sure she didn't have time to beat him to the location or to get anyone else there first.

Suddenly, Stella had doubts. She was basically being reeled to her death. The killer was calling her, and she was doing his or her bidding.

I'm starting to wonder why I should meet you after all.

Why would I do that?

At first, there was no reply. She waited, staring at the screen. Then another email appeared. The subject line was: *I was going to surprise you, but...*

She opened it. It was an image. Clicking on the jpeg, a picture appeared. It was a picture of Jamie's baby, Keira.

A second later, her phone rang. It was Stella's mother. She ignored the call and her mother kept calling. Stella knew why. The killer had the baby. Her heart began pounding with fear.

Okay, she typed hurriedly and hit reply.

Strapping on a holster, she tucked her pistol into it. She threw on her beat-up leather jacket and laced her steel-toed boots. Grabbing her phone and keys, she headed out, slamming the door behind her. In the back of her mind, she briefly wondered if she'd ever see her place again. The killer she was up against was no joke. He—or she—had already killed her teammates who were the best of the best. And most definitely better than she was.

It only took ten minutes to get to the building the killer had named. Stella knew it well. They had studied it in school. The Larson House was in Chinatown, it had been on the West Coast's underground railroad. Beginning in the late 1800s, a woman named Geraldine Larson had turned the large home for girls into a refuge for the Chinese girls she and others rescued from trafficking and servitude. Stella remembered being fascinated hearing about the series of underground tunnels under Chinatown that served as a way for the girls to hide and escape when corrupt policemen came with search warrants to the home. They were with men who claimed they "owned" the girls.

And this was where the killer wanted to meet. With the baby. Stella was sick with worry.

As she drove, her phone rang nonstop. Her mother must be frantic, but Stella couldn't risk telling anyone what she knew. Knowing the killer was ruthless, she didn't want to spook him into killing Keira before Stella could rescue her.

She wished she had someone to call. Anyone. But there was nobody. All the people who could help her in a dire situation like this were dead. There was nobody to call. Nobody to confide in who could understand her life and the dangers it held. Nick had been the one. He had known all her darkest secrets. He had known, and often been by her side, the few times she'd had to take another life.

And he'd loved her. He knew everything about her and loved her anyway.

Stella had never felt so alone in her life.

If she didn't get to Keira in time, she wouldn't be able to live with herself. The Larson House was on the far end of Chinatown, opposite from the lively strip clubs that lay near the border of North Beach, the Italian section. It was also off the main drag. Stella parked directly in front of the building and peered at its windows. They were dark.

Sticking her phone and keys in her jacket pocket, she locked her car and headed toward the door. When she twisted the knob, it opened. She stepped inside, wary, listening intently. There were no sounds. She drew her pistol and began to walk stealthily through the building, slowly and methodically, her head swiveling as she moved looking for anyone.

As she made her way to the back, there was another door, this one was wide open. A set of steps lay before her in the darkness. Stella turned on the flashlight on her phone and pointed it at the stairs. They went as far as she could see. The killer was luring her with the promise of her rescuing the baby, but this murderer was ruthless. The baby might already be dead.

Even as she tried to talk herself out of it, Stella knew she had to go down the stairs. She could do it. The stairs weren't that bad. It wasn't ideal, but the ceiling was high, and the stairs were wide. She'd pretend like she was going from the second floor to the first. Stairs didn't bother her in general. Only if she thought about them leading underground. That's when cold fear raced down her limbs.

Glancing one last time behind her, she began to make her way down the stairs. They creaked loudly no matter how gingerly she stepped upon them. A dank, musty smell rose in the air. The stairs led to a utility room. It was empty, but there was a large hole cut out of one wall at about shoulder height. Beyond it was blackness.

She shone her flashlight inside. It looked like a small coal tunnel. She froze. There was no way in hell she could crawl into that space. Might as well just shut her up in a coffin and tell her it would be okay. Tears pricked at her eyes.

Her claustrophobia was her Achilles heel. It would kill her one day.

She stood there for a few seconds and willed her body to move. Willed herself to at least stick her head in the hole and look around again. But she froze. Cold sweat dripped down her temples. It was impossible. She'd go get help. She couldn't do it on her own. The thought of crawling into that death trap was too much.

Stella began to turn around, but then she heard it. The faint wailing of a baby. All the moisture was stripped from her mouth. Taking a deep breath, she counted down from five. On "one" she plunged through the hole. She tucked and rolled and came up to the squealing of a rat that she'd startled. She shone her light on it as it scurried away further down the tunnel.

What if it got to the baby? What if there were many more of them? That sent her adrenaline pumping, and she began to run. As she did, it felt like an unseen ghoul was on her heels, breathing down her neck, but she knew it was only her own terror.

Suddenly the tunnel grew closer and curved at a sharp ninety-degree angle. She heard soft crying sounds. She maneuvered around the corner and felt the wide-open space before her flashlight bounced off the higher ceilings. She shone the light from her phone at the floor, looking for the baby. It was in a car seat and some black boots were beside it. Reaching for her gun with her other hand, she raised the light slowly up the body to the person's face.

For a few seconds, the breath was taken out of her lungs. Her knees grew weak. Her pulse pounded and her face grew white hot. Stella's mouth dried, and she felt as if she were going to collapse in a puddle right there on the floor. Her blood rushed to her ears. She must be delusional.

"Impossible," she managed to whisper.

"Stella."

As soon as she heard the voice, she knew she wasn't hallucinating.

It was Nick.

44

HE FLICKED ON A LANTERN HANGING FROM A HOOK ON THE wall, and she saw him clearly then.

"I don't understand." It took her a few seconds to realize the hot stinging on her cheeks came from an endless stream of tears. "What's going on, Nick?"

Distantly, she realized that her reaction was off. She knew she should be running to hug him and never let him go. But the other part of her brain was telling her what she didn't want to admit. What she couldn't wrap her mind around.

Nick.

The baby.

Her focus turned to the baby. "Give me Keira," she said and took a step forward. He lifted a hand and she saw a pistol dangling from his fingertips.

"Not yet. We've got a lot to talk about."

"I thought you were dead."

"Clearly. But you were looking to replace me before my so-called body was even cold."

"What are you talking about?"

241

"How could you, Stella? Or should I just call you by your code name?"

She frowned. "What? What did I do except love you?"

"You said you would love me forever, didn't you?" he said. "But you slept with Harry the day you got out of the hospital."

Cold terror ran down her back. "How do you know?"

"I was there. I was watching you. Hell, I was waiting for you to leave. I was going to tell you everything—why I was still alive and how I had to pretend I was dead. I wanted to run away with you. That's why I saved all that money, but the minute you thought I was dead, you slept with Harry."

"You don't understand," Stella said in a pleading voice. "I was out of my mind with grief over you. Where have you been? Why didn't you come find me?"

"And then you moved back here, and you slept with every man who looked at you, Stella. It just proved you never loved me."

"I never stopped loving you, Nick," she said. "Not until this moment when I saw what and who you truly are."

Nick acted like he hadn't even heard her and continued.

"Even after Harry, I was willing to forgive you," he went on. "I was willing to still see if you wanted to join me. If I'd have told them I could get the Black Rose on my side, they wouldn't hesitate to let us work together. We would have been a formidable team. We were good together. The Black Rose. Do you remember her? You were deadly. Now? Now you're pathetic."

"I'm not that woman anymore, Nick. That's your fault. When you died, or when I thought you died, I lost my taste for it."

"You can't quit. Once you're a killer, you're always one," he gave a short laugh. "Don't you realize that? Your little cop boyfriend, if he ever wakes up, would be disgusted by you if he knew what and who you really are."

Stella flinched. He was right.

"Stella, just admit it, as a team we would be unstoppable. The best out there by far. I just needed to wrap up some loose ends and then we could even have been independent and taken only the jobs we wanted, pass on the ones we didn't."

"Loose ends?" Stella nearly shrieked. Quickly she glanced at the baby who was watching her. She told herself to focus, but she was horrified. "You call the people who loved you most in the world, loose ends? Bellamy? Jordan?"

"Don't forget Matthew," he added through gritted teeth. "Thank you for leading me to him. I thought you were smarter than that. Everything you did on the Headway computer was available to me. Come on, Stella. You are really slipping."

Stella thought she was going to throw up. He had been her "source" emailing her, but really fishing for information that had led him to Matthew. More blood on her hands. Closing her eyes for a few seconds, her breath came out in a shudder when she opened them again.

"Nick, you're insane," she said in horror. At the same time, her grief was fresh and sharp. The man she had loved was dead for all intents and purposes. But he wasn't done.

"Then, you slept with that cop last year and you must love him because you slept with him again. And now you go see him every day."

"You hurt him too, didn't you, Nick?"

"I was ordered to. But I would have anyway."

"Well, he's awake now, and he knows it was you."

"Stella. Get back against the wall! Now!" It was Tommy Mazzoli. "San Francisco P.D.! Put your hands up!"

"He's got a gun!" she shouted.

It was too late, Nick had trained his gun on the cop. Whirling, she saw that Mazzoli had his own gun pointed back at Nick.

"Nick, let him go. He's not part of this. This is between you and me. He doesn't know anything. He was just following me to make sure I got home safe."

"You're wrong, Stella. Again. He knows everything."

Stella began to creep forward toward Keira as Nick moved away from her toward the back of the tunnel. Stella saw a door there and knew what his plans were. She'd worry about that after she got the baby.

Nick still had his gun pointed at Mazzoli.

"You know if I let you live, you're going to tell people who I am, aren't you?" he asked the cop.

"Who are you kid?"

"Don't play dumb. It's unflattering."

"Yeah. I know who you are, Nick Gold."

Stella winced. Now Mazzoli was dead for sure. "Please let him go. I'll come with you. I'll put my gun down and come with you," she said to Nick. "It's not too late for us."

"I'm not worried about this punk kid," Mazzoli said.

"You should be," Stella said. "He's not what he appears. He's a former SEAL Team Six member. But much, much more and much, much worse."

Nick smirked. "She's right about that."

"Drop the gun," Mazzoli said. "I don't want to have to shoot you, kid."

"What you don't understand is that I'll shoot this baby before I shoot you," Nick said and took a step toward the car seat. "You won't get off a round in time."

He lifted the gun just as Stella roared and charged, throwing herself toward the car seat. As she dove, she fired at Nick. A burst of gunfire from several directions echoed in the stone chamber. White hot pain bloomed in her left shoulder. She watched as a bullet struck its mark and Nick's wrist went limp. Blood blossomed on his arm and his pistol clattered uselessly to the floor.

The relief she felt at her own body stopping the bullet from reaching the baby immediately dissipated when she heard a loud thud behind her. Mazzoli. She winced.

But her focus was getting Keira out of harm's way. She swung her body in a wide arc with the car seat underneath her and managed to push it toward the corner of the wall out of range of Nick's aim.

On the ground, Nick reached for his pistol with his other hand. She gritted her teeth and crawled forward toward her own gun. As soon as she did, Stella executed a precise roll onto her back and with arms pointed straight out fired at Nick. She'd supported her weak arm with her other hand, but her aim was wobbly. He ducked with lightning-fast speed and her shot went high knocking some rock down from the ceiling. Before she leaped to her feet, she fired again. But he had turned to run.

To her surprise in the dark behind him was another passage. She jumped to her feet and ran after him. Then she stared in disbelief. The opening he had disappeared into was on the ground and as big as a rectangular sewer drain in a big city. Her heart thudded in her throat, looking down at it.

He knew. Nick had always known about her claustrophobia. This was his plan. He knew he could escape this way if things went bad.

Stella heard a small whimpering, and then Keira began to wail. She couldn't leave the baby alone to go after Nick. But she was nearly certain where she could find him.

She would have to hurry.

She ran toward the car seat. Looking back, she saw Mazzoli in a heap in the corner. He wasn't moving. A sob escaped her throat.

Scooping up the car seat with the baby, she ran.

Stella knew just where Nick was headed and if she didn't hurry, another cop would be dead within the hour.

45

STELLA MANAGED TO SHOVE WADS OF TISSUES INTO THE shoulder wound in the car, and then wrapped an old scarf around her forearm, tying it with her teeth as she drove. Keira, in her car seat in the back, watched her carefully in the rearview mirror. Stella knew she had lost a lot of blood, but she also needed to stop Nick.

A sob left her throat as she thought about the kind-hearted Tommy Mazzoli who had followed her to keep her safe and ended up dead. She had to stop Nick from killing yet another innocent person.

When she had told him that Griffin was alive, something had flashed across Nick's face. She'd known him long enough to know that it had been fear. Something she'd only rarely seen. Now he was going to take out the last threat. Was going to try to kill Griffin before the cop could identify him as the assailant. She was sure of it.

Stella parked illegally near the front of the hospital and left her car running as she shoved her gun into the back waistband and then scooped Keira out of the car seat and hoisted her onto her hip. Rushing inside, she punched the elevator button for the ICU unit.

Keira looked up at her and smiled, and Stella smiled back. "What am I going to do with you? I can't take you in with me." She shook her head. She couldn't have left the baby in the car, either.

The door opened suddenly. She saw a male nurse standing there waiting for her to exit. It wasn't the ICU floor. It was the wrong floor! She punched the elevator close button at the same time she thrust the baby into his arms. "Take her and call 911. Tell them there's a man with a gun in the ICU."

As the door slid shut, she saw his astonished face. The next time the door opened she was ready and rushed onto the floor of the ICU. Immediately, she knew something was wrong. The entire floor was deserted. Heart pounding in her throat, she ran toward Griffin's room. The two chairs that normally contained the armed policemen acting as guards were empty.

She drew her gun and raced into the open door of the room. The first thing she saw was Griffin. He was awake and staring at her. His arms, torso and legs were bound to the hospital bed with duct tape.

"Run, Stella!" he screamed.

Then she saw Nick. Off to the side in the corner, he had a gun dangling from a hand at his side.

"Why?" Stella gritted the word out as she stepped into the hospital room holding her own gun at her side, also facing down. She saw Nick's eyes flicker toward it.

"Isn't it obvious? You are in love with him."

She glared. "I mean why all of it? Why? I thought I knew you. Who were you all that time? Was it all an act? Or did something happen to change you? I don't understand."

"I was the one who recruited you. I was told to get you on our side."

"You never had feelings for me? You're lying."

He looked away for a second.

"I knew it. You can't look at me and lie. No, that's wrong. You looked at me and lied the entire time we were together. Every single second."

"I didn't care at first. But yes, I started to care about you."

"Care?" Stella scoffed.

"But that didn't matter when it came to doing my job."

"What the hell was your job, Nick? Killing civilians?"

He didn't deny it.

Disgust filled her. That day in Syria came back in flashes. The parade of caskets. So many tiny ones. So many children. She'd watched it on the news later. The entire world had watched, horrified. The team had been disgraced and disbanded. Quietly and quickly.

"You ran back in there to save them, so what happened?" she said, and her eyes narrowed in confusion.

She saw his Adam's apple bob.

Bile filled her mouth. "You ran back in there, not to save them, but to kill them?"

The words came out of her own mouth, but she couldn't believe them.

"They were in the way." His tone was matter of fact.

"They were innocent," Stella said and hated that her voice cracked. She rubbed her forehead with the hand that didn't hold the gun. "Fathers. Mothers. Children. They were civilians. Why? Why? Tell me why and how they were in the way?"

He shrugged. "Does it really matter?"

"Yes," she nodded fervently. "It matters to me. I need to know why. Just tell me why."

She was also stalling, hoping that when the police arrived, they didn't come with sirens blasting. But they might. She was running out of time.

"They were the ones who were going to inherit the oil fields," Nick said and sighed, seemingly bored with the conversation. "They were holding up the sale."

"The sale?" Her voice was filled with astonishment. Mind racing, it all clicked into place in stark horror. The sale. The merger. The oil fields.

The team had been used. They hadn't been misled by terrorists. They had been purposely directed to go in and kill Syrian civilians to clear the way for the sale of oil fields. But they had balked when they had discovered early on that the people they'd been ordered to assassinate were not terrorists but civilians. This entire time, they had thought they had been set up by terrorists, but they had been set up by their own government.

And Bellamy had found out somehow. He'd been about to expose everybody.

"How did Bellamy find out?" She choked back the emotion in her voice from saying her friend's name.

"He saw me. In Thailand. He was there with some woman. He did a double take. I was on a boat, and he was on the shore. He stood up and called my name."

"He's dead for that? For seeing you? Anyone could have told him he was crazy and seeing things. You didn't have to kill him, Nick."

"He didn't let it go," Nick said. "The next thing I knew he was back in Syria questioning the family members of the people I killed. They admitted to him that they had been paid handsomely to say their family members had died in an explosion."

"But they didn't. You assassinated them one by one, didn't you? Women. Children. Grandfathers and grandmothers. You are a son of a bitch," Stella said, her voice dripping with disgust.

"You're the only one left, now," Nick said, and turned toward Griffin. "You and your cop lover. He goes and then you. But I want to see your face when I kill him."

"Put your gun down, Nick," she said, her voice low and deadly.

Griffin raised an eyebrow. Stella didn't know if it was some sort of signal and didn't wait to find out. The second Nick raised his gun, she roared and charged.

Nick pivoted and fired a shot, missing her by inches. She whirled and aimed a reverse back roundhouse that landed squarely on his chest, sending him plummeting into the wall, knocking medical equipment over. But he recovered with ease and sprang forward, his fists a blur. He managed to land a few powerful blows that sent Stella reeling back, crashing into the wall. Her pistol clattered to the floor.

Then he was on her, his hand on her neck, pressing her head against the wall as she gasped for air. There was a sound behind them from Griffin's bed. Nick turned slightly and Stella took advantage of the distraction to wedge enough space between them for her knee to thrust up and into his pelvis.

He grimaced but didn't let up on his grip on her neck. Her body fought desperately for the air it needed. She knew she was running out of time. She had both hands on his forearm, trying to dislodge his grip when she saw her chance. There was a blood pressure cuff on the wall beside her. She looped the tubing through a small gap between the wall and his arm and then yanked. His arm was pushed away.

As she wriggled out of his grasp, she aimed her elbow up sharply and connected with his nose with a sharp cracking sound. He howled and staggered back. She dipped and scooped up her pistol as she saw him raise his hand with his gun in it. A cut on his eyebrow was gushing blood across one eye.

They both fired. Nick's shot went wide, striking the wall behind her. Nick fell to the ground.

Stella stood there with the gun still pointed out, her hand shaking. And then she fired again. And again.

"Stella?"

It was Griffin. She looked over at him, blinking.

"He's dead."

Nodding, her arm dropped to her side.

The sound of shouting and pounding footsteps filled the corridor and several police officers rushed in with guns aimed at Stella.

"Drop your weapon!"

"Code 4! Code 4!" Griffin screamed. "Don't shoot!"

The cops didn't shoot, but they also didn't lower their weapons. Just then, Mazzoli walked in. Stella stared.

"Bulletproof vest. Even off duty," he said and thudded his chest. "Hit my head when I fell. Knocked me out cold."

46

A̲L̲E̲C̲ W̲A̲L̲K̲E̲R̲ H̲A̲D̲ J̲U̲S̲T̲ S̲A̲T̲ D̲O̲W̲N̲ A̲T̲ T̲H̲E̲ D̲I̲N̲I̲N̲G̲ R̲O̲O̲M̲
table to eat his breakfast.

His dining room screamed old world money more than almost
any other place in the house. It was furnished with dark wood and
busy wallpaper, and a sideboard held family heirlooms of silver and
rare China. He'd even had a small button installed under the table
at his seat where he could buzz the kitchen if he needed something
from Bruce.

Bruce had the day off today. Something about a doctor's
appointment, but Walker suspected he was up to something else.
Walker always wondered if Bruce was one of those funny guys who
liked other men. Maybe. It wouldn't surprise him. One of these
days, he'd get the gumption up to let that fellow go. It was hard
though because Bruce knew some of Walker's secrets. No matter.
Money talked. He could pay him handsomely to sign an NDA,
right?

Margaret set the plate of eggs, bacon, and buttered toast in front
of him and then hurried away with a sob swiping at her tears.

Walker sighed loudly.

He was trying to be sympathetic. He really was. But when he'd thought about getting rid of the kid, he didn't know he'd have two grieving women on his hands at home. It was getting old. Frankly, he was sick of making the sympathetic clucking noises and hugging Margaret and Isabel, patting their back, and saying, "It's okay. It's okay."

They would sob into his shirt until it was wet with tears and who knows what else. He didn't want to think about it at breakfast time.

Isabel had immediately taken to her bed on hearing the news. She lay there rocking back and forth with her hands clamped over her ears while somehow managing to emit a glass-shattering wail for hours on end until he'd marched into the hall where Margaret was pacing and told her to call the doctor before he moved into a hotel. Margaret had glared at him as if he were a monster, but she'd called the family doctor who'd come over and shot Isabel up with something that made her quiet down. Now Margaret forced some type of pills on their daughter that made Isabel walk around like a shadowy zombie, lurking in corners or curled up on the sofa with a blanket over her and tears streaming down her face.

She barely spoke. It was the most disturbing thing Walker had ever dealt with, but Margaret reassured him they would get their daughter back in due time—that she just needed some time to grieve Rory's loss.

As he was sopping up some of his egg with the last bite of toast, he heard the doorbell ring. He glanced at his watch with irritation. Who would be rude enough to come over this early in the morning? Then he heard Margaret's exclamation and the sound of deep male voices and heavy footsteps. He started to stand, still holding a piece of egg-sodden toast in his hand, and then froze when the men entered the dining room.

Police officers. Several.

He blinked.

Has something happened in D.C.? Were these men sent as a

protection detail? He recognized the short one in front. The guy was a doorknob. Short man complex. This one walked up to him.

"Alec Walker, you are under arrest on suspicion of murder, extortion, treason, and tax fraud," the officer said.

Walker understood immediately. The gig was up. But what the? Four officers to take him in? Like he was a dangerous killer.

The short cop ordered him to put his hands behind his back.

Walker had always hated that guy. Every time Walker went to get coffee at the diner in his neighborhood, this dumbbell would stare. Walker knew for sure the little shrimp hadn't voted for him.

"Daddy!" Isabel was crying and screaming, tugging on his arm. "Please don't leave me! I can't bear to be alone. First Rory and then you? I can't bear it."

It was the first time in days she seemed like her old self. At least his arrest had knocked some sense into her again.

"Buck up, buttercup," he said. "You'll be fine."

Margaret was holding Isabel back, her eyes wide as she gave Walker a pleading look.

The cop was still droning on reading his Miranda rights, which Walker was tuning out. "Anything you say can and will be held against you in a court of law."

"Yeah, yeah, yeah. Margaret, call my attorney. Right now!"

They shuffled him out of his own house like an animal. He groaned as they stuffed him into the back of the squad car. Turning, he saw Isabel, the ding dong, standing there with her mouth open.

Shaking his head, he turned back toward the front of the vehicle. He should've known this would happen. Of course, he'd be the only one who would go down for this. It didn't matter what he said. He had no proof. It was his word against a billionaire's word.

He would lose. Money talked.

Nobody liked politicians anyway. But before he went down, he'd threaten to expose everyone he knew. If he were going down, they would go down with him.

* * *

Walker had been in jail for about a week when a man he didn't recognize came to visit him. He walked into the visitor's room and understood right away.

The man was nondescript—brown hair, brown eyes, average height, average weight, no distinguishing features. In other words, an every man who would defy specific description by witnesses. But he was wearing an expensive suit. Walker immediately knew who had sent him.

"What do you want?" Walker said and scowled.

"Our friend wanted me to remind you that a lot worse things can happen to a man than a life in prison."

"Yeah, yeah, yeah. I know."

"Good," the man said and stood up.

"You know that article that ran?" Walker said. "By Stella Collins? You guys were ready for that and had your stories lined up to point straight to me, right? But here's what you don't realize. That girl? She's going after you next. Tell your boss that."

47

For some ridiculous reason, Garcia had forbidden Stella from going to work for a week after the shooting, so by the time she stepped foot into the newsroom that Monday afternoon, she was ready to be back.

A week alone in her apartment had been torture. She'd fled and hid out at her parents' house where her mother treated her like a little kid and that silly dog slept with her all night long. To heal, she slept. Didn't stay up later than midnight and yet found herself sleeping until four in the afternoon on most days. When she awoke, her mother would fix her comfort food—pasta fagioli, pasta with butter, Italian wedding soup with homemade bread.

One night, she found herself hugging the dog like a doll and the darn thing was on his back snoring. He was adorable. Her mother would open the bedroom door to let the dog out or feed him and then the dog would come back in and hop up onto the bed and curl up against Stella. It was as if the dog knew that Stella needed him.

Her mother spoke softly to her and somehow managed to keep her dad and all the other relatives far away, especially Stella's uncle.

Sometimes her mother would come into Stella's room and just give her a hug or rub her back or brush her hair.

"Stella, *mia cara*, your mama is here for you always."

Stella would hug her back. "Thanks, mama. I love you."

Her mother didn't know that Stella was torturing herself over the knowledge that she had fallen stone cold in love with a killer who had fooled her. To her surprise it was a worse feeling than the grief she'd felt when she'd thought he'd died trying to save those children. At least then he was a hero in her eyes.

Now, he was a monster. He was pure evil who had conned her and betrayed her in the worst possible way. Now she doubted herself on a level she never had before. She would need some time to regain her faith in her instincts.

It was disconcerting. And humiliating. Even though nobody was still alive to know just how foolish she had been to fall for Nick's deceit.

Finally, it was Sunday night. She set her alarm and was able to make herself somewhat presentable to head to the newspaper.

Her mother kissed her on the forehead. "You can quit, you know. You can find another job."

"I know, mama."

"You could do something safe like be a secretary. Your uncle has lots of businesses that need help."

Stella smiled wanly. Her mother had the best intentions, but just didn't understand. She never would. And that was okay.

On her way, Stella stopped at the gas station for a coffee and grabbed one for Garcia. As soon as she stepped inside the newsroom, both hands holding coffee, she froze. The entire news staff—editors, reporters, copy editors—all stood there.

Garcia in the front. He began a slow clap, and the others followed.

"Oh, hell. This is embarrassing," Stella said, handing Garcia his coffee, and walked past them.

"The publisher bought us all beer and pizza because of your story," Marilyn said.

Stella raised an eyebrow. "Really? The story the publisher told me not to write? Huh?"

She scooped up a piece of pizza as she passed the desk with the open boxes on her way to her desk. The other employees dispersed, and Stella grumbled as she logged into her computer.

Garcia was suddenly at her side. "Nice work, Collins."

"Thanks," she said around a bite of the pizza. "Hey, this stuff isn't half bad."

"I had a talk with Caitlin Archer. The publisher's rep. They're going to back off on micromanaging what we do around here."

"Thank goodness," Stella said.

"And they're submitting your story to the Pulitzer committee."

"Nice," Stella said. "Listen, I've got to get to work on this child trafficking story. If you don't mind."

Garcia grinned. "Ha!"

"What?" Stella said and frowned.

"You're embarrassed."

She shook her head but couldn't stop grinning.

"You're acting all tough girl, but you are happy as hell aren't you?"

Stella shrugged. "I don't know."

"Ha!" Garcia said. "You are."

Laughing, he walked back to his desk.

Stella just shook her head and sighed. Then she pulled up her story and began to write. She filed the story right on deadline and then packed up to leave. Garcia was busy on the phone, but he winked and waved goodbye.

When Stella stepped outside the building, there was a figure waiting for her in the dark. She reached for her bag. She'd taken to carrying a pistol with her.

The man put his hands up over his head.

"Just me."

It was Griffin.

"Okay if I walk you to your car?"

Stella hadn't seen him since she'd shot Nick in front of him. "Sure," she said.

They began to walk, Stella noticed he was a little slow.

"How you doing?"

"I'm okay. A little shaky, but they said that will go away. I'm doing some occupational therapy and some other stuff before I go back to the streets. They have me on desk duty."

"Boring," Stella said.

"Tell me about it."

When they got to her car, she turned, leaning back on it. "Glad you're awake," she said.

He laughed. "I'm glad I'm awake, too."

"Listen, how are you doing? I know it's tough, well, that's an understatement, it's devastating to take another life. Are you in counseling for it?"

Stella stared at him. Of course he didn't know. Of course, he thought she should be in therapy. The only thing that would have sent her to therapy was the fact that the man she killed was the love of her life. The killing itself was a blip to her. The reality of that fact, that she hadn't even thought about the gravity of taking another life, made her sick to her stomach.

After all that time away, she was still the Black Rose. Nick had been right. And he'd also been right about Griffin. If the cop knew who and what she was, he would despise her. She was the opposite of everything he stood for.

"How's Mazzoli?" she asked, trying to change the subject.

"He submitted his resignation today."

"No, kidding?"

"He's done. Too many crooked cops on the force, he said."

"That's a fact. I've been here less than a month and even I know that."

"I didn't really wait for you tonight so we could talk about another guy."

"Really?" Stella said and looked away.

Griffin grabbed her hand and pulled her into a dark doorway. He pulled her to him and kissed her long and hard.

"Good to see you again, too," she said when she pulled away.

"How far is your place from here again," he asked coyly, in a husky voice.

"No."

"No?"

"It's not that I don't want to."

"Okay. Do you mind if I ask why?"

Stella thought about it long and hard as he watched her. She could never tell him why. She could never be with him because she was a killer. Even if she stopped killing for the rest of her life as she planned, the fact was she had been an assassin working for the U.S. government on a covert team that had gone terribly, horribly wrong and ended in a blaze of fire when they'd been responsible for the deaths of families and children.

She shook her head sadly. "You're a good guy, Griffin. But I only like you as a friend."

Ouch. Even saying the words hurt. They were utter lies. There was no future for them. It was doomed before he even began. He stopped killers. She was one.

Something flashed across his face, and Stella felt a pang of guilt. Then he smiled.

"Well, I need a friend right now." He let go of her hand lingeringly. "A friend who likes Ethiopian food especially."

"In that case," Stella said and smiled. "I'm your girl."

48

THE HOUSE THIRTY MILES OUTSIDE OF AUSTIN, TEXAS, seemed innocuous. From the outside, it was a somewhat typical rambler. Sprawling across a large, cleared space, it then was surrounded by a small forest of poplars. The only thing someone might find odd was that all the windows—and there were at least a dozen large ones—reflected the land around them. There was no way to see inside.

A large carriage house behind the rambler housed half a dozen vehicles, including a motorhome with all-terrain tires and bullet-proof sides and glass. The roof of the rambler was lined with solar panels and a small greenhouse to one side grew hydroponic produce. Another small shed contained small farm animals, including a pig and chickens.

The house did not appear special to outsiders. But it was.

Outside of a select few, the only person who really knew all its secrets was a builder and his crew. Shortly after construction, a terrible accident at a job site had killed the builder and his foreman. It was believed that the rest of the crew, mostly illegal immigrants, had scattered after the accident, worried about deportation. But the truth was tragedy had also befallen them.

It behooved the man to have the secrets of his house remain secret, since he didn't trust anybody. Even the men who had now gathered in his underground den, had only an inkling of where they were. All they knew was that when the van they were in arrived at the driveway to the house, they were blindfolded. After they left the van, they were taken inside and then told to step inside a room that was clearly an elevator. They were then led through a series of rooms that grew increasingly colder.

That's why they were so confused when the blindfolds were taken off, and they ended up in the same den they had visited before without being blindfolded. They just chalked it up to the man's eccentricities. But looks were exchanged.

It wasn't like anyone would ever make it to the main house, anyway. The gated driveway was on an old road that few people traveled or even knew about. That is, if you made it past security and down the long, winding driveway that snaked through the woods. At the end of the driveway was yet another gate and yet another set of guards. The house was essentially a fortress.

What the man's visitors didn't know—and what he had made sure nobody else knew—was that the room they were in was deep underground. They were standing in a den that was a replica of the one two stories above them. In fact, the entire home they were standing in was a replica of the house above. It was a bunker that would withstand a nuclear explosion.

The place had its own greenhouse powered by grow lights, a small chicken coop in a replica outdoor space, its own plumbing system, well water set up, generator and even air filtration system. The man could live down here for twenty years if it ever came to that.

The reason he was conducting the meeting down there was because shortly before the men had arrived, the head of his security team had reported a drone hovering above the property. He couldn't be too careful. He was starting to think that high-tech surveillance equipment had listened in on his conversations in the house on the ground level.

The men he had gathered could be silenced easily. He could don a gas mask he kept in a nearby closet and hit a switch, and the entire room would immediately be filled with lethal fumes. It was an emergency measure he'd put into place in case enemies ever infiltrated his space. It could happen. One couldn't be too careful. Not with the power he wielded. His enemies were many and powerful. It was a fact he'd learned to accept at a young age.

And so the other three men were taken underground and seated in the den. He sat in the big red leather chair facing them. They sat on a large couch that was so deep their knees rose higher than their waists. He liked having them feel childish and at a disadvantage in that way.

Clearing his throat, he began: "I thought this was over."

He looked pointedly at one man, the crooked F.B.I. agent he'd had on payroll for the past two years.

"It is essentially," the agent said.

"Essentially isn't good enough."

"It's too dangerous to take her out now," the FBI agent said. "Since her story ran, they would have to do a thorough investigation and so many people know about it that I'm not sure we could pay everyone off to keep their mouths shut."

"How did she get away?" the man in the red leather chair asked. "We had the best of the best go after her."

Another man, a recognizable top military leader, answered. "We think it was the emotional bond the two used to have that made him weak."

The man in the red leather chair thought about that for a few seconds and then said, "If that's the case, then we can't be certain he didn't tell her about the mission. I don't care how risky it is. She has to go."

"We need to wait for it to cool down a bit," another man said.

He was from the White House. A kingmaker. And the man in the red leather chair wanted to be a king. So, he trusted this bit of advice, despite his impatience.

Still, he thought about it for a few moments before he answered. Silence was power. It always would be, so he paused. The rest of the room waited. They had learned to be patient when he was thinking.

Most of them had.

"He was going to kill her, but she killed him first. There is no way he told her what he knew," the crooked F.B.I. agent insisted, breaking the silence.

"You're defending a dead woman," the man in the red chair said as he reached over and pushed a button. The wooden panels on the far wall parted and a movie screen appeared. The lights in the room dimmed and small lights on the floors lit up. Then the movie screen flickered to life. It was a live satellite feed.

At first it was so far away it was unclear what was on the screen. But then the image became clearer. The satellite was looking down at a cemetery. Soon, the screen was filled with green grass dotted with white tombstones. In the center of the screen was a woman with dark hair dressed in black.

Then the image cut out for a second and when the screen flickered back on, it was a close up of the woman. Her body filled the screen. Wearing a black trench coat, huge black sunglasses, and red lipstick, her dark hair blew in the breeze. She swiped a strand away with her hand. Her other hand held a black rose.

She stood in front of a fresh grave for a few moments. Then she reached down and placed the black rose on the dirt. The headstone read *"Nick Dalton. 1985-2023."*

Then the screen was filled with the back of the woman, her trench coat flapping behind as she walked away.

* * *

Stella LaRosa returns in *Red Ink*, coming soon. Pre-order now:

https://amazon.com/dp/B0CY67YVZY

Join the LT Ryan reader family & receive a free copy of the Rachel Hatch story, *Fractured*. Click the link below to get started: https://ltryan.com/rachel-hatch-newsletter-signup-1

Also by L.T. Ryan

Find All of L.T. Ryan's Books on Amazon Today!

The Jack Noble Series

The Recruit (free)

The First Deception (Prequel 1)

Noble Beginnings

A Deadly Distance

Ripple Effect (Bear Logan)

Thin Line

Noble Intentions

When Dead in Greece

Noble Retribution

Noble Betrayal

Never Go Home

Beyond Betrayal (Clarissa Abbot)

Noble Judgment

Never Cry Mercy

Deadline

End Game

Noble Ultimatum

Noble Legend

Noble Revenge

Never Look Back (Coming Soon)

Bear Logan Series

Ripple Effect

Blowback

Take Down

Deep State

Bear & Mandy Logan Series

Close to Home

Under the Surface

The Last Stop

Over the Edge

Between the Lies

Caught in the Web (Coming Soon)

Rachel Hatch Series

Drift

Downburst

Fever Burn

Smoke Signal

Firewalk

Whitewater

Aftershock

Whirlwind

Tsunami

Fastrope

Sidewinder (Coming Soon)

Mitch Tanner Series

The Depth of Darkness

Into The Darkness

Deliver Us From Darkness

Cassie Quinn Series

Path of Bones

Whisper of Bones

Symphony of Bones

Etched in Shadow

Concealed in Shadow

Betrayed in Shadow

Born from Ashes

Return to Ashes (Coming Soon)

Blake Brier Series

Unmasked

Unleashed

Uncharted

Drawpoint

Contrail

Detachment

Clear

Quarry (Coming Soon)

Dalton Savage Series

Savage Grounds

Scorched Earth

Cold Sky

The Frost Killer

Crimson Moon (Coming Soon)

Maddie Castle Series

The Handler

Tracking Justice

Hunting Grounds

Vanished Trails

Smoldering Lies (Coming Soon)

Affliction Z Series

Affliction Z: Patient Zero

Affliction Z: Abandoned Hope

Affliction Z: Descended in Blood

Affliction Z : Fractured Part 1

Affliction Z: Fractured Part 2 (Fall 2021)

About the Author

L.T. RYAN is a *Wall Street Journal, USA Today*, and Amazon bestselling author of several mysteries and thrillers, including the *Wall Street Journal* bestselling Jack Noble and Rachel Hatch series. With over eight million books sold, when he's not penning his next adventure, L.T. enjoys traveling, hiking, riding his Peloton, and spending time with his wife, daughter and four dogs at their home in central Virginia.

* Sign up for his newsletter to hear the latest goings on and receive some free content ➜ https://ltryan.com/jack-noble-newsletter-signup-1
* Join LT's private readers' group ➜ https://www.facebook.com/groups/1727449564174357
* Follow on Instagram ➜ @ltryanauthor
* Visit the website ➜ https://ltryan.com
* Send an email ➜ contact@ltryan.com
* Find on Goodreads ➜ http://www.goodreads.com/author/show/6151659.L_T_Ryan

***

Kristi Belcamino is a USA Today bestseller, an Agatha, Anthony, Barry & Macavity finalist, and an Italian Mama who bakes a tasty biscotti.

Her books feature strong, kickass, independent women facing unspeakable evil in order to seek justice for those unable to do so themselves.

In her former life, as an award-winning crime reporter at newspapers in California, she flew over Big Sur in an FA-18 jet with the Blue Angels, raced a Dodge Viper at Laguna Seca, attended barbecues at the morgue, and conversed with serial killers.

During her decade covering crime, Belcamino wrote and reported about many high-profile cases including the Laci Peterson murder and Chandra Levy disappearance. She has appeared on *Inside Edition* and local television shows. She now writes fiction and works part-time as a reporter covering the police beat for the St. Paul *Pioneer Press*.

Her work has appeared in such prominent publications as *Salon*, the *Miami Herald*, *San Jose Mercury News,* and *Chicago Tribune*.

Instagram ➜ Instagram.com/kristibelcaminobooks
Facebook ➜ facebook.com/kristibelcaminobooks

Made in the USA
Las Vegas, NV
22 March 2024

87609834R00154